PRAISE FOR KATIE ASHLEY
AND HER NOVELS

"A mixture of funny, sweet, tender, and sexy. . . . [Ms. Ashley has] got me good and hooked."
—Fiction Vixen

"*Wow* is all I can say. . . . So if you are new to Katie Ashley, treat yourself. I promise that you will not be disappointed. . . . [It] will definitely warm your heart, make you laugh, and have you smiling long after you finish."
—Guilty Pleasures Book Reviews

"It was all fabulous. Steamy, romantic, swoon-worthy, adorable!"
—Smitten's Book Blog

"Had me laughing while it tugged at my heartstrings. . . . You know how much we loves us a HOT read, and there is plenty of heat here, ladies."
—Flirty and Dirty Book Blog

"Full of everything I love in a romance book. A sexy, scared-of-commitment leading man . . . a very relatable, beautiful woman . . . drama to last for days, and a scorching love story that left me wishing this book would never end."
—The SubClub Books

"This book was emotionally wrenching, funny, and sexy. It has a bit of everything."
—Romance Lovers Book Blog

D1016227

Also by Katie Ashley

Vicious Cycle

REDEMPTION

ROAD

A VICIOUS CYCLE NOVEL

KATIE ASHLEY

A SIGNET ECLIPSE BOOK

SIGNET ECLIPSE
Published by New American Library,
an imprint of Penguin Random House LLC
375 Hudson Street, New York, New York 10014

This book is an original publication of New American Library.

First Printing, October 2015

LIBRARY OF CONGRESS CATALOGING-IN-PUBLICATION DATA:

Ashley, Katie.
  Redemption road: a Vicious Cycle novel / Katie Ashley.
          pages cm.—(Vicious Cycle; 2)
  ISBN 978-0-451-47492-6 (softcover)
  1. Motorcycle clubs—Fiction.   2. Motorcycle gangs—Fiction.
3. Man-woman relationships—Fiction.   I. Title.
  PS3601.S548R43 2015
  813'.6—dc23   2015015628

Printed in the United States of America
10 9 8 7 6 5 4 3 2 1

Set in Bulmer MT Std Regular
Designed by Spring Hoteling

Penguin
Random
House

In loving memory of the strong, beautiful women who
have influenced my writing, especially this book, by being the
Steel Magnolias they were:

my mother, Ginger Ashe, my grandmother, Virginia Jackson,
my aunt, Janet Davis, and my second mother and friend,
Elizabeth McDilda Martinelli

ACKNOWLEDGMENTS

First and foremost, thanks go to God for blessing me with the most wonderful career in publishing, along with the gift of storytelling.

To my agent, Jane Dystel, who always has my best professional and personal interests at heart and who is always in my corner with support and help regardless of whether it's night or day!

To Kerry Donovan, my editor at NAL: I can never thank you enough for your understanding and consideration on this manuscript when I was sidelined by intense pregnancy nausea. You've been an absolute pleasure to work with on this series.

To the team at Penguin/NAL, thank you for making the release of *Vicious Cycle* so amazing and for all your promotional help on the series.

To my supportive street team, Ashley's Angels, your enthusiasm, encouragement, and support mean the world to me. Thanks for loving me and my characters so much!

Kim Bias: Thanks for being my handler once again and checking in daily to make sure the book was coming along. Thanks for

Acknowledgments

all your help making Rev and Annabel's story the best it could be. I appreciate your support and friendship!

Marion Archer, my wonderful friend and editor from Down Under, you know I cannot put a book out without it first being seen by your eyes and having your plotting magic worked on it. Thank you for working me in with my extreme procrastination and writer's block! Love ya hard!

Cris Hadarly: Thanks for being such a dedicated friend and book supporter. I couldn't make it in this business without you! Thanks for the fan art and promotion for my books.

Jen Gerchick, Jen Oreto, and Shannon Furhman: Words are inadequate to say how much I appreciate your friendship and support. You guys are the best book pimpers ever!

Michelle Eck and Karen Everett: Thanks for all your help on making *Vicious Cycle* and this series a success.

To all my author buddies who are too numerous to list: I love you hard for your friendship and support!

The ladies of the Hot Ones and Smutty Mafia: You have my eternal love and admiration!

REDEMPTION ROAD

PROLOGUE

The whirring sound of his mother's ancient hand mixer drew Nathaniel's attention away from his homework. He sniffed the chocolate-scented air appreciatively. Glancing over his shoulder, he watched as his younger brother, Benjamin, leaned on the counter, eyeing the mixture and waiting for just the right moment to stick his finger in and get a taste of the icing.

"Don't think I don't know what you're doing," his mother said, with an amused smile.

"But you said we could lick the spoon," Ben protested.

"That's *if* you get your homework done."

With an exasperated sigh, Benjamin trudged across the worn linoleum floor and back to his chair next to Nathaniel. After he flopped down, he reluctantly took up his pencil.

"There. This one is done," his mother announced. She had just put the final touches on one of the chocolate cakes she had spent the better part of the afternoon baking. He and Benjamin would have to wait until she was completely finished to devour the remaining icing.

His mother glanced over at Nathaniel. "Honey, would you do me a huge favor and run this down to Miss Mae's?"

"Sure." He rose from his chair and went over to the counter. "But you better save some of the icing for me."

Smiling, she reached over and ruffled his hair. "Of course I will." After putting the cake into a container, she thrust it into Nathaniel's arms. "Thanks, sweetheart."

He headed out the kitchen door and down the back steps. Mae Sanders lived three houses up the road from them on the right. All twelve of the houses in the semicircular lane, or compound, as people called it, belonged to members of his father's church. At the top of the hill sat the old cotton mill office that now housed Soul Harbor, the church where his father was the pastor.

Carefully balancing the cake tray in his hands, Nathaniel made his way up Miss Mae's flower-lined front walk and then up the three steps onto the porch. After he pounded on the door, it swung open. But it wasn't the blue-haired, grandmotherly Miss Mae standing there. Instead, it was the tall, lanky figure of Kurt Miller, one of the homeless men from his father's church whom Miss Mae had taken on to help her with work around the house. She had a soft spot for the less fortunate and always had one or two people living with her.

"Well, if it isn't Nate the Great," Kurt said, with a wide smile.

Nathaniel felt his cheeks warm under the attention. No one at church ever paid much attention to him. Compared to his two rambunctious brothers, he was quiet, the well-behaved and obedient one. But since Kurt had arrived two weeks ago, he had gone out of his way to make Nathaniel feel special.

Amusement flickered in Kurt's dark eyes. "You brought me a cake? But it isn't even my birthday."

Shaking his head, Nathaniel replied, "No, my mama sent it to Miss Mae to take to the VFW for bingo night."

Kurt stroked his chin. "That's right. Tonight is bingo night." Stretching his arms wide, he motioned for Nathaniel to come in. "She just left for the beauty shop and won't be back for an hour. But you can leave the cake for her so you don't have to make two trips."

"Okay, thanks," Nathaniel replied as he stepped over the threshold. All the houses in the compound were alike, so he knew the way to the kitchen. They had once been part of the row houses belonging to the cotton mill before it had gone out of business.

After setting the cake on the counter, Nathaniel turned to go, but Kurt stopped him. "What's your rush?"

Nathaniel shrugged. "Just need to get back to my homework."

"Ah, it ain't goin' nowhere. Why don't you sit down for a minute?"

Even though he knew a spoonful of chocolate icing was awaiting him at home, Nathaniel felt it would be rude if he refused to sit for just a minute. Or at least his mama would think it was rude, and the last thing he wanted was to disappoint her.

After easing down into one of the straight-backed kitchen chairs, he looked expectantly at Kurt.

"How about something to drink?" Kurt asked.

"Um, okay. Sure."

"How's school?" Kurt asked as his footsteps creaked along the worn floorboards.

"It's fine. Got all As," Nathaniel replied.

"Good for you." With his back to Nathaniel, Kurt glanced at him over his shoulder. "Got a girlfriend?"

Fiery embarrassment filled Nathaniel's cheeks. "N-No, I—I don't," he stammered in reply.

"Don't worry about it. With your looks, in a few years the girls will be all over you."

"I hope. I mean, I guess I want them to be," Nathaniel murmured.

He couldn't imagine a girl ever being interested in him, and he was too shy to talk to them. He wished he could be more like his older brother, David. At fourteen, he always had a steady girlfriend, with others waiting in the wings.

Kurt set a mug down in front of Nathaniel. "Here's some coffee to warm you up before you have to head back out into the cold."

Nathaniel fought the urge to protest that his mother didn't allow him to drink coffee, as he was afraid of looking uncool in front of someone like Kurt. So he took the mug and blew ripples across the dark surface of the steaming liquid. When he thought it wouldn't burn his tongue, he took a sip.

Wrinkling his nose, Nathaniel eased the mug away from his lips. He surveyed the contents curiously. "This sure doesn't taste like coffee."

"I put a little nip of Jack in there," Kurt replied, with a wink.

Nathaniel widened his eyes. "You put . . . *alcohol* in my coffee?"

"Sure. Why not? I was your age when I had my first drink."

As Nathaniel continued studying the mug, he could feel the familiar tug of his conscience that happened whenever the angel and the devil on his shoulder waged war against each other. He was pretty sure his mother would fall to her knees in prayer for him if she knew, and then his father would tan his hide. Even though he should've poured out the mug's contents, he couldn't help wanting to taste a little more. "You won't tell, will you?" he questioned in a whisper.

Kurt flashed him a toothy smile. " 'Course not." He nodded at the mug. "Drink up. Make it count."

Shrugging away his doubt, Nathaniel took several more hearty sips. The more he drank, the more terrible the mixture tasted. He didn't want to have any more, but Kurt urged him on. Once he had finished it, he set the empty mug down on the table.

"How do you feel?" Kurt asked.

Furrowing his brow, Nathaniel tried to make sense of what was happening to him. His head felt like it might fly away from his body. Within seconds, the room started spinning like it had the time he'd been caged in on the Tilt-A-Whirl at the county fair. He'd desperately wanted to get off, but he'd been forced to endure the entire ride. At the moment, he wanted to stop the way his body was feeling.

A cold hand on his cheek caused him to jump. "Nathaniel, how are you feeling?"

"I . . . I can't make it stop," he murmured, his eyelids fluttering closed.

"Don't try to."

The next thing he knew, his body was being lifted out of the chair. He was dragged into Miss Mae's bedroom. After the door slammed and locked behind him, his face was forced down onto Miss Mae's frilly pink comforter.

"What . . . are . . . you . . . doing?" he questioned. It was a struggle getting each word out.

When hands fumbled with the button of his jeans, he tried to push them away. "I'm going to make you feel good, Nathaniel." Kurt's voice came from behind him.

Nathaniel didn't want to feel good. He just wanted to go home. He wanted to be in the safety of his kitchen, arguing with Benjamin over who got more icing.

As he faded in and out of a dark, shadowy consciousness, harsh hands roamed over his body. Just when he thought things couldn't be any worse, pain like he had never experienced tore through him. Tears welled in his eyes, then streaked down his cheeks. His suffering seemed to go on and on, and he began to fear that it would never end.

But then, through the hellish haze, he heard someone come through the front door. From the loud clomp of the boots on the floorboard, he knew it was his father. His mother must've sent his dad to look for him. Just as he got the strength to raise his head to call for help, Kurt's hand clamped over his mouth. His harsh whisper came at Nathaniel's ear. "If you even think about screaming, I'll cut your throat and all of your family's. You got me?"

Nathaniel wanted desperately to scream. He wanted the nightmare, the pain, the humiliation to end. And yet even though he didn't care whether he lived or died, he didn't want anything to happen to his family.

But when his father didn't appear at the door, Nathaniel let his hope die. He buried his face in the soft folds of Miss Mae's comforter and wept. At the sound of a loud bang, he jerked his head up.

His father stood in the doorway. The unadulterated horror mixed with rage on his face caused Nathaniel to shudder with fear. He barely had time to brace himself for his father's wrath before the gun came up and a blast came out of it so loud that the windows rattled.

And then, as his father called his name in a ragged breath, Nathaniel realized he had just traded one hell for another.

ONE

REV
THE PRESENT

I came awake to find someone shaking the hell out of me. Flipping open my eyelids to escape my tormented unconsciousness, I stared up into the concerned blue eyes of my brother Bishop. His hands gripped my shoulders so tightly I figured there would be marks. "What the fuck, man?" I questioned, slinging him away.

He tumbled back on the mattress. "You were having one hell of a nightmare."

I sighed and rubbed my shoulders where his hands had been. "Yeah, well, that doesn't mean I want to wake up to your ugly mug with morning breath in my face," I replied, trying to ease the palpable tension in the air.

Bishop didn't laugh. He didn't make a move to get off the bed, either. He continued staring at me like he hoped he could somehow will me into talking. He'd been giving me the same stare for the past few days while we'd been on the road. Whenever we'd stop for food or to gas up our bikes, I would find him staring at me, chewing his bottom lip like he wanted to say something. He had been desperate since three nights ago, when a personal tragedy within our club allowed him a tiny glimpse at my long-buried secret.

Breaking the silence between us, I asked, "What time is our meeting with the El Paso Raiders?"

"Seven."

I glanced over my shoulder at the glowing digital clock on the nightstand. "That doesn't give us much time to make it across the state. Better get crackin' and hit the road. You want the shower first?"

"Nah, you can have it." As I rose off the mattress, Bishop said, "I'll go grab us a quick breakfast."

"Thanks, brother."

When I started across the threadbare carpet to the bathroom, Bishop's words froze me. "Rev . . . you know it doesn't matter to me what the fuck happened to you—it ain't gonna change a damn thing about the way I feel about you. No matter what, you're my big brother and my prez."

Since I was both too emotionally conflicted and too stubborn to respond, I ignored him and pushed on into the bathroom. After locking the door behind me, I gazed at my reflection in the mirror. Two days of driving across Georgia, Alabama, Mississippi, and Louisiana with minimal sleep had taken its physical toll. That, coupled with emotional stress, had left dark circles under my eyes. We'd packed up to leave so abruptly, I hadn't bothered with a razor, so my beard was growing in. I looked like the hell that raged inside me.

Turning on the water full blast, I stepped into the shower. I placed my palms flat on the tile and stood with my head under the stream. Rolling my shoulders, I tried to ease my tense muscles.

Two days ago felt like two years and another world ago. It was hard to imagine just forty-eight hours ago I'd been dancing and drinking at my brother Deacon and sister-in-law Alexandra's wedding. Then one phone call from the Raiders' unofficial doctor, Bob "Breakneck" Edgeway, had changed everything.

Whenever I closed my eyes, one of two faces would haunt me. It was either the sinister visage of my rapist or the fresh-faced, innocent countenance of Breakneck's daughter. It had been five years since I had seen Sarah at any of the Raiders events. She'd been an awkward thirteen-year-old girl in braces who had spent most of the BBQ fawning over Eric, the teenage son of our then-president, Case. Now she was a freshman at Texas A&M. From the picture Breakneck had texted me, I could see she'd grown into an auburn-haired beauty with an innocent smile.

The kind of girl that low-life traffickers were always jonesing for.

The criminal profiling of the scum who bought these women indicated they didn't want fake-breasted, slutty types. They could pay for those any day on the streets or at the strip clubs. No, they seemed to want the unattainable female—the one who would never give them the time of day, unless she was forced. And sadly, Sarah fit that bill.

We didn't have much to go on other than that it was the Highway Henchmen who took her and were making financial demands on Breakneck to get her back. Apparently, she had spilled the beans that her old man was a biker. Usually, girls kidnapped for trafficking never got a chance of being ransomed back to their families. Instead, they were sold to the highest bidder, into a life of sexual slavery. The thought that Sarah now faced that future turned my stomach and enraged me.

After scrubbing off yesterday's grit and grime with the hotel's cheap soap, I made fast work of rinsing. The moment I turned the water off, I heard my phone ringing in the bedroom. Throwing a towel around my waist, I hurried out of the bathroom to grab it. When I saw who was calling, I grimaced. "Yeah?"

"Where the hell are you?" Deacon demanded without even a hello.

"I'm touched that you thought to call me while you're on your honeymoon."

Deacon's low growl came in my ear. "Don't fucking change the subject, asshole."

"I was just trying to be nice."

"Yeah, you're just being a prick is what you're doing. Now I want a fucking straight answer."

"Last time I checked, big brother, *I* wore the president's patch." I knew my words were the equivalent of poking a rattlesnake ready to strike. Regardless of whether I was the president of the Hells Raiders, I still owed Deacon an explanation.

"Fine, motherfucker, then answer me as your newly patched vice president, why my two brothers bailed on my reception to hit the road and are now in Texas."

Defeated, I leaned back against the counter. I knew I couldn't evade his questions anymore. "It's complicated."

"I'm listening."

Slowly, I began unraveling the story of Sarah's abduction, and how we were going to get her back from the Henchmen.

When I finished, Deacon merely muttered, "Fucking hell."

"Yeah, that pretty much sums it up."

Deacon exhaled a long sigh into the phone. "Man, I can't believe you just left here without taking it to the table. You're the president, for fuck's sake. While it's admirable of you to do this for Breakneck, this situation isn't just about you. It involves the entire club."

"You're not telling me anything I don't already know. Just tell the guys I'll deal with any repercussions when I get back."

"I just hope it doesn't get any worse."

Pushing off the counter, I demanded, "Are you questioning my judgment?"

"Look, I know you and your code of honor. You'll do whatever you have to do to get Sarah back."

"You say that like it's the wrong thing to do."

"It is when the Raiders are trying to go legit."

Even though he couldn't see me, I shook my head in disbelief. "What the fuck is wrong with you? We're talking about an innocent girl's life here—one of our brother's kids. Have you forgotten that Raiders protect their own regardless of the cost? You would do anything if someone had Willow or Alexandra. Hell, you have before."

"Do *not* bring my wife and kid into this," Deacon hissed.

"Don't question me, and I won't. Try for a moment to remember that Sarah is Breakneck's kid, so for his sake, I'm willing to do *anything* to get her back. If that means some blowback on the club, then I'll fucking deal with it."

"No, we'll *all* end up fucking dealing with it."

I exhaled a frustrated breath. "I know you have a lot of pressure from Alexandra for the club to go legit. But I guarantee if you told her what was happening, she would be behind me all the way, regardless of what the repercussions might be on the club."

When Deacon cursed under his breath, I knew I had finally gotten through to him. "You're a stubborn motherfucker," he grumbled.

With a laugh, I replied, "I learned from the best, brother."

Deacon snorted. "Yeah, well, just be careful."

Since I knew Deacon wasn't an overly emotional guy, I couldn't help feeling a little touched at his concern. "I will. But at the end of the day, this is something I have to do."

"Trust me, I get it. I don't have to like it, but I sure as hell get it."

"We'll be back as soon as we can."

"Call me the minute you have her."

"I will."

After Deacon hung up without a good-bye, which was so his style, I went to get dressed. But no matter how hard I tried, I couldn't shake the overwhelming feeling of dread crisscrossing its way over my skin. Although I would never have admitted my fears to him, I knew Deacon was right. Getting Sarah back was going to have blow-back on the club.

At the time, I had no idea how severe.

Bishop returned with breakfast, and we were back on the road within half an hour. After a quick stop for lunch and gas, we pulled into the outskirts of El Paso a little before seven. We had been asked to meet our Texas brothers at a gentleman's club they owned, which was located in one of the seedier areas of town.

When I pushed down the kickstand and eased off my bike, every muscle in my body screamed in agony. It had been a long time since I had done such an extensive run. The distance, coupled with the stress hanging over me, made me feel positively decrepit. I wanted nothing more than a hot meal and a cold beer. But as I gazed up at the blinking, half-naked woman on the Rising Phoenix sign, I realized I would be short on the hot meal, and in its place would be a lot of hot ass.

"Man, are we fucking lucky or what?" Bishop questioned as he slipped off his helmet.

I chuckled. "Only you, little brother, would find any luck in this situation."

"Oh, come on. We've been on the road for three days. What better way to unwind than to have a lap dance and a cold one?"

"Do I have to remind you that we're here on serious business?"

Bishop rolled his eyes. "Jesus, you're always such a hard-ass."

Ignoring him, I started across the gravel of the parking lot to the building. Two muscular men outfitted in Raiders cuts stood guard at the front door. At the sight of Bishop and me, smiles stretched across their hardened faces. The taller one stepped forward. "Prez said to be on the lookout for you guys."

Returning his smile, I threw out my hand. "I'm Reverend Malloy, and this is my brother Bishop."

"Snake, and that's Weasel," he replied, motioning to the other guy. "Great to meet you guys. Ya know, I slept over at your clubhouse a few years back after a run." He winked at me. "You Georgia boys sure know how to show your brothers a good time."

With a chuckle, I replied, "We sure as hell do."

Stepping in front of us, Snake pushed the door open. "Let me take you to Prez."

"Thanks, man."

As we entered the club, it reminded me of the Lounge—the strip club the Raiders owned back home. While it had once been a favorite hangout of Deacon's and it still remained one of Bishop's, I had never been overly fond of it. Maybe it was because it harbored bad memories for me. When I should have been old enough to know better, I had gone there searching for love and companionship. What I found was a girl who didn't just break my heart but shredded it with her claws. She saw me as her one-way ticket out of the stripping life and played me like a fool. It's one thing to be told your girl is cheating on you, but to walk in on her being hammered by one of your brothers is a whole other level of fucked-up. She got fired from the club and fled town, the brother got sent to another chapter after I worked him over good, and I got left with a whole lot of pain. Almost three years had passed, but I still wondered if I would remain alone forever.

There was only so much that could be done to an already broken and battered sense of trust.

Among the other patrons sitting at the bar were three men in Raiders cuts. At the sight of us, they rose off their barstools and started our way. One man, not much older than myself but with a head of white hair, stepped away from the others. "This is our president, Ghost Phillips," Snake said by way of introduction.

"Rev Malloy," I replied.

Ghost pumped my hand up and down. "Good to see you, man. I sure as hell wish it was under better circumstances."

"So do I."

Jerking his thumb behind him, Ghost said, "That's Undertaker and Chulo, our vice president and sergeant at arms."

I nodded at them. Ghost motioned to a table. "Have a seat. Let me get you two set up with some drinks."

Before I could argue that we didn't have time for drinks, Ghost had waved over a waitress. Reluctantly, I eased down into one of the chairs. Within seconds, I felt a hand on my shoulder. I glanced up as a leggy blonde dropped onto my lap, pressing her ample cleavage into my cut. When she began to grind her core against my crotch, my breath involuntarily caught in my chest. She flashed a smile at me. "Hey, baby, you look good enough to eat," she mused.

I jerked my gaze from her back up to Ghost. He winked at me. "We wanted to show you boys a little El Paso Raiders hospitality, so the girls are on the house. Besides, I figured you guys could use some unwinding after being on the road so long."

"Hell yeah," Bishop replied as he appreciatively took in the attention of the brunette girl rubbing against him.

I didn't share in Bishop's approval of the Raiders' show of hospitality. It angered me that Ghost and his men couldn't see the irony in the situation. Somewhere Sarah was being passed around to strange men for their enjoyment. Sure, the difference was these women were being paid and doing it of their own volition, and Sarah had no choice, but it still didn't sit well with me.

Shaking my head, I eased the blonde gently off my lap and onto her plastic heels. I took a few breaths to ensure that I could respond without alienating Ghost and his men. "That's kind of you, Ghost, but when it comes to Breakneck's daughter, I'm afraid we don't have any time to waste."

Ghost gave me a grim smile. "I get it, brother. I was just trying to make what I had to tell you a little easier to take."

My brows rose in suspicion. "You mean the news about Sarah is worse than we thought?"

He nodded. "Come on, let's go somewhere we can talk."

After Bishop reluctantly released his girl, we fell in step behind Undertaker and Chulo and made our way through the tables to the back of the club. Another hulking biker stood guard at the door. He jerked his chin at Ghost, and then stepped aside for us.

We followed Ghost down the dimly lit hallway to the last door on the left. When we got inside, I found an impressive mahogany table with ten chairs that must have worked well for short-notice meetings. After taking a seat across from Ghost, I began rapping my knuckles anxiously on the table.

"After hearing from you the other day, I immediately put out some feelers for our informants with ties to the Henchmen."

From inside his cut, Ghost produced a manila folder. He took out a glossy black-and-white picture and then shoved it across the table at me. I sucked in a breath. It was of Sarah. She was at some college bar, having drinks with friends. Across from her on a stool at the bar was a guy in a cut. I would've needed a magnifying glass to prove it for certain, but I was sure he was a Henchman. Apparently she had been on their radar if they had taken the time to photograph her.

After I flashed the picture at Bishop, he asked, "Can we use the picture to trace the guy?"

Ghost shook his head. "While it was one of the Henchmen who took her, she's no longer with them."

I leaned forward in my chair. "What do you mean she's not

with them? They're demanding ransom money from Breakneck for her return."

"The Henchmen don't make it their usual business to deal in human trafficking. But they have been known to abduct a girl or two to sell when they get into a bind with a rival club."

"Which club?"

Ghost winced. "The Diablos."

"Jesus Christ," I spat. It was one thing for Sarah to have been taken by the Henchmen. Although they were dangerous, they were still a low-ranking club in membership and without many allies. The Diablos, however, were in a whole other fucking realm.

Out of the top five mega clubs in the world, the Diablos were up there in the ranks with the Hells Angels and the Mongols. They were considered dangerous, not just by the FBI and the ATF—the department of Alcohol, Tobacco, Firearms and Explosives—but by other clubs as well. They drew their strength from their ties to some of the most powerful drug cartels in Mexico. They got off on the most extreme forms of torture, and they didn't give a shit if they had to take out women or kids to get what they wanted.

This was a game changer of epic proportions. "Are you absolutely sure she's with the Diablos?" I asked.

Undertaker nodded. "I have a contact at the border check. He confirmed that a girl matching Sarah's description was taken into Juárez yesterday morning."

Ghost took out another photograph and slid it across the table. "We received this photo earlier this afternoon."

Once again, Sarah's black-and-white image appeared before me. But this photo showed a shadow of the girl who had been talking and laughing in the other photo. Her eyes were cast down to her lap where her hands were clasped. Even through the photograph, her fear was palpable.

"But I thought the cartels were trafficking girls out of Mexico, not into it," Bishop said.

"This is the part you're not going to like," Ghost answered.

I grunted before telling him, "There's not one fucking thing about any of this that I like."

Ghost nodded at Chulo.

"It appears that upper-class white girls have become a growing commodity with high-ranking cartel members. The Diablos' El Paso chapter has been targeting college bars and campuses. Somewhere outside of Juárez, they have a camp where they house the girls before selling them to the highest bidder," Chulo said.

"Who owns the camp?" Bishop asked.

Chulo took a long swig of beer before replying. "Guy named Mendoza. He's one of the Rodriguez cartel's *lugartenientes*." At Bishop's and my blank expressions, he winked. "That's 'lieutenant' for you gringos."

I furrowed my brow in confusion. "Wait—so he's one of their soldiers?"

Shaking his head, Chulo explained, "Being *lugarteniente* makes him the second-highest position in the cartel. He supervises the lower levels like the hit men."

My mind whirling with questions, I couldn't help asking, "So if he's some second-in-command in the drug world, where does selling girls come into this?"

"Because of the recent crackdowns on the narcotic trade, human trafficking has become an easy way to supplement their income," Chulo replied.

As I digested this new information about Sarah's capture, I momentarily had to cradle my head in my hands. This was way beyond anything I had ever experienced as a club member, least of all as president. Not even Preacher Man or Case had ever come up against one of the cartels. They'd rationalized that the risks outweighed the benefits and steered clear of anything involving drugs.

"So we're pretty much fucked, huh?" Bishop said beside me.

Raising my head, I shot a hard glare at Bishop. "Maybe for the moment, but we're not letting Breakneck down."

"Glad to hear you say that," Undertaker replied.

I cut my gaze over to him. "What do you mean?"

With a wicked gleam in his eyes, Undertaker replied, "I mean, we're going to help you guys go in and get your girl."

I cocked my brows at him. "You're serious?"

"Fuck yeah."

Shaking my head, I replied, "While we appreciate it, we can't ask you to do that."

Chulo snorted. "And we're not asking for your approval. Besides, we have our own reasons."

"He's right," Ghost said before I could argue any further.

"What reason could you all possibly have for going up against the Diablos and the Rodriguez cartel?" I countered.

Ghost eased back in his seat. "For the last six months, the Diablos have been putting the heat on clubs throughout Texas and Louisiana to patch in with them."

"I guess I can assume that you all don't want to patch in," I said.

Ghost's blue eyes narrowed at me. "We would die first before we wore any other patch but the Raiders."

"Trust me, I can understand. But at the same time, I have to remind you what you're committing to."

"We're fucking aware," Undertaker replied.

I surveyed the stalwart expressions on the faces of the three men, and I realized then there was nothing I could do or say that was going to change their minds. Finally, I smiled at them. "Then I have to say I'm very grateful for your help."

Beside me, Bishop shifted in his chair. "Since Rev and I are fucking clueless about what to do, I sure as hell hope you guys have a plan as to how we're going to get into Mexico and go up against some second-in-command cartel lord."

Ghost chuckled. "Yeah, we have a plan."

"It better be some old-school A-Team or SEAL type of shit," Bishop countered, his expression saying he wasn't convinced of the El Paso Raiders' abilities.

Rising from his seat, Ghost narrowed his eyes at Bishop. "Trust us. We have a fucking plan."

TWO

ANNABEL
TWO MONTHS EARLIER

With a chart in my hand, I hurried down the hallway. As I opened the waiting room door, heads jerked up and anxious eyes met mine. "Herschel Greene?" I said after glancing once again at the chart.

An elderly woman in a faded pink polka-dot dress rose from her chair. At her feet, a pudgy American bulldog grumbled at being roused.

I smiled at the pair. "Come on back."

Mrs. Greene returned my smile, and then she and Herschel followed me down the hallway to one of the examining rooms. "I don't believe I've ever seen you here before. You must be new," she stated as her heels clicked steadily on the tile.

It wasn't the first time I had faced that question from one of the regulars since being hired at AMC (Animal Medical Center) in College Station. Each time I had to answer it, I felt a little more homesick. After all, I'd spent twenty-four years practically in the same place and among the same people. Mainly it was my group of friends I missed the most.

Back home in Virginia, I had never faced scrutiny for being a newcomer simply because everyone knew who I was. It's almost inescapable when your face is plastered all over campaign literature from the time you're a baby. Annabel Lee Percy, granddaughter of Hamilton Mullinax—former two-term governor, and daughter of Emmett Percy—current incumbent senator.

Pushing my homesickness aside, I replied, "You're right. I am new. This is my third week. I've just moved here to attend veterinary school at Texas A&M."

"Oh, how lovely."

I closed the exam room door behind us. "And what seems to be the problem today?"

With her lips turning down in a frown, Mrs. Greene gazed adoringly at the bulldog. "My Hershie is terribly sick. He can't seem to keep anything down."

As I started to make a note in the dog's chart, something caught my eye that made the rising apprehension fade and had me biting back a smile: "Mrs. Greene needs to be reminded that Herschel should not be fed high-fat treats like cake. Otherwise, no gastrointestinal problems can be found after extensive barium testing."

Glancing up at Mrs. Greene, I nodded. "Let me get Herschel's temperature and weight, and then one of the doctors will be in to see you."

"Herschel sure does like that Dr. Jenkins."

I smiled as I prepared the rectal thermometer. "Yes, Dr. Jenkins has a great bedside manner." After I realized that I sounded partial, I quickly replied, "Of course, doctors Santini and Baldwin do as well."

"Yes, but Dr. Jenkins is awfully handsome, isn't he?"

Her words caused me to freeze just before I violated Herschel with the thermometer. When I looked up at her, she gave me a knowing smile and then a wink. "Um, yes, I do suppose he's handsome." I quickly focused my attention on taking Herschel's temperature, which earned a yelp from the bulldog. Once the reading had been made, I said, "One hundred and one on the dot." When I met Mrs. Greene's apprehensive gaze, I smiled. "That's absolutely perfect."

She exhaled a relieved breath. "I'm glad to hear it."

After getting a reluctant Herschel on the scales, I recorded his weight. "It'll just be a moment for one of the doctors."

"Thank you, Miss . . . ?"

"Percy. I'm Annabel Percy."

"A lovely name for a lovely girl."

Now it was my turn to say thanks. Then I told her, "Be right back." Just as I started out the door, I literally ran into Dr. Jenkins. "Oomph," he muttered as I slammed into his chest.

"I'm so sorry," I said.

He chuckled. "It's okay, Annabel. I was actually coming to look for you."

My brows shot up in surprise. "You were?"

"I have a potential sedation case for vaccines. I was wondering if you could work your magic."

"Um, I can try."

"I would appreciate it, and I'm sure the owner would as well."

As I followed him down the hallway, I couldn't help feeling slightly empowered that Dr. Jenkins had sought me out. At the previous place where I'd worked, they jokingly called me the Pet Whisperer for my ability to calm animals down. Although I was often asked what my secret was, I wasn't actually aware of anything special that I did. I just seemed to connect with them when they were afraid or in pain.

When I entered the exam room, a kind-looking golden retriever was backed into the corner. At the sight of Dr. Jenkins and me, he bared his teeth and growled. Without another word from Dr. Jenkins, I went over to the dog and crouched down on his level. When I met his wary but aggressive gaze, I held it. Silently, I willed him to be calm, to relax, and to trust the doctor.

As the dog continued holding my stare, Dr. Jenkins picked up the syringes on the exam table and then slowly walked around to the dog's back flank. He was able to administer the shots without a growl or even a whimper from the animal. When the doctor was done, the dog backed away.

Tentatively, I reached out my hand. After the dog sniffed it, I started to pat the top of his head. His tail wagged appreciatively. "There. You're all done."

"That's amazing," the owner said, wide-eyed.

Dr. Jenkins smiled. "It certainly is. I've never seen anyone with such a gift."

Like a true redhead, I wore my embarrassment on my cheeks. "I'm just glad I could help."

After seeing a handful of four-legged patients, it was time to leave for the day. Grabbing my purse, I headed to the door, only to find Dr. Jenkins blocking my exit.

He gave me a genuine smile. "Annabel, I just wanted to say thank you again for today. You have become such an asset to this practice."

I fought hard not to start blushing again. "Thank you, Dr. Jenkins. It means a lot to hear you say that."

"Josh," he said. "You can call me Josh."

With a smile, I replied, "Thank you, Josh."

We stood in an awkward silence as we seemed to tiptoe along the line of whether to continue being professional or shift into more personal territory. It had been this way almost since the day I first met Josh Jenkins. He didn't look at me the same way the other doctors did, and to be truthful, I looked at him differently, too.

Dr. Jenkins finally cleared his throat and stepped aside. "Well, uh, have a good evening."

"Thank you. Same to you."

Once I escaped through the door, I had to fight the urge to skip out to my car. All my life I had dreamed of becoming a veterinarian, much to the disapproval of my parents. Coming from a political family, they didn't see how being a vet could benefit my father's career or my future husband's. It went without saying that said future husband would come from one of the finest social circles. My parents would have found my interest in Dr. Jenkins appalling.

I hadn't been groomed for future political office like my older sister, Lenore. After graduating top of her class from Harvard Law, she would be the next senator or political representative from our family. Conversely, I was the pretty face whose soft-spoken charm was considered far more Jackie Kennedy than Hillary Clinton. In my parents' eyes, my one goal in life should have been to marry well and offer support to my future husband's political career.

But while they had always underestimated my talents, I had silently pursued them. After graduating with a 4.0 in biology from the University of Virginia, I shocked my parents by going through with graduate school applications in veterinary medicine. While I had originally been accepted and begun coursework at the University of Virginia, I found myself itching to spread my wings and be independent. At first my parents would hear nothing of the sort. The only way I had finally convinced them to pay for my continued education away from home was to appease them by going to Texas A&M. Their choice had nothing to do with the fact that it was one of the top ten veterinary schools in the country. No, it was about what a politically important state Texas was.

As I slid into my car, my phone began to ring. Glancing at the caller ID, I groaned. "Speak of the devil," I muttered. It was the one person sure to kill the happy buzz I was feeling. "Hi, Mother," I said, forcing myself to sound pleased to talk to her.

"Hello, darling. I just wanted to call and check in. Daddy and I were wondering how Texas was treating you." Regardless of the miles and miles between us, I could still register the fake concern in my mother's voice. Considering that she had yet to call me to see how I was doing after the move, I knew there was a more self-serving purpose for her call—one that involved my plans for the evening.

"You mean you just wanted to call to make sure Preston Bradford and I were still going out tonight."

My mother's trill of a laugh grated on my last nerve. "Okay, fine, you caught me. I was dying to know if it was still on."

My parents, along with their close friends the Bradfords, who lived in Houston, relished the fantasy that Preston and I were going to get married, not only uniting two political powerhouse families but also producing the marriage of the future president and first lady. I'm not sure how they had made the quantum leap from Preston and me merely talking to wedding bells, but if it kept them off my back for any length of time, I was willing to indulge them.

"Yes. He's picking me up at seven."

"That's absolutely wonderful. I knew there was a spark between you two at the Bradfords' Fourth of July party."

I snorted. "The only spark between us at the party was when he accidentally caught my bathing suit cover-up on fire." If Preston were ever elected president, he would probably outdo Gerald Ford in the clumsy department. It had been far too early in the party for him to use the excuse of being drunk. Instead, he could only blame himself for tripping over a chair and collapsing on a table, which knocked off a candle that hit the hem of my caftan. The only reason I hadn't entirely written him off that day was because of how sincere he was when he apologized and how kind he was by looking after me for the rest of the party.

"For goodness' sake, don't mention that tonight. He gets enough teasing from his family about his clumsiness. The last thing he needs is to hear it from a date."

Rolling my eyes, I said, "I wouldn't dream of it, Mother. You know, I do know how to carry on a meaningful conversation with a man. You do remember sending me to summer finishing school, don't you?"

"Yes, yes, of course. I just don't want you saying or doing anything to turn him off. He's already so accepting of the fact you plan to have a career."

"I *will* have a career," I corrected.

My mother's exasperated sigh told me she was maxed out with me being "petulant," as she called it. "Yes, well, just have fun. Okay?"

"Thank you. I'll try."

"And let Daddy and me know how it went as soon as you can."

"Mother, I'm twenty-four, not sixteen."

"Annabel"— my mother's voice rose an octave—"just humor us, okay?"

"Fine, fine," I muttered, feeling the onset of the usual headache that accompanied talking to my mother.

"Good-bye, then."

"Good-bye." I hung up and tossed the phone onto the seat.

I battled rush-hour traffic across town to my apartment, then hurried inside to get ready. After a quick shower, I stood in front of my closet, trying to decide what to wear. Normally a first date called for something sexy, but in this case I didn't figure Preston and his overly conservative background would appreciate it. I decided on a pair of jeans, a dressy green top, and heels, and had just finished with my makeup and hair when the doorbell rang.

When I threw open the door, Preston, looking preppie and

polished in a polo shirt and khakis, gave me a beaming smile. "Annabel, it's so good to see you again."

Returning his smile, I said, "It's good seeing you again, too."

His blue eyes surveyed me apprehensively. "You know, after our first disastrous meeting at my parents', I was afraid you might not want to ever be seen with me again."

I groaned inwardly but managed to wave my hand dismissively. I had to wonder how socially inept he was to even bring that up. "That was nothing. I'm glad to have a chance to get to know you better."

Preston seemed to appreciate my well-thought-out answer. "Let's go to dinner, then. I was thinking Pacey's."

I was a little surprised at his choice, but I didn't let my expression reflect it. Pacey's was a college bar and hot spot right off campus. It didn't exactly scream romance, but I guess it was a safe bet for a first date. He knew his way around campus since he was a political science major.

"Sounds great."

Once we got to Pacey's, a waitress led us to a somewhat secluded booth. Just as I picked up my menu, I felt a prickly sensation run up my spine that someone was looking at me. When I glanced up at the bar, I locked eyes with a drop-dead good-looking guy. His jet-black hair was cut short, highlighting his chiseled jaw, covered in scruff, along with a pair of full, highly kissable lips. Even though he was sitting down, I could tell he was impossibly tall by the way his legs folded on the barstool. His chest muscles bulged under the white T-shirt he wore.

Over the shirt was a leather vest of some kind. I think they were called cuts. I had seen them before on television but never in person. The cut, with its sewn-on patches, was something bikers wore. Before I could stop myself, I licked my lips. My reaction caused a sexy grin to stretch across his face. When he winked at me, I quickly ducked my head and went back to examining my menu.

"What sounds good?" Preston asked. And it was then that I had the reality check that I was ogling some strange man not five feet from the man I was out on a date with. I vowed then and there to keep my attention on my date.

But as soon as the appetizer came and conversation between us became stilted, I found my gaze returning to the stranger at the bar. Each time I looked at him, he was looking at me. The more I took in his bad-boy appearance, the more I couldn't help thinking about what it would be like to kiss him.

When it came to men, I'd always played it safe. I'd dated the good guys—the future-husband types. But deep down, I'd never really been satisfied by those types. The number of sexual partners I'd had could be counted on one hand—and none of them had ever made me lose my mind in the bedroom. The one thing I fantasized about was having one uninhibited sexual experience so that in years to come, I could look back on it with a blush on my cheeks and a rush of warmth between my legs.

As dinner progressed, I realized Preston would never be the one to deliver that mind-altering sexual experience. So I was more than a little relieved when the waitress brought our check.

"Yo, Preston," a booming voice called behind us.

Preston whirled around and his face broke into a wide grin. "Hey, guys." He rose to do the manly hug/backslap thing with the three guys standing there. "Perfect timing. Annabel and I just finished dinner."

My brows furrowed at his statement. "I'm sorry?"

A slight flush tinged Preston's cheeks. "Oh, um, you don't mind hanging out a little longer to watch the game, do you? The guys and I kinda have a Monday-night tradition."

Nibbling on my lip, I fought the urge to either laugh maniacally or burst into tears at the situation I found myself in. Instead of having an actual date, I had been worked in to accommodate Preston's schedule. If I had had any ideas about Preston's and my romantic future, they would have fled in that moment.

Forcing a smile, I said, "Sure. That will be fine. As long as we're not out too late. I have an eight o'clock class in the morning." I held my tongue on the fact that I hated football with a fiery passion.

"Of course," Preston replied.

"Okay. Sounds good." As I rose from the booth, I once again caught the stranger's gaze. Cocking his brow at me, he seemed to be issuing some sort of challenge. I cut my eyes away from his and looked at Preston. "Give me a few minutes. I'm going to run to the bathroom."

"No problem." He leaned in and bestowed a chaste kiss on my cheek before turning to follow the guys to the game room. With a sigh, I picked up my purse and started for the bathroom.

Just as I was passing the sexy stranger at the bar, his arm reached out and grabbed mine. "Excuse me?" I demanded as I slung his arm away.

"Don't let that uptight prick ruin your evening. Sit down—have a beer with me. You deserve a night with a real man."

The tug-of-war between politeness and temptation raged in my mind. "Thank you for the offer, but I don't think so."

"You know, I haven't been able to take my eyes off you all night."

My brows shot up, and with a teasing smile, I said, "You should work on your pick-up lines because that one is kinda creepy."

He threw his head back and laughed. "Yeah, I guess it is." His dark eyes twinkled. "You're a ballbuster, aren't you?"

I shrugged. "Maybe."

"You know what, ballbuster?"

"What?"

"You've been checking me out just as much." A wicked gleam burned in his dark eyes. "Since I'm not a gentleman, I would say you've been eye-fucking me all night."

I crossed my arms over my chest. "Oh, is that right?"

When he leaned in closer to me, his breath scorched my cheek. Almost involuntarily, my eyes closed at his proximity. I hated the feelings he was eliciting in me, but at the same time I wanted to savor them and explore them. "You want to know what it's like to be with someone like me—a biker. A good girl like you wants to know if all the rumors are true."

"You're pretty sure of yourself."

He grinned. "As sure as the wet panties you're sporting right now."

My eyes widened, and I stared at him. "No one has ever talked to me that way before." Secretly, I loved the boldness of his filthy talk. It made me wonder what would come out of his mouth next.

"And you love it." When I started to protest, he shook his head. "Come on and let me buy you a drink, ballbuster."

Nibbling my lip, I stared at the entrance to the game room. Everything in me said this was a bad idea. That I should make my way back to Preston as soon as possible. But I had always taken the safe route, and I was sick of it.

"Don't worry about him. He's already so into the game he's forgotten he had the finest piece of ass he'll ever have sitting across from him."

"Do you have a bike?"

His brows rose in surprise. "Hell yeah, I have a bike. A fucking Harley-Davidson Dyna Super Glide Sport."

This was it. Now-or-never time. "Then take me for a ride."

"You're serious?"

I nodded. "I've never been on a motorcycle before."

He laughed. "That doesn't surprise me at all, babe."

Thinking about Preston's disregard for my feelings gave me fuel to keep going. "So will you take me home?"

"You're not waiting on your boyfriend?"

"He isn't my boyfriend. And no, I'm not."

The guy rose from the barstool. "Then let's get the hell out of here."

"Wait—I don't even know your name."

"It's Johnny."

"And I'm Annabel." As I fell in step behind him, I couldn't help wondering whether this decision was a good one.

THREE

ANNABEL

My anxious feelings quickly disappeared. I'm not sure I had ever felt anything so freeing as being on the back of Johnny's motorcycle. Any fear I'd had about riding on a bike faded. With the wind rippling through my hair and clothing, I closed my eyes and snuggled closer to Johnny.

In that moment, I enjoyed the freedom of the open road. I didn't allow myself to worry what my parents would think about me being with some blue-collar stranger or how appalled they would be by my reckless behavior. Inwardly, I chuckled at what Preston's face would look like when he realized I had ditched him. Would he even acknowledge he had been thoughtless? I wondered if he would buy some lame excuse that I'd had a friend take me home.

When the bike started to slow down, I raised my head from Johnny's back. My brows furrowed in confusion as we pulled into the parking lot of a run-down motel. I had given him directions to my house, so I wasn't sure what we were doing in this part of town.

After Johnny eased up to the curb, he killed the engine and put the kickstand down.

I slipped off my helmet. "What are we doing here?"

Johnny glanced at me over his shoulder. "Thought we'd go inside and get to know each other a little better."

Instantly, my stomach twisted into apprehensive knots. The reality of the repercussions of my decision crashed down on me. While I might have been extremely attracted to Johnny, I certainly wasn't ready to sleep with him. Deep down, I should have known he would have expected more for taking me for a ride. "I really don't think that's a good idea."

"Why not?" Johnny asked, his brows shooting up in surprise.

"Because I barely know you."

"Then give me a chance to get to know you."

I shook my head. "No, you don't understand. You see, I don't have sex with a guy I just met."

Giving me his most seductive smile, Johnny countered, "Maybe I can change your mind."

I swallowed the rising fear in my throat and willed myself not to panic. "Look, I'm sorry if I led you on, but you were just supposed to take me for a motorcycle ride and then take me home." My eyes scanned the desolate parking lot, and more than anything, I wished that there were people around. "So I would really appreciate it if you would take me home now."

Johnny's dark eyes narrowed at me. "I'm afraid I can't do that, darlin'."

"W-Why not?" I asked as a chill ran down my spine.

At that moment, the door to the room in front of us swung open. Three hulking men loomed in the doorway. They all wore motorcycle cuts like Johnny's. "Whatcha score tonight?" one guy with waist-length dark hair called.

I glanced from them back to Johnny. "What's going on?" I

questioned lamely. In the back of my mind, I had already come up with the frightening answer. More than anything, I knew I needed to get away from Johnny. I needed to get my phone and call 911.

"Sorry, darlin'. But you're going to make me an awful lot of money."

Without further thought, I scrambled off the motorcycle and started sprinting away from Johnny and his friends as fast as I could. Although I could barely run in my heels, my fear pushed me harder and harder. I'd almost reached the motel office when strong arms grabbed my waist. As I was jerked back against Johnny's body, his breath burned in my ear. "Don't you even think about running again, bitch!"

I opened my mouth to scream, but the bite of a needle pierced the skin on my neck, silencing me. The raging fight I'd had within me succumbed to the drugs pumping through my system. As my eyelids drooped, I felt my feet leave the pavement, and I began to float.

My body felt like a buoy bobbing along the ocean waves. One minute I was outside gazing up at the darkened sky and the next I was in a hotel room. As I was lowered down onto something hard, my eyelids fluttered, but no matter how hard I tried, I couldn't wake myself up.

Conversation floated above me. I began to feel like I was in a coma— that level of consciousness where you are aware of your surroundings, but you can do nothing about it.

"I did good tonight, right, boys?" Johnny asked. Just the sound of his voice now caused my skin to crawl. Gone was any attraction I had once felt for him. Instead, I loathed him for the monster he was—a true wolf in sheep's clothing.

A hand gripped my jaw and roughly turned my head from side to side. "She's a little older than the usual pick," a different man said.

Johnny grunted. "Yeah, well, she was at Pacey's like all the other girls. I don't take the fucking time to ask if they're eighteen. I go on looks and personality, and she's the best looker I've picked in months."

A cruel laugh came from my left side. "I'll agree with you on that one. Mendoza's gonna cream his pants when he sees her. Just his type. Probably keep her all for himself."

"Then I suggest we take some now while we still have the chance," I heard Johnny say.

In that moment, I floated outside of myself. Self-preservation? It felt as if I were standing on train tracks, staring down a charging locomotive. With one foot stuck in the tracks and the other scrambling to find freedom, I could do nothing but watch my impending demise.

Then rough hands were all over me—stripping me of my clothes, touching me in intimate places that brought stinging tears of humiliation to my eyes. Excruciating pain soon replaced the humiliation as I was physically torn and battered. There seemed to be no end—I was trapped in a strange alternate universe of degradation and assault.

And there, in a seedy hotel room while I was gang-raped repeatedly by four strange men, the old Annabel died in a nightmare she never could have fathomed. Her broken spirit slipped away while her ravaged body was forced to go on in a horrific world, alone and hopeless.

FOUR

REV

The van jolted and jostled us over the uneven terrain as we drove farther and farther into no-man's-land. Glancing out the window, I took in the moonless night and our dark isolation from civilization.

It seemed unbelievable that less than forty-eight hours ago I had sat at a table in the Rising Phoenix and listened to the El Paso Raiders' attack plan. While I had first been skeptical that they had the resources to take on a cartel lieutenant, they had quickly made me a believer. I had felt more than confident in tonight's mission and was sure that soon Breakneck would be reunited with his daughter.

Now I threw a glance over my shoulder into the third row, where Breakneck sat next to Bishop. He had flown in yesterday to be a part of the rescue mission. At first, Ghost hadn't wanted him to come along. "He's too emotionally invested—it'll fuck things up." But Breakneck had gone toe-to-toe with him to veto any ideas about him staying back at the Raiders' compound. In the end, I didn't know what physical condition we were going to find Sarah in, so it made sense to have someone with medical training along.

Because we couldn't just go storming into a cartel compound half-cocked, it had taken a full day of further research and planning before we felt ready to move. Thankfully, the El Paso Raiders had set the wheels in motion while Bishop and I were on the road. They also had a lot of allies who were willing to get us intel. The room in their roadhouse where they held church looked more like something out of a Pentagon war strategy session as we spent hours poring over maps, aerial images, and printouts from Google Earth.

What we had learned from the Raiders' sources was that Mendoza ran a relatively small-time trafficking operation. He never housed more than five or six girls at a time before "unloading" them, as it was known. Because of the low numbers, he had fewer than ten men working for him at the compound. With our group of nine in the mission, we were pretty evenly matched.

The location of Mendoza's slave camp was about fifty miles from any semblance of civilization. The gravel road we now found ourselves on seemed to stretch into a desert oblivion. Close on our tail were two other identical, black-paneled vans. One carried the remaining members of our mission, and the other was loaded down with enough explosives to take out the wired, steel-enforced gate at the front of Mendoza's compound.

"Fuck, I wanna claw my skin off. I think I'm allergic to this fucking war paint!" Bishop exclaimed, breaking the tense silence. As a form of camouflage, each of us had slathered black shoe polish onto his face, neck, and arms.

Despite the tense mood, I chuckled. "Jesus, you're as bad as when you had the chicken pox. Mama and Pop didn't sleep for three days trying to make sure you didn't scratch yourself to death."

"Whatever," Bishop grumbled.

When the van began slowing down, I sat up a little straighter. Chulo turned around in the passenger seat to face us. "Okay, guys, here is where we leave the vans for safekeeping. We'll do the last half mile on foot. Then once the front gate is blown, the reserve vans will pull up to wait for us."

With a nod of my head, I reached for the handle of the door. Once I slid it open, I dropped out onto the soft desert floor. Breakneck came next, with Bishop behind him. They were followed by Ranger and Nero, two of the El Paso Raiders who had been appointed to come with us based on their skills.

At six foot five and three hundred pounds, Ranger got his road name from his time with the Army Rangers. After two tours in Afghanistan, he came home to his MC brothers and worked out his extreme PTSD by beating the hell out of anyone who crossed the Raiders' path. Like a true Army Ranger, he was our lead man into the compound.

Nero, a scrappy Italian originally from Jersey, had stepped forward to be our explosives expert. With his bottlecap-thick glasses, he looked more like a tech nerd than a tough biker. But any doubt I had in his abilities faded the first time he showed us a test run of one of his homemade bombs. I knew then he was truly an asset to have along.

"He stays with the vans," Chulo said, pointing to Breakneck.

Even in the darkness, I could see Breakneck's fists clenching at his sides. "I'm going to find my daughter."

"You won't be any help to her if you get your ass shot," Chulo challenged.

I placed my hand on Breakneck's shoulder. "It's for the best if you stay here. If this goes bad, we're all going to need you in one piece, not just Sarah."

"Fuck," Breakneck muttered under his breath. After a few tense seconds, he nodded and then slipped back into the van.

Once we checked our weapons and were ready, Chulo ordered, "All right. Let's go."

As I ran across the rugged desert terrain, it brought back memories of my one tour in Afghanistan. Just out of high school, I had signed on for a two-year term in the army. It was the shortest one I could do where I actually got out of town, but I would still not be gone long from the Raiders. It wasn't so much a great sense of patriotism or that I felt I needed molding into a man as it was about getting money for school. Of course, in the end, I got only a two-year degree at the local technical college before Preacher Man was on me to step up and take more responsibility in the club.

As far as suffering from PTSD, the lifestyle I had known before I went into service had prepared me to deal with the horrors of war. That said, it didn't mean I didn't occasionally have a nightmare that brought me shouting up off the bed in a sweaty mess. In the end, the nightmares were just a few more to add to an ever-increasing pile. I was pretty sure any shrink who ever got a look inside my fucked-up head would make a run for it.

Just ahead of us was the row of tightly woven shrubbery that sat about twenty feet from the front gate. After seeing it on a map, Chulo had decided it would be our rendezvous point. Once we were all accounted for, Chulo radioed the weapons van. As I gripped my assault rifle tighter, I tried to still the erratic beating of my heart. Adrenaline had it pumping overtime. There was nothing left to do now but wait for the van to arrive and for the explosives to truly set our plan in motion.

When the van came into view, I drew in a sharp breath. Just as it got to the line of shrubbery, the driver's side door was thrown open and one of the El Paso Raiders jumped out. The van's gas pedal was rigged to keep accelerating. Just as it was about to hit the gate, gunfire broke out, riddling the hood with bullet holes. But it was all in vain.

The moment it smashed into the steel, the van exploded in an orange ball of fire, taking out a section of the gate.

"Now!" Chulo shouted.

I sprang out from behind the shrubbery to get behind Ranger. With his gun cocked, he kicked down another part of the gate that was hanging precariously by one hinge. As it collapsed, he motioned us to follow him. The moment I entered Mendoza's courtyard, I felt like I had been transported back into the service. Everything seemed executed with military precision.

Immediately gunfire rained down on us. Crouching, we returned fire until we took out the two targets and the only sound in the compound was the bellowing alarm.

"Go on. I'll cover you guys," Ranger said.

"Rev, you, Nero, and Snake take the house," Chulo ordered.

"Okay."

"We'll take the back bunker," Chulo said, nodding at Bishop and two others.

With Nero and Snake at my side, we hurried across the courtyard. When we got to the veranda, gunshots went off behind us. Glancing over my shoulder, I saw Ranger taking out three men who were rushing toward him. I had no idea how, with those odds, the fucker managed not to get hit.

Using brute force, Snake kicked in the front door while Nero and I covered him. When we met no opposition, we headed into the foyer. With its marble floors, crystal chandeliers, and expensive art, it was evident what drug money could buy, and Mendoza certainly enjoyed the finer things in life. Nero cleared his throat, then said, "Okay, how about I make a sweep of the front. Rev, you take the hallway and bedrooms, and Snake, you take the middle."

"Sounds good," I replied.

I advanced out of the foyer and past the living room. When I started down the hallway and came around the corner, a hail of gunfire met me. I ducked into an open bedroom. In the darkness, I took a knife out of my belt. Pressing myself against the wall, I listened to the sound of boots clomping down the hallway. As the gunman entered the doorway, I plunged the knife into his chest. The hit momentarily disabled him. Grabbing him by the shoulders, I shoved him against the wall and wrestled away control of his weapon.

"Where is the American woman?" I demanded.

"Fuck. You."

Pressing my knife against his throat, I growled, "The *gringa* with red hair. Where is she?"

When he shook his head defiantly, the seething anger racing through me reached a volatile point—one where I no longer saw reason. Since he was of no use to me, I plunged the knife into the man's throat. After severing his artery, I released him, letting him drop to the floor.

Sputtering and convulsing, he began to bleed out over the white marble floor. As I stared down at the man in disgust, rage filled me. Although I should have reined myself in, I couldn't stop myself from kicking him over and over again in the gut and groin.

Once the man was still, I jerked my knife out of his neck. Since I could always use another weapon, I took his rifle and swung it over my shoulder. Just as I started out of the bedroom, a low moan caused me to whirl around. The room had appeared empty when I looked inside. As my gaze flicked around the room, another moan came from the other side of the room. With my finger on my gun's trigger, I started slowly across the marble floor. When I got around the side of the bed, I was met with the sight of a pool of blood and a female body.

"Jesus Christ," I muttered at the sight of the crumpled form in front of me. Shifting my guns, I dropped to the floor. It was a woman wearing only a man's white dress shirt. Besides the blood, her body was black and blue with bruises. Someone had done a real number on her. It was obvious she had been left to die.

My hand froze after I'd reached to push the strands of auburn hair out of the girl's face. Sarah had auburn hair. Was it possible that I had unknowingly found her? Could it be this easy?

"Sarah?" I questioned. "Sarah?" My tone had grown frantic. Her swollen eyelids fluttered at the sound of my voice. "Are you Sarah Edgeway?"

"Annabel," she whispered.

It felt like a harsh kick to the gut that it wasn't Sarah. But at the same time, I knew I had to save this girl. Drawing her to me, I slid one of my arms under her back and the other under her legs. When I eased us off the floor, she cried out in pain. "I'm sorry. I'm going to get you help. I promise."

She surprised me by opening her eyes and gazing up at me. "J-Jesus?" she croaked.

It took me a moment to process that with my unkempt hair and beard I'd made her think of the religious figure. At the hopeful look in her bloodshot eyes, I felt terrible for having to let her down. "No, I'm Rev," I said lamely.

My words seemed to be of little comfort to her as she grimaced in pain. "Hurts."

"I know. Stay with me. I'm going to get you out of here."

When I got to the doorway, I stuck my head out and peered left and right. It appeared to be clear, so I started out of the bedroom. Cradling the girl in my arms made it a little more difficult to make our way through the maze of rooms.

Just as I got to the doorway of the house, the stinging bite of a bullet pierced my left calf. "Motherfucker," I groaned before whirling around. The moment I saw it wasn't one of our guys who might've shot in mistake, I started firing. I clipped the guy in the shoulder, sending him crashing to the ground.

Throwing open the front door, I waited for any gunfire in response. When everything remained silent, I eased out onto the veranda. Peering into the night, I saw one of the relief vans sitting outside the gates. My left leg dragged slightly behind me as I hustled as fast as I could. I was halfway across the courtyard when an explosion rocketed through the compound, sending me crashing to the ground.

The next few seconds ticked by agonizingly, as if the world had slowed to a crawl. The blast had robbed me of my hearing, and I struggled with the feeling of having cotton in my ears. Gradually, I heard a chorus of agonized screams along with various voices yelling.

"Come on, Rev," someone said at my side. I glanced up to see Chulo standing over me. He grabbed my arm and helped hoist me up. I then bent over and picked up the girl. "Fuck, man. You've been hit."

"It ain't bad. She's in worse shape," I replied.

"You sure you got her?"

I nodded. "You just cover our asses, so I don't get nailed again."

"You got it."

Carrying Annabel with my wounded leg seemed to take forever to get through the gate. Just as we reached the van, Breakneck came running over to us. "You found her?" he asked, his face lighting up.

His question caused my chest to tighten in agony. I didn't know how I was going to kill his hope. Finally, I shook my head. "No, man, this isn't Sarah. I found her in Mendoza's private quarters. She's been beaten almost to death."

Breakneck's face fell. "It's not my Sarah?"

"I'm so sorry. Maybe one of the others has her."

Shouts and gunfire tore our attention to what was happening beyond the gate. Our group of men came around the corner of the house. Some were running, while others were barely limping along. Most were covered in blackened soot and ash.

"What the fuck happened?" I demanded.

"The bunker where he kept the girls . . ." Bishop shook his head. "It was rigged with explosives. The second we got through the alarm system, someone blew it all up."

I closed my eyes. It was a fucking coward's defense strategy. Destroy the evidence of your crimes when you were about to get caught. In this case, Mendoza sacrificed the lives of the young women for no reason at all.

When I opened my eyes, I saw that Breakneck was staring wide-eyed at the flames billowing into the night sky. It was painful to watch as the realization washed over him. An agonized cry tore from his lips as he sank to his knees on the ground. To come this far only to lose Sarah in the end was brutal.

"Okay, boys, let's get the fuck out of here before the reinforcements arrive," Chulo ordered.

With anguished eyes, Breakneck whirled around. "No. We can't leave. Sarah's still in there."

Bishop placed a hand on Breakneck's back. "I'm sorry, man. She's gone."

"You don't know that. We don't know unless we find her body."

Chulo grunted in frustration. "Listen, man, you forget any idea about going back for her body because there ain't nothing left. That place was wired so tight the feds won't find a scrap of anything. You get me?"

Although a look of defeat flashed across Breakneck's face, he didn't respond. He once again resumed staring at the flames.

Glancing down at the girl in my arms, I said, "Chulo, we need a hospital for her."

"And for you," he replied.

"You were hit?" Bishop questioned.

"It's nothing."

"Yeah, well, that nothing looks like it's bleeding pretty bad," Nero observed.

"Whatever." With the girl weighing heavy in my arms, I went to get her settled in the van. When I started to ease her down on the seat, I noticed the blood pooling down her thighs. "Jesus," I muttered. Whirling around, I grabbed Breakneck's arm. "Forget about me. She's hemorrhaging or something."

Breakneck threw a glance at Annabel before returning his stare to the inferno at the compound. "I . . . I can't."

Grabbing him by the shoulders, I shoved him into the side of the van. "Listen to me. I'm sorry we didn't get to Sarah in time. I'm sorry that you lost her. But you can't shut down. We've got a girl who needs your help."

Breakneck shoved me away. "Fuck you!"

"Guys, we gotta move. *Now*," Chulo said.

The second van cranked up its engine. I shook my head at Breakneck. "What about your fucking Hippocratic oath, huh?"

Breakneck glared at me. "My little girl was just murdered, you bastard. I don't give a shit about anyone else. You can fucking bleed out for all I care."

"You think this is what Sarah would want? You think she would be proud her old man was refusing to treat someone—a girl who had been through the same hell she had?"

Breakneck refused to look at me. Instead, he was staring at something on the girl's hand. He brushed past me to go over to her. He took her hand in his and then brought it closer to his face. "This was Sarah's."

My brows rose in surprise. "Maybe this girl and Sarah were friends."

Breakneck gently laid the girl's hand on her chest. He exhaled an anguished breath. Glancing over his shoulder at Chulo, he said, "We need the closest hospital or clinic. With that bleeding, coupled with whatever internal injuries she's sustained, she's got maybe an hour. I need to get in and stop the bleeding."

Chulo glanced from Breakneck to me. "Thirty miles up the road there's a hospital. It ain't much, and it sure as hell ain't no trauma center."

"I'll make do," Breakneck replied.

"One good thing is most of the staff can be bribed, and we're going to need that for sure," Chulo said.

"Fine. Let's go," I replied.

As we started the van, I surveyed Breakneck one last time. With muscles taut throughout his body, the heart-wrenching agony was written over his face as well. His baby girl was dead. Murdered. It was likely that the finality of Sarah's death would leave him a broken man. For our mission not to have been completely in vain, Annabel had to live.

With a swift nod in his direction, I tried to convey to Breakneck all my unspoken sympathy along with my thanks.

He shook his head. "Don't be thanking me yet. She's got a helluva long way to go to survive." Although there was doubt in his voice, there was also a hint of firm resolve.

FIVE

ANNABEL

As I floated back into consciousness, a sigh escaped my lips. The excruciating pain that had cloaked me was gone. While I appreciated the blessed relief, a sudden panic seeped into my pores. Did the newfound peace mean I was dead?

Prickly fear crept from the top of my head down to my feet, and I shivered. My groggy mind whirled with questions. Where was I? What had happened to me? When I tried desperately to widen my eyes to see where I was, they would only open halfway. They felt too swollen to fully open.

Just as I struggled to remember what had caused my eyes to swell, the events of the last few hours came racing back to me. Mendoza's face masked in rage, his fists flying in fury, and his harsh words, "I'll kill you for letting another man's name come off your lips."

When a bright, blinding light snapped on above me, a hoarse scream broke across my busted lips. Any peace I had felt was fleeting as I realized I wasn't in heaven. Instead, I was surely back in hell. But as I started thrashing around, I realized I wasn't in Mendoza's quarters. I was laid out on a hard table. Once an antiseptic smell entered my nose, I couldn't help wondering if I was in a hospital.

"It's okay, sweetheart. No one is going to hurt you."

I froze at the kind words, which were spoken with such care. Fluttering my eyelids, I managed to open my eyes enough to see someone I didn't recognize in front of me. He didn't wear a Diablo's cut. Instead, he was outfitted in medical scrubs. As if he could sense my fear and the questions I had racing through my mind, he said in a low, kind voice, "My name is Dr. Edgeway. One of my men found you back at the compound. You were hurt badly, and you needed surgery to save your life."

Vaguely I remembered men arriving at the compound. Even though I had been in such agony, I remembered the chaos around me—the screaming, the explosions, the loud, threatening voices. But Mendoza had beaten me so badly I couldn't do anything but lie on the floor and await my fate. Just as I felt myself fading, I had seen Jesus. He had gotten me out of Mendoza's quarters. My savior had told me his name. I racked my brain to try to remember it. Finally it came to me.

"Rev?" I questioned.

The doctor's brows shot up in surprise. "He's just outside. If you want him, I'll have him come in."

For reasons I couldn't understand, I wanted the stranger with me. "Please."

He nodded. As he turned to the door, the room began to grow darker. I fought hard to stay awake to see my savior. When I saw him framed in the doorway, I couldn't fight any longer, and I once again fell under the harsh tide.

When I resurfaced, I found myself in a darkened room. Relief flooded me as I imagined I must've made it out of surgery. When I shifted in bed, pain tore through my abdomen, causing me to gasp. A warm hand met mine, and I immediately jerked away, recoiling from the touch. I could hear the panic in the muffled cry of apprehension that escaped my lips. Who was touching me? Where was Dr. Edgeway? I didn't like the nearly constant uncertainty I now felt.

"Shh, Annabel, it's okay. I'm not going to hurt you."

That voice. It didn't belong to the doctor from before, but somehow it was still familiar to me. Slowly I turned my head on the pillow, searching through the darkness for him. A light flicked on over my head, and I was finally able to see him. His kind blue eyes met mine, and they instantly eased some of the fear. The striking color seemed such a contrast to his mahogany hair. He sat in an uncomfortable-looking chair pulled up against the bed. In the silence, I drank in his comforting appearance—his long, jeans-encased legs, the T-shirt that appeared to be covered in blood or dirt, his shoulder-length hair that was swept back from the face that gave me a reassuring smile, his broad chest.

When I realized we were alone in the room, sharp jabs of fear prickled over my skin. My rational mind told me to be frightened of him. He was a stranger—a strange man at that. He towered over me with muscles that could inflict great harm. But everything I needed to know about him was in his eyes. Searching them showed me that he was a gentle giant, and he seemed like someone that I could trust.

At what must've seemed like my continued apprehension, Rev held his hands up. "I'm not going to hurt you, I swear. As long as I have a breath in me, no one is ever going to hurt you again. You're safe."

I stared at him, weighing his words. "Y-You saved me," I whispered.

"I guess you could say that," he replied. I was shocked when he shyly ducked his head. The reaction seemed so foreign from the tough-guy persona he exuded.

"You got me away from Mendoza and that horrible place."

"Yeah, I did."

"So you saved me, and I'd like to thank you."

He glanced up to give me a sad smile. "You're welcome."

When I tried pushing myself up in bed, pain once again charged through my midsection like a locomotive, causing me to wince. "Do you need more pain medicine?" Rev asked.

"No!" I answered a little more loudly and emphatically than I should have. I felt embarrassed at Rev's raised brows. "I'll be fine," I added more calmly. The truth was I didn't like feeling woozy and incapacitated. The last time I had been drugged was when I had been kidnapped.

Once I had ridden out the pain, I asked, "How long have I been out?"

"A day."

I gasped. "I was out that long?"

"After being beaten and going through surgery, you needed it."

"How bad was I?"

Rev grimaced. "Breakneck wasn't sure you would make it through the surgery."

"Breakneck?"

Rev chuckled. "I mean, Dr. Edgeway."

"He was very kind to me when I woke up before surgery."

"He's an amazing doctor. If anyone could have saved you, it was him."

Staring into Rev's face, I recalled more of what had happened before I went into surgery. "I asked him to get you, didn't I?"

He nodded. "And I came to you."

"Yes, you did," I murmured as I vaguely remembered his standing in the doorway before I'd slipped into unconsciousness again.

"I stayed by your side the entire time you were in recovery. It's probably good we are in Mexico because I'm pretty sure an American hospital wouldn't have allowed me to stay."

I couldn't rationalize why I found myself so drawn to him or why I had felt the need to have him with me during surgery. After all, he was a stranger to me. Sure, he had proven himself to some degree by rescuing me from the depths of hell, but I still knew so little about who he was. Was Rev really a knight in shining armor or had I once again met a wolf in sheep's clothing?

When I shook myself free of my distracting thoughts, I found Rev staring at me. I hadn't cared about my appearance since I had been kidnapped. Although I had been forced to look good for Mendoza, I didn't seek his approval. For some strange reason, though, I now found myself worrying about what Rev thought of me. I brought my hand, which was currently tethered to an IV pole, to my hair. "I must be a mess."

"No. I was just thinking how much better you already look since the surgery. I was so scared for you when I found you in the compound."

"I thought you were Jesus," I murmured, alluding to what I had said at the compound.

"I'm still just Rev," he teased.

For some reason, I found myself smiling at his response. It felt good to smile again and to have someone tease me. It made me think of the past, before everything that had happened to me with Mendoza. "So, what kind of name is Rev?" I asked.

"Road name."

I jerked my hand from his in revulsion. *No, it can't be true.* Surely someone as kind and caring as Rev couldn't possibly be like Johnny and his friends.

When I continued staring at him, Rev said, "It's not what you think."

"You're a biker, right? What else is there to think?"

"I'm a Hells Raider. We're *nothing* like the Diablos."

"You sure about that?" I countered before I could stop myself.

A defiant look flashed in his eyes. "I've never laid a hand on a woman that wasn't consensual. And I've sure as hell never beaten one. Even if I'd wanted to, my club would have taken my cut if I did. One of our bylaws is that no man is ever to abuse his old lady or any other woman."

"Really?"

He nodded. "It was a wedding gift our former president gave to his wife. She'd had a rough go in life. Lots of men had hurt her over the years."

Even though I didn't know her, I felt a strange affinity with this former president's wife. We had both found ourselves members of a club no one would ever want to join. "He sounds like a good man."

A pained expression came over Rev's face. "He was."

"Was?"

"He got killed a few months ago."

"I'm so sorry," I replied. My heart went out to Rev because I could feel the sorrow emanating from him.

"Thank you."

Grimacing, I pushed myself up in the bed. "And I'm sorry for accusing you of being like the men who . . . hurt me."

"Don't be sorry. You can't help the way you feel. And I know what you went through."

Cocking my head at him, I asked, "So what's 'Rev' short for?"

"Reverend."

My brows shot up in surprise at the thought of Rev having a religious calling. "You're a minister?"

"No, but my father was." At what must have been my continued inquisitive expression, he drew in a breath. "When my brothers and I patched into my father's club, we took road names that bound us as a family and honored his former life as a minister."

"Former life?"

Renewed grief etched its way onto Rev's face. He didn't respond for a few moments. Staring down at his hands, he said, "When I was eleven, he left the pulpit and went back to the biker world. My two brothers and I followed in his footsteps, much to our mother's disappointment."

Feeling guilty for dredging up his pain, I said, "I'm sorry. I seem to have a special gift today for bringing up things that make you feel bad."

He gave me a small smile. "Don't apologize," he replied. "Speaking of fathers, I'm sure you'll want to get in touch with your family. Although we found out your identity, we thought it would be better for you to contact them."

A pang of regret stabbed me at the thought that it had been Rev who brought up the subject of my parents and not me. The truth was I had forced myself to bury any thoughts I had of them in the deep recesses of my mind. In those early weeks as Mendoza's captive, I'd thought about my parents a lot. I wondered what they were doing and how they had reacted to my abduction. I fantasized that they had pulled strings and dispatched some Special Forces unit that would arrive at any minute to save me. But as time went on, the weeks turning into a month and then two, and no one came for me, I had to force myself to stop thinking about them. I had to reason that I had left them little to go on when it came to tracking me down.

Focusing on something else Rev had said, I questioned, "You know who I am?"

He nodded. "Annabel Lee Percy, originally from Virginia but living in Texas."

My brows rose in surprise. "You were able to find all of that just by me telling you my name?"

Rev smiled. "My fellow Raiders have talents. Of course, it wasn't that hard going through the missing persons reports for girls named Annabel."

"I see."

Reaching into his back pocket, Rev took out a phone. "Would you like to call them now?"

"No. Not right now."

Rev's brows furrowed in confusion at the panicked note in my voice. But at that moment I didn't have the energy to try to explain my complicated family. I'm sure it sounded strange that I didn't demand the phone from him to have a tearful reunion. Trying to lessen the abruptness of my reaction, I said, "I'm just a little too tired right now. Maybe in the morning when I've had more rest."

Although he nodded, I could see he was confused. Fortunately, just then my attention was drawn away from Rev by a gentle knock at the door. When I turned my head, I saw Dr. Edgeway standing in the doorway. He smiled. "I see you're awake."

I nodded, and he started into the room. "Mind if I check to see how you're doing?"

"No, that's fine."

Rev stood up from his chair. "I'll step out."

While I knew that I needed privacy for the exam, my chest tightened at the thought of him leaving. He must've sensed my apprehension because he said, "I'll be right outside if you need me."

"Thanks."

Once we were alone, Dr. Edgeway came over to me. Instead of beginning the exam, he stood awkwardly beside the bed, his hand shuffling some loose change in his pocket.

"Is something wrong?"

He gave a slight jerk of his head. "Before I examine you, there's something I need to ask you about."

"Okay," I replied apprehensively.

Dr. Edgeway then pulled something out of his pocket. When

he held it up to me, I gasped. It was the emerald and diamond ring I had briefly worn. I hadn't even realized it was gone. I wondered if they had taken it off me before surgery. "My ring."

"*Your* ring?" he questioned in an accusatory tone.

Shrinking back in the bed, I said softly, "Yes, it's mine. It was a gift from someone, and I'd like to have it back."

"Who gave it to you?" he demanded.

"A—a girl." I swallowed hard under his intense stare. "Yesterday or the day before. I don't remember."

His anger slightly dissipated. "Did she have red hair?"

My brows shot up in surprise. "How did you know that?"

A wounded look appeared on his face. "Because she was my daughter."

My chest clenched in agony. "She was?" He gave a brief nod. I had first seen the redheaded girl from the window of Mendoza's bedroom. She arrived with two other girls the day after three girls had been sold. Her appearance after a barrage of blondes and brunettes made me wonder if I might have new competition for Mendoza's affections. I guess I hoped it more than anything. But when she wasn't brought into the main house, I realized I was to have no relief.

Suddenly it all began to make sense. "So that's why Rev and his men stormed the compound: to get your daughter back."

"Yes. It is."

A horrible feeling overcame me. "Didn't she make it out?"

Dr. Edgeway closed his eyes in pain. The torment on his face spoke volumes of the level of his grief. "No. She didn't."

"I'm so sorry," I whispered. I had only had a brief meeting with the girl. Ten minutes, maybe fifteen. But in that moment, I mourned her as if we had been lifelong friends.

Dr. Edgeway didn't respond. Instead, he stared down at the ring. "This was a high school graduation gift to Sarah from her mother and me. She had always wanted an emerald ring like her mother had." He shook his head. "I can't imagine why she would have given it away."

I knew that what I had to say was only going to make Dr. Edgeway feel worse. "She didn't want to give it away. She only asked me to hold on to it for her in case she could one day get it back."

His silver brows furrowed. "What do you mean?"

Now it was my turn to close my eyes in pain. "The day after I arrived at the compound, Mendoza immediately made me his favorite. Besides being with him, one part of my job was to help acclimate the new girls who were brought in. Since I could speak English, I had to inform them of what was expected of them. Anything they had on them was taken. Jewelry was allegedly used to pay for their food until they were sold."

Bile rose in my throat as I thought of the frightened girls I had been forced to talk to. I understood their fear even though I hadn't received the same treatment. Instead, I had received my induction straight from Mendoza. Of course, mine was far different from that of the other girls, since I was selected to stay at the compound.

Focusing on Dr. Edgeway again, I continued. "I guess it was just two days ago when I met Sarah, and she asked me to take the ring and keep it for her. Since none of the other girls had been so attached to what they had, I felt I had to do as she asked. So I took it. And when Mendoza noticed it on my hand, I lied and told him I had wanted to pretend it was a present from him." Revulsion rose in me at the memory of having to play those survival games. "After he beat me, he let me keep it."

Dr. Edgeway cursed under his breath. "I'm sorry you endured that just to make Sarah feel better."

Tears stung my eyes. Tears of anger. Tears of anguish. Tears of desperation. While I should have been touched by Dr. Edgeway apologizing for the physical pain I had endured, the blackened part of my soul wanted to lash out at him. How could he possibly think his sorrow could ever take away the degrading and deplorable things that I had experienced? Words only minimalized the suffering I had been through. But just as fast as the rage had risen up inside me, the more rational side of my mind reasoned that the man before me was a grief-stricken father trying his best to wade through the quicksand he now found himself in. "I'm just sorry I never got the chance to return it to her." My voice hitched as I in turn minimalized his suffering with mere words.

"So am I," he replied. With an agonized sigh, he slipped the ring in his pocket. "I suppose we better get to the task at hand before Rev wonders what is going on in here."

"Okay," I replied as I wiped the tears from my cheeks with the back of my hand.

He eyed the machines I was hooked up to and the IV bag. "While I should be grateful there was a hospital to bring you to in this godforsaken place, I'm not impressed with their level of care compared to back in the States," he remarked.

When he reached for the sheet, I involuntarily gripped the edges tighter. Closing my eyes, I shook my head. "I'm sorry."

"Don't apologize. It's to be expected after what you've been through, especially with a male doctor."

After I released the fabric, Dr. Edgeway pulled the sheet down and then eased my gown up over my abdomen. "The incision looks like it is healing well, no signs of infection." When he lightly tapped my stomach, I flinched. "It's not surprising that you're sore. Besides the surgery, you had been worked over quite extensively."

"What exactly did you have to do?"

Dr. Edgeway didn't immediately respond. Instead, he put my gown back in place and pulled the sheet up. Finally, after what felt like an eternity had passed, he cleared his throat. "The blunt force trauma you sustained caused your spleen to rupture. If Rev hadn't found you when he did, you would have died from internal hemorrhaging in another hour."

Bile rose in my throat as I painfully recalled my last hours in the compound. "I'm not too surprised that Mendoza left me to die. . . . He wanted me dead."

"It was pretty evident from your injuries that's what he intended."

"So you just had to take out my spleen?"

After glancing down at the tile floor, Dr. Edgeway shook his head. "The blunt force trauma also caused a miscarriage—" My gasp of horror forced his gaze to meet mine.

"I was . . . pregnant?"

"Yes. You were."

I could barely wrap my mind around such a thought. Of course, I had long been denied my birth control pills while in captivity, and since I was owned by Mendoza, he didn't bother with condoms. I guess nature had taken its course. But the thought of carrying that monster's child made my stomach roil in revulsion. At least there were some small mercies, and I had lost the baby. As much as I loved children and wanted them someday, I didn't think I could have withstood raising a child of Mendoza's.

"But I'm afraid that's not the worst of it."

"I'm sorry?"

"The miscarriage caused a tear in your uterine lining that couldn't be repaired. The only way to stop the bleeding was to perform an emergency hysterectomy."

Although Dr. Edgeway appeared to continue speaking, I couldn't make out anything else he said. Absently, my hand came to rest on my abdomen. *My now-barren abdomen.* "I can't have children," I whispered in disbelief. I suddenly hoped and prayed that at any moment I would wake up from the nightmare, even if it found me back at Mendoza's compound.

"You can't carry a child, but you can still have a child of your own."

"What?" I questioned absently.

"Annabel, look at me," Dr. Edgeway instructed. When I finally met his gaze, he said, "You still have your ovaries. With today's modern fertility treatments, you can have your own child via a surrogate. It isn't impossible, especially for someone from your background."

I know he didn't intend it, but it sounded like Dr. Edgeway thought that I should be grateful for the wealthy background I came from. Allegedly it would be my salvation—the only way I could ever have a child of my own flesh and blood. But at that moment, money, status, or prestige didn't mean shit. It sure as hell hadn't saved me from Mendoza. And there was no way financial wealth could reassemble the fractured pieces of my life. There were some things that money simply could not buy.

"Annabel, you will heal and move on."

"But I'll never have life within me," I challenged.

He shook his head slowly. "No. You won't."

I felt like I was being pummeled with new waves of grief and loss. After all I had endured, now I had survived only to learn I could never carry a child?

Why?

For the thousandth time I asked myself that one question.

Why?

Why me? Why did bad things keep happening? It struck me in that moment that while I might've physically escaped from my nightmare, I would be forced to continuously endure the emotional aftershocks. I became so overwhelmed with dark and desperate feelings then that I didn't think I could keep my head up. "I'm very tired. I think I need to rest."

"I'm sorry, Annabel. If I could have gotten to you sooner and under different circumstances, maybe I could have repaired the tear without having to remove the uterus."

Even though he was sincere, I didn't want his apology. Nothing he could say or do could ever make things right for me. No one could. At that moment, I realized I had traded one hell for another.

From this day forward, I would never be anything more than a shameful burden to my parents. As a woman who had been defiled by criminals, I would be considered damaged goods. Preston would never date or marry me, and for that matter neither would any other man in our social circle. Even if someone did, I couldn't bear the picture-perfect family for him. No political propaganda commercial would want to feature a couple along with their surrogate.

There would be no going back to the life I had had before. The future that spread out before me was desolate and bleak. As I closed my eyes, I wished that Rev had never found me, and instead had allowed me to die on the floor of Mendoza's compound like the worthless trash I was.

SIX

REV

When Breakneck came out of Annabel's room, he was ashen. Since he had been in there a long time, a surge of concern that something had gone wrong overwhelmed me. Grabbing his arm, I asked, "Is she okay?"

His agonized eyes met mine. "No, she's not."

My heart clenched. "Wait, did she—"

"After her examination, I had to explain to her the severity of her injuries and the course of action I had to take."

Crossing my arms over my chest, I asked, "What do you mean?"

"I had to do a partial hysterectomy."

"Jesus," I muttered.

"She isn't taking the news very well." He shook his head. "In fact, it's devastated her."

I couldn't even begin to imagine what Annabel was going through. Having children was something so intertwined with being a woman, and now she had lost that. If she was someone who had always wanted kids, I'm sure the news was a complete blow on top of everything she was already dealing with. "I'll go and talk to her."

Breakneck nodded and then walked farther down the hallway. When I opened the door, Annabel didn't even look up. Instead, she kept staring straight ahead. "Hey," I said softly as I walked over to the bed. A chill shuddered through me at the visual evidence of how much the news had affected her. It was like seeing an entirely different girl. Not that she didn't deserve to be a basket case after what she had been through, but it was certainly alarming.

"I thought you might want to talk," I said.

A single tear slid down her cheek. "I just want to be alone."

"Okay. We don't have to talk. But why don't I sit here with you for a while?"

"Whatever," she muttered, closing her eyes.

With an uneasy feeling, I sat down in the chair beside the bed and kept quiet, but it was a long time before she fell into a fitful sleep. When one of the nurses came in to check her vitals, she brought back a sedative. Once the liquid seeped from the IV into Annabel's veins, she finally found a peaceful sleep. Then it was my turn to toss and turn in the chair.

In what was becoming our on-the-road ritual, Bishop shook me awake the next morning. Sometime during the night, a roll-away bed had been brought in, but I didn't even remember moving from the chair. Rubbing my eyes, I asked, "What time is it?"

"Little after seven. I brought you some breakfast."

"Thanks, man." I pulled myself into a sitting position. As I glanced around the room, my gaze focused on the rumpled sheets of the empty bed. "Where's Annabel?"

"She wasn't in bed when I got here. Pretty sure she's in the bathroom."

A prickly feeling like nicks from barbwire went through my chest. I strode across the room and pounded on the bathroom door with my fist. "Annabel? Are you all right?" When there was no reply, I pounded harder. "Annabel, answer me!" I commanded in a voice harsher than I meant to use.

"Leave me alone, Rev," came the weak reply.

As if I possessed Superman's X-ray vision, I knew exactly what was transpiring behind the door. If I strained my ears, I could hear the almost inaudible dripping of blood. Taking several steps back, I ignored Bishop when he asked, "Rev, what the hell are you doing?"

Instead, I focused all the strength I had on the obstacle in front of me. At a full gallop, I lunged at the door, busting the lock and sending it swinging open. The scene before me was just as I had imagined. Annabel sat hunkered down on the toilet with a crimson river pooled around her. The razor blade she'd used to slit her wrists lay in the midst of the carnage.

"No, no, NO!" I shouted as I barreled forward into the room.

She lifted her battle-worn green eyes to mine before sadly shaking her head. "Don't you understand? They've taken *everything* from me—my innocence, my will to live . . . even my ability to bear children." Tears streamed down her face. She brought a blood-streaked hand up to swipe them away. "I have nothing left."

Jerking my T-shirt over my head, I ripped it down the center, then began to tear it into wide strips. "This is not fucking happening. Not on my watch."

When I knelt down beside her, she attempted to scramble away from me. "Don't you dare save me! This is my choice, dammit. I finally have a choice, and I'm ending it."

I shook my head at her while I continued tearing the fabric. "I won't let you do that, Annabel."

As I reached for her bleeding wrist, she shot up off the floor, trying to escape me. A feral gleam burned in her eyes before an agonized scream escaped her lips.

"You fucking bastard! Stop being a hero. Just let me die!"

Ignoring her, I pinned her against the wall. Like a caged animal, she began to fight me, kicking and clawing. Bright red blood began to paint us both. I couldn't imagine how she even had the strength to fight after all she had been through.

Bishop appeared behind me. "Jesus Christ!"

"Get out," I commanded.

"Should I get Breakneck or one of the nurses?"

"Just get the fuck out."

"Rev, she needs fucking sedation not only before she shreds you, but before she bleeds out."

"Get. Out!" I bellowed.

Grumbling under his breath, Bishop stomped out of the bathroom. With my thighs bracing Annabel's, I pinned her in place with my hips. I grabbed one of her wrists. Winding the ripped shirt around and around, I managed to cut off the bleeding. As I surveyed the wound, I silently thanked God she had made a novice's mistake and hadn't cut too deep. She would need stitches, but it was nothing life-threatening. After tying the makeshift bandage tightly in place, I moved on to the next hand just as the palm was about to come in contact with my face.

When I was done, I exhaled the breath I'd been holding. The roar in my ears and the pounding in my chest slowly began to dissipate.

Defeated, Annabel sank slowly down the wall and onto the floor. Staring at the bandages, she questioned, "Why? Why couldn't you just let me die?"

"Because it's not your fucking time. If it was, you would have gone up in that blast with the rest of the women." I raked a shaky hand through my hair. "Besides, you're twenty-four years old. You've got your whole fucking life ahead of you."

Shaking her head, she replied, "A tormented life of unfulfilled dreams."

"You don't know that. You can't let this defeat you. You can't let *them* defeat you. You take your life and Mendoza wins."

"Easy for you to spout out all the self-help bullshit."

"Actually, it isn't."

Her brows came together in confusion as inquisitive eyes met mine. "What do you mean?"

In that moment, as the hellish ghosts of my past closed in around me, the pressure to breathe had my lungs feeling like a squeezed accordion. I had never spoken of my rape—the actual words had never left my lips. My father knew because he had witnessed the end, and Breakneck knew because he had experienced the aftermath. It had been a horrible secret we kept from my mother and brothers.

Annabel was a complete stranger to me—someone I'd known less than forty-eight hours. The reason why she deserved to know, and my blood family didn't, escaped me. But in my heart, I also knew there was a purpose to telling her. In the macabre room splattered with blood, it seemed almost effortless to unburden myself of the sordid details I had tried to bury for so long.

The intense burden of the secret I was about to divulge weighed on me physically, and I began to sway back and forth. My left leg gave way, and I found myself collapsing onto the floor. I shifted my leg with a grimace.

"What happened to you?"

"I got shot leaving Mendoza's."

"When you were carrying me?" Annabel questioned.

"Not that it makes any difference, but yeah."

"I'm sorry," she whispered.

"You have nothing to be sorry for."

Annabel snorted contemptuously. "I got you shot. It's just one more thing to make me feel horrible about myself."

"Hear me when I say you *can't* keep thinking like that."

"And what makes you an expert?"

"Look, I can't say I understand exactly how you feel because I didn't experience the same torment as you." Holding her gaze, I continued. "But when I was eleven years old, I was raped."

Annabel's eyes widened in shock. Any old animosity on her face was replaced by shock and sympathy. As the deafening silence hung heavy around us, I drew in a ragged breath and began my story. The walls of the hospital bathroom melted away as I traveled across the years, back to a bedroom with a pink bedspread. As I unburdened myself, the shackles, which had once bound me in a long silence, fell away, and I experienced a freedom I'd had no idea existed anymore.

When I finished speaking, I stared down at the floor, unable to look at Annabel. It wasn't that I was ashamed of what she might have thought about me. It was more the fact that I was physically and emotionally overwhelmed. I was almost twenty-eight years old, and it had taken me sixteen years to say the words out loud.

A rustling sound finally drew my stare from the bloodstained tile. I looked up to see Annabel slowly inching toward me. Just as our bodies touched, she stopped. "I don't know what to say," she whispered.

With a shrug, I replied, "You don't need to say anything."

She shook her head. "How could I hear a story like yours and not have something to say?" She wet her dry, cracked lips. "I would say I was sorry, but that simple word seems so insignificant."

More than anyone I knew, Annabel truly understood the meaning of her words firsthand. "I guess so."

Tears welled in her sad eyes. "You were so young. Just a baby. Me . . . I was old enough to know better. In some ways, I got what I deserved. I walked right into the lion's den."

"Don't you fucking say that!" I shouted, my fists clenching at my side. My words and tone caused Annabel to shrink back. She didn't deserve to be yelled at, but at the same time, I had to get through to her. And I didn't know how many chances I would have to get this right. It wasn't like I had a whole lot of experience consoling broken women.

Tentatively I reached my hand out to touch her cheek. When she didn't pull away, I brushed my thumb along her jawline. "I'm sorry for yelling at you."

"It's okay."

"Annabel, I want you to understand that you should never, ever think like that."

A mirthless laugh tumbled from her lips. "Honestly, Rev, you're too forgiving. I'm twenty-four years old, not fourteen. I knew better. But still I asked a man I'd never met to take me on a motorcycle ride. I allowed myself to become a victim."

"Yeah, well, maybe I spent years blaming myself for drinking that coffee when I knew I wasn't supposed to have any. I wasted so many nights lying in bed thinking I deserved what happened to me because even though I was drugged, I hadn't fought back hard enough. That there was something I had done wrong to make Kurt want me over my brothers." I shook my head. "It's all bullshit, Annabel. Letting those kinds of thoughts eat away at you won't get you anywhere."

She remained silent for a few minutes and I could tell she was deep in thought. "After you were . . ." She swallowed hard as she met my eyes.

"*Raped,*" I enunciated the word for her. "I've been a fucking coward about the word long enough."

She gave a quick nod of her head. "After you were raped, did you ever want to hurt yourself?"

Her innocent question sent the walls of the room spinning and closing in on me. My breath quickened to harsh pants, and I knew

I was dangerously close to hyperventilating. *No, I can't lose it. Not here. Not now.*

Closing my eyes, I pictured myself far, far away from the blood-soaked room. I waded into the crystal-clear waters of a stream. As the cool liquid encased my body, peace began to hum through my veins. The farther I went into the water, the greater the relief became.

I opened my eyes to find Annabel staring at me openmouthed. "What did you just do?"

"A visualization technique Breakneck taught me many years ago."

"You calmed yourself down right in front of me. One minute it was like you were going over the edge, and then the next . . ."

"I had peace," I finished for her.

"Yes," she murmured.

"I was pretty volatile there for a while after what happened to me. The emotions coupled with preteen hormones made me explosive. I was throwing punches at my brothers, at kids at school. It was when I took a swing at Breakneck that he realized I needed an outlet."

"Will you teach me the technique?"

"Sure. If you think it will help."

"Yeah, I do." She gave me a small smile. "Thank you, Rev."

We sat in silence for a few minutes. Then I braced myself to unburden myself even further. "The answer is yes."

"Excuse me?"

"Yes, I tried to hurt myself."

Her green eyes widened. "What did you do?" she questioned in a whisper.

"I tried to hang myself in my closet."

Although she had tried slitting her wrists not a half hour ago, Annabel's hand flew to her mouth in shock. "Oh no."

"The months after the rape were almost as bad as the day itself.

The man who raped me was just a drifter, so no one came looking for him or had any questions about what happened to him. I guess it would've been even worse if my father had gone to prison. Within just a few weeks, my old man left his church. He started drinking again, moved out of the house. My mother cried all the time. My brothers had no clue what had caused the seismic shift in our family, but I did. It was all my fault. I had caused my father to kill a man, to leave his wife and family, and to leave his church."

"You poor thing," Annabel whispered.

"So I took a belt, tied it to the rack in the closet, and then tied it to my neck. I didn't leave a note. I just climbed up on the chair and stepped off—" Annabel's gasp of horror caused me to momentarily pause. "But my weight was too much for the rack, and it collapsed to the floor." For a moment, I was that scared, devastated little boy all over again. I could feel his pain and desperation just as strong as when I was first experiencing it.

"You never tried it again?" Annabel asked.

I shook my head. "No, it was around then that Breakneck reached out to me. As a member of the Raiders, I guess he saw a change in me—one that was worse than my brothers. Maybe he had a soft spot for cases like mine because he had experienced something similar in the past. Or maybe he just wanted to help out a brother's kid. At first, I wondered if he was just some other pervert like Kurt. But then I remembered how kind he had been the day my father had taken me to him. So when I was just twelve I started going with Breakneck when he worked at the free clinic down in Atlanta. I got to help out doing small chores, which kept my mind occupied, and at the same time, I got to see people who were far worse off than me."

"And that's what eventually helped you move on?"

"That and time. The old adage about it healing all wounds is true. Of course, the pain is never completely forgotten. It's more like it lies buried below the surface. Certain sights, smells, or sounds can bring it back."

Annabel raised a bloodstained hand to tenderly touch my cheek. "Thank you for saving me. Again."

My brows shot up in surprise. "You really mean that?"

Cocking her head to the side, she remained contemplative for a moment. Then her eyes once again met mine. "Yes, I do."

It was at that moment that Breakneck appeared in the doorway. "Jesus Christ," he muttered with wide eyes.

Annabel snatched her hand away from my cheek and then ducked her head from Breakneck's stare. Shielding her from the barrage of questions I knew he wanted to ask, I said, "Annabel needs you to take a look at her wrists. She may need stitching. I'll clean up in here."

When he realized exactly what had transpired, his lips pinched together tightly. I could imagine that inside he was silently seething.

With a wince, I pulled myself off the ground. Unsteady on my wounded leg, I weaved back and forth for a moment. Once I was stable, I reached down to help Annabel up. She couldn't bring herself to look me in the eye, so I gently put my finger under her chin and tipped her gaze to mine. "You let Breakneck take care of you while I clean up. Then, if you're feeling up to it, you can take a shower, or we can get one of the nurses to clean you up. Okay?"

She nodded and then padded barefoot out of the bathroom. With an agitated sigh, Breakneck turned to go, but I grabbed his arm. "Don't," I hissed under my breath.

"Don't what?" he demanded.

"Don't be hard on her."

His eyes flashed with rage before he pushed me inside the bathroom and shut the door. "You want me to coddle a girl who almost threw her life away this morning? A girl who should be fucking grateful she's alive at all when so many aren't?"

I shoved him against the blood-spattered wall with more force than I'd intended. "For one minute, leave Sarah out of all of this. Think back to that eleven-year-old kid you stitched up one day and then weeks later tried to put back together when he fell apart." Breakneck blinked in acknowledgment. "You cannot and will not discredit her pain. She has every fucking right to want to take her life. That's not our place to judge. Our part is to help her see there's a reason to go on no matter how hard it seems right now. You feel me?"

"Yeah, I feel you," he replied.

After releasing him, I took a step back. "Glad to hear it."

His gaze dipped down to my leg. "Are you all right?"

"Just a little tender, that's all."

"Maybe I should have a look at it."

"Take care of Annabel first."

"Chivalrous to a fucking fault," he muttered before turning and leaving me.

I didn't want to alert the medical staff to what had transpired with Annabel, so I ducked out of the bathroom and then stole a bucket and mop out of the supply closet. I also grabbed a pair of scrubs so I would have something to change into once I finished cleaning. After a quick sweep of the floor and walls, I returned the supplies, then took a long, scalding shower.

My calf still hurt like a motherfucker, but at least the stitches hadn't popped and there was no bleeding. I slipped the scrubs on and took one last inspection of the bathroom before going outside.

Breakneck had finished up with Annabel's stitches. Annabel's and Bishop's attention was drawn to the television while Breakneck stared at his phone. At the sight of me, Annabel jerked her gaze to mine.

"Shower's all yours now."

She nodded and then turned to Breakneck. "It's okay if I get the stitches wet?"

"The gauze should protect them. Just don't stay in long. And if you start to feel light-headed, call out for one of us."

"Okay," she replied. After taking the spare hospital gown from the side of the bed, she went into the bathroom.

Bishop glanced between me and Breakneck. "You think it's safe for her to be alone in there?"

"I did a sweep of the bathroom. There's nothing in there she could use, even if she was so inclined."

"Where the fuck did she get a razor to start with?"

I shrugged. "Maybe she asked one of the nurses for it. Since she wasn't on suicide watch, they probably didn't think a thing about it."

"You don't think she'll be a repeat offender and ask them again?" Bishop asked.

Before I could reply, Breakneck said, "No. I think she's going to be all right." When I shot a questioning look at him, he gave a brief jerk of his head. "For a first-timer, she did a number on her wrists, but the wounds weren't deep enough, and after talking with her, I don't think she needs to be put on suicide watch or anything like that."

Bishop snorted. "With us on round-the-clock duty, we're watching her enough as it is. She doesn't need anything else."

"I'm not taking any fucking chances on Mendoza being alive or the Diablos hunting her down. Those cocksuckers are psychotic," I argued.

Breakneck rose from his chair. "She'll be discharged tomorrow. We need to start planning how to get her back to the States."

Crossing my arms over my chest, I said, "For starters, we're going to be riding out of here. No way can we be flying. Annabel doesn't have any ID, and whatever paperwork the Raiders concoct to get her over the border, it won't hold up with TSA. Besides, we don't need any record that we were even here."

Breakneck shook his head. "With the extent of her injuries, there's no way in hell she can ride on a motorcycle. She needs four to six weeks recuperation from the hysterectomy at least."

"Okay. So I'll rent a car and drive her," I replied.

"Then how does your bike get home?" Bishop questioned. As I paused to consider that issue, Bishop said, "Maybe Breakneck should drive her home."

"No way," I answered adamantly.

Bishop looked at me in surprise. "You got a better suggestion?"

"Rev's right," Breakneck said.

"He is?" The doubt was clear in Bishop's tone.

With a nod, Breakneck added, "For whatever reason, Annabel has bonded with Rev. For her continued mental stability, she needs him right now, especially during a long car ride. I can ride his bike back." At Bishop's incredulous expression, Breakneck snapped, "Wipe that fucking look off your face. I can still ride a Harley."

Bishop held up his hands defensively. "I never said you couldn't."

"I'm not that old."

I chuckled. "If anyone can pull off that long a haul, it's you, man."

Breakneck finally smiled. "Besides, I think it'll do me some good to be on the open road."

"Have you talked to Betsy about funeral plans for Sarah?"

Betsy was Breakneck's ex-wife and the mother of his three children. While they had divorced years ago, they had somehow managed to keep an amicable relationship. He cleared his throat. "Yeah. I've spoken with her. She wants to wait until I get back to plan anything." He gave me a pointed look. "Whenever that is."

"Take all the time you need."

"Thank you," he replied, his eyes momentarily appearing glassy.

After a few seconds, he cleared his throat. "I'm assuming Annabel has yet to speak to her parents."

I shook my head. "When I mentioned calling them, she was pretty evasive."

"That's understandable. Her father is a real dick."

"You know him?" I questioned incredulously.

"Not exactly. Just heard him speak on CSPAN before. Real right-wing nut job. The kind that hides a million secrets and shady dealings behind a picture-perfect smile."

"Regardless of all that, I'm sure they're desperate to know she's all right," I argued.

"You might be surprised. But in spite of all that, she needs to call them this afternoon. Should her identity be discovered crossing the border, we'll have a hell of a hard time explaining why she's with us."

I nodded. "Okay. I'll have her call them when she gets out of the shower."

"I'm going to head out for now," Breakneck said. He turned to Bishop. "Why don't you come with me, and we can feel out the Raiders for help with a car?"

"Sounds good," Bishop replied.

"I'll come back later this evening to check on Annabel. Make sure she gets plenty of rest."

"I will."

Breakneck cocked his brows at me. "I don't guess there's any chance of you going back to the hotel tonight and letting Bishop or me stay?"

I shook my head and told him, "I'm fine right where I am. Besides, I think she would rest easier with me."

With a smile, Breakneck replied, "Yes, she would. She seems to do everything better with you."

His words stayed with me long after he and Bishop had left the room. My mind couldn't help drifting to Deacon and Alexandra. I thought of how much she had needed him, physically and emotionally, after she had been tortured and almost raped by one of the Raiders' enemies. While it was an honor to help Annabel through her dark times, I couldn't chase away the nagging feeling that she was growing too attached to me. What would happen to her when it was time for us to go our separate ways?

SEVEN

ANNABEL

As I reached to turn off the shower, my gaze froze on my battered wrists. For a few moments, I could only stand there, staring at the marks I had made on them. I could almost hear my mother's disdainful voice remarking on how the gashes would leave such unattractive scars. To be scarred in our world of superficial perfection would be as bad as having leprosy. I would now be forced to remember my moment of weakness and despair each and every day of my life—a physical testimony to a place and time when the weight of the world became too much to bear.

They would be there when I woke up in the morning and would remain throughout the day until I laid my head on my pillow at night. I would never play the piano again without seeing the scars, nor would I examine one of my furry patients without the glaring reminder. During spring and summer when I wore short sleeves, people's attention would be drawn to the scars, and their minds would whirl with the possibilities of what had happened to me. Mostly, I knew, they would look disapprovingly at me because I had once tried to take my life.

While part of me was horrified at the thought, the other part relished the truth of the battle scars which adorned my body. Soldiers and police officers often were injured in the line of duty, and they wore their scars with pride. In a small way, mine would also be a testament to what I had been through and *ultimately* survived.

It was the small incision on my abdomen that caused the greatest emotional pain. It would be the one I *couldn't* wear with pride. It would be a constant reminder of my physical shortcomings. While deep down I clung to the hope that I would someday be a mother, there was no gray area when it came to me experiencing pregnancy.

As a fresh wave of grief washed over me, I leaned back against the shower wall and thought about how I found myself now in a strange, otherworldly place. A place born of living three lifetimes in less than three months. There had been the Annabel I was before the kidnapping, the Annabel I was during my enslavement in Mexico, and the Annabel I would be now. *And who was she?*

After living such a controlled life both under my parents' thumb and in captivity, I found myself alarmed at the thought of what tomorrow might bring. Questions of how to proceed with my life inundated my brain at almost warp speed. Once I started down that train of thought, I didn't know how to stop it. I knew I was supposed to take only one day at a time as I recovered, even as little as one step, but I couldn't help but wonder what would happen now.

A gentle knock came at the door. "Annabel? Are you okay?" Rev asked.

Realizing I must've been in the shower longer than I'd intended, I quickly turned off the water. "Yes, I'm fine," I called.

After I toweled off, I realized I was too tired to dry my hair, so I combed it out and left it wet. I slipped into another hospital gown and what were apparently the post-op granny panties I was mandated to wear. When I came out of the bathroom, I found that only Rev remained. I wasn't sure where Dr. Edgeway or Rev's brother had gone.

"Hi," I said softly.

He glanced up from the book he was reading. "Hello. Feeling okay?"

I nodded. "Much better now. Little tired."

"I was worried about that. You need to get some rest."

With a yawn, I replied, "I plan on it." When I eased into the bed, Rev stood up to help pull the sheet and blanket over me. "Thanks."

My head had barely touched the pillow when I fell into a deep sleep. I awoke to the unappetizing aroma of the dinner trays being brought around. I had always heard the jokes about American hospital food, but if there was anything worse, it had to be Mexican hospital food.

When I glanced over to where I had last seen Rev, he was still sitting in the chair beside the bed, watching TV. "Hey," I said.

He turned his head to grin at me. "Hey there, Sleeping Beauty. I was wondering when you might wake up."

His term of endearment made me smile. "I can't believe how long I slept," I said as I pushed myself into a sitting position.

"You needed it."

An aide appeared with my food and set it down without a smile. "*Gracias*," I murmured as she turned to leave. I opened the lid and then quickly shut it.

"You need to eat," Rev urged, when I pushed the tray away.

"I'd like to see you try that."

With a smile, he rose from his chair. He took the lid off my tray and then picked up a fork. He cut a piece of the pale, overbaked chicken cutlet. After he took a bite, his expression soured, and he quickly turned to spit the food into the trash can.

"That's horrible."

"I tried to tell you."

"I'll call Bishop and ask him to bring us some food that's a little more appetizing."

I smiled at him. "That sounds like a plan."

After Rev made the call, he didn't put his phone away. Instead, he kept looking at it and then at me. The expression on his face told me he was apprehensive about something. "What's wrong?"

"Nothing's wrong."

"Are you sure? You look funny."

A teasing smile played on his lips. "That wasn't a very nice thing to say."

I laughed. "I didn't mean it like that. You look like something's bothering you. Like you need to tell me something you really don't want to."

Rev's smile faded. "You're very perceptive. You're being discharged in the morning, so we'll be leaving for El Paso." Then he proceeded to tell me the plans that I assumed Breakneck and he had made earlier. "But before we leave, I need you to talk to your parents."

My stomach churned at the prospect. "I tried to kill myself earlier today. Must I endure that as well?" I said, knowing I sounded bitter.

He stared at me, his dark brows furrowed. I could tell the wheels were spinning in his head about what kind of heartless girl I must be not to want to put my worried parents' minds at ease. In the vast scheme of things, it didn't matter what he thought of me, but at the same time, I couldn't bear to have someone as good and kindhearted as he was thinking I was a bad person.

"Rev, I'm sure this all seems strange to you, but just like I don't understand the world you come from, you don't understand mine, either."

His expression softened a little. "Trust me, I get that people have fucked-up families. But no matter what happened before with them, they have a right to know."

Nibbling my lip between my teeth, I contemplated his response. I finally relented. "What if you called them?"

"Seriously?"

I nodded. When he still seemed unconvinced, I said, "Please?"

He exhaled a long, almost defeated sigh. "Do you want to speak to them after I have?" When I shook my head, he groaned. "Fine. I'll call them." He then wagged a finger at me. "But you owe me."

"You're right. I do. But for more than I can possibly repay."

"Some things are on the house," he replied, with a tender smile that made my chest tighten with emotion.

"I'll give you my father's private number. That way you won't get the run-around from his aides."

To my surprise, Rev put the phone on speaker. My father picked up on the third ring. "This is Emmett Percy." Hearing his voice should probably have brought me some form of comfort, but it didn't move me at all. When your parents have kept you at arm's length your entire life, even a catastrophic event doesn't change the way you feel. The only person I would want to talk to at the house was Connie, my former nanny, who was now employed as my mother's assistant.

"Mr. Percy, you don't know me, and I don't know you. The only thing you do need to know is your daughter Annabel is safe."

My father sucked in a harsh breath. "What do you mean? Who are you? Where is my daughter?" he demanded.

"The fewer details you know of her kidnapping and rescue, the better. That can be said for all parties involved. She is safe and recuperating, so any search efforts you had should be canceled. She will be returning home to you in Virginia in a few days."

"I don't believe a fucking word you've said. I want to speak to my daughter this instant."

Rev thrust out the phone to me. His no-nonsense look told me I had no choice but to speak to my father. With a resigned sigh, I said, "It's me, Father."

"Annabel? Annabel, are you really okay?"

"Yes, I am. I swear. And I'm not being coerced into saying that, either."

"Where are you?"

"You don't need to know that."

"The hell I don't! Is that man the one who kidnapped you? I'll have the CIA and the FBI on his ass in seconds."

"Father, please. He saved me from something pretty horrible. He doesn't need to be harassed by you or your minions."

"I want you home—immediately. It's been a media circus since you left—"

Rage boiled inside me at his comment. Gripping the phone tighter, I spat, "I didn't just leave. I was *kidnapped* by a group of traffickers. Do you understand what that means? I had no choice. In anything that happened or anything that was done to me."

My father remained silent for a moment as if he was trying to process the horror of what I had just said. But he wasn't focusing on my torment—the unspeakable pain his daughter had gone through. No, I was certain he was worrying about how my family could find a way to get out of this unscathed both politically and socially. "I will send the plane for you right now. Wherever you are in the world."

"No. It isn't necessary."

"Annabel, be reasonable. Your mother has barely slept in the two months you've been gone. Both of us are wrecks."

Once again, he was thinking only of himself. It didn't matter what I had gone through, the sleepless nights I had endured. "I'm sorry, Father. But that's all you need to know right now."

A humorless laugh came through the phone. "Fine. I see this experience hasn't humbled you and has only made you even more headstrong. So if that's the way you want to play it, I'll just find your location from the phone tracer. Or have you forgotten that all my calls are traced?"

"This is a GoPhone. Good luck with that one," I replied, before disconnecting the call. I tossed the phone back at Rev. "Happy now?"

He didn't look happy. In fact, he appeared horrified at what had transpired between my father and me. "They had to know, Annabel."

"Now do you understand why I didn't want to call them?"

He jerked a hand through his hair. "Yes, I do. And I'm sorry— not for making you call, but I'm sorry that's the family you have to go back home to."

"It is what it is. My parents are horrible, my sister is tolerable, but at least I have a really good group of friends. They're the ones I would want to know I was okay."

His expression turned suddenly contemplative. "Do you have a boyfriend back home?"

For some reason, the very innocent question didn't seem so innocent. "Why would you ask me that?"

He shrugged. "Just wondered who else there might be in your life worth getting back home to."

"No, there's no boyfriend."

His brows shot up in surprise. "How is it possible a girl as pretty as you doesn't have a boyfriend?"

The compliment seemed so foreign coming from him. In spite of that fact, warmth flooded my cheeks. "That's sweet of you to say."

Even though he looked slightly embarrassed, he said, "I mean it."

"No, there's not been a boyfriend for a while actually." As I thought about the old Annabel's life, I found myself almost smiling. "There was a guy I liked back in College Station."

"A guy you went to school with?" Rev asked.

"Actually, he was a vet at the animal hospital I worked at."

"Is that what you were in school for? To be a vet?"

I nodded. "I can't imagine doing anything else. I've loved animals practically since I was born." With a sly smile, I added, "I guess I found them to be much nicer than my family."

Rev laughed. "I can see how you might believe that."

I absently flicked away a piece of fuzz on my blanket. "I was in my first semester of veterinarian school. I've missed so much that I guess I'll just start over in the fall."

"I think you'll be an amazing veterinarian," Rev said encouragingly.

"And how can you tell?"

Cocking his head, he stared at me for a moment. "There's something about you that says you have a caring nature."

"Except when it comes to my parents."

"Don't be so hard on yourself about them. Lots of people have complicated relationships with their families."

"Do you?"

Rev smiled. "How quickly you forget—my father killed my rapist, gave up his church, and divorced my mother. I would say that makes for complications, doesn't it?"

I shook my head. "But you still got along with your father, didn't you?"

"Yeah, I did. He was a good man despite his faults."

"You seem to get along well with Bishop."

Rev grinned. "Ah, yes, my dear, sweet baby brother who should have been here half an hour ago with dinner." After he laughed, he added, "Yeah, he's my best friend. Along with our older brother."

"What about your mother?"

The amusement in Rev's face was replaced with such a look of admiration and tenderness that it caused an ache in my chest. "She's my hero. Everything good and decent that I am is because of my mother."

His endearing words, along with the conviction with which he spoke, momentarily left me speechless. I couldn't help wondering just for a moment what it might be like to have such a woman as my mother. "She sounds like an amazing person."

"She is." The corners of his lips turned up in a smile. "She's probably one of the reasons I'm still single. She's spoiled me too much."

"So there's no girlfriend or wife back home?"

"No. There isn't."

Although I couldn't explain why, his answer gave me a sense of relief. Hitting him with his question from earlier, I asked, "How is it that a man as handsome as you is still single?"

He grinned. "Stop it. You'll make me blush."

I couldn't help laughing at his teasing remark. He was such a paradox—a tender, gentle soul wrapped up in a handsome, yet hard and gruff exterior. "Seriously, though. I might've only known you for a few days, but I can tell what a good, decent, and caring man you are. Not to mention the easy-on-the-eyes bit."

Rev ducked his head shyly. "I don't know why other than I got my heart broken a couple of years ago."

My fists clenched at my sides, and for the first time in my life, I wanted to scratch the eyes out of a girl I'd never met—the girl who had dared to break Rev's heart. "That's a shame, because you deserve someone who makes you happy, not someone who hurts you."

Rev's head shot up at my comment. His intense stare made me regret what I said. He opened his mouth to say something, but the hospital room door burst open and silenced him. Bishop blew in laden with food bags.

"Finally. What took you so long?" Rev asked. He stood up and started to reach for some of the bags, but Bishop jerked them away.

"Oh hell no! Don't you even begin riding my ass about how long it took. Do you know how fucking far we had to go to find a car?" He paused dramatically. "An hour."

"I'm sorry—" Rev began, but Bishop shook his shaggy blond head wildly back and forth.

"Did I mention how during that hour I had to ride bitch with Ghost so that I could drive the car back?"

The corners of Rev's lips twitched like he was fighting not to smile. "That sucks, man. I'm sorry. I really am."

"You better fucking be," Bishop muttered. He then sidestepped Rev to come over to the bed. He plopped a McDonald's bag down in front of me. "The only good thing about driving an hour away was fucking civilization." His blue eyes narrowed on mine. "I hope you like McDonald's."

I could tell he was just waiting for me to complain. "I love McDonald's, and I haven't gotten to have it in forever. Thank you, Bishop," I said sweetly as I reached for the bag.

His shocked expression was somewhat comical. "Yeah, well, you're welcome."

As I unwrapped a cheeseburger, my stomach growled noisily. The moment I bit into it, I moaned in delight. "This tastes amazing."

Bishop grinned. "Glad you like it."

Rev came over to the bed. "You got anything for me?"

"There's at least five cheeseburgers in there," Bishop replied before he went over and plopped down in the chair Rev had been sitting in.

With a wink, Rev asked, "Mind if I have a cheeseburger, or do you think you'll devour them all?"

I laughed. "You can have three. I think two will be my limit." I glanced over at Bishop. "Unless you want one."

He shook his head as he rubbed his stomach. "I ate on the drive back."

With Bishop taking the only chair, Rev surveyed the room to figure out where to sit. "You can sit on the bed if you want," I suggested.

He contemplated my words for a moment before he finally eased down on the edge. A few minutes went by with just the sounds of rustling wrappers and chewing.

"So what happens when we get to El Paso?" I asked around a mouthful of cheeseburger. It struck me in that moment that my manners would have appalled my mother.

"You get on a plane home to Virginia, and we get our asses back to Georgia," Bishop replied.

My hand froze as I was bringing the cheeseburger to my mouth for another bite. "Back to Virginia? But what about College Station?"

Rev started to answer me, but he was interrupted by Bishop snorting contemptuously. "Sorry, sweetie, but there is no College Station for you anymore."

Rolling his eyes, Rev said to Bishop, "Did anyone ever tell you that your tact sucks?"

Bishop shrugged. "Truth is the truth."

I swallowed. "But I have an apartment in College Station and a life."

"Well, that life is over. As for your apartment, I'm sure we could get some of the Texas Raiders to pack it up for you."

Now it was my turn to snort. "You have got to be kidding. A bunch of strange bikers pawing through my things? I don't think so."

"Fine. Since you're too good for bikers' help, get some of your daddy's people to do it. The only sure thing is you're not staying in Texas on our watch."

"Why not?" I challenged.

He sat up straight in his seat. "You really don't get it, do you?"

"Bishop," Rev growled.

My gaze flicked between the two brothers before I narrowed my eyes at Bishop. "No, actually, I don't get it. I guess you could say my view of things is a little skewed after being in captivity for the past two months." I added, "So why don't you enlighten me?"

Bishop stared at me for a moment. Then a grin stretched across his face. "You know, I think I like you."

"Lucky me," I snapped before I could stop myself. I wasn't sure what had come over me. In the past, I never would have given attitude to someone like Bishop.

He laughed. "You remind me of my sister-in-law, Alexandra."

"Why is that?"

"Because unlike the club wh—women, she doesn't take any shit from me."

"I like her already."

Rev chuckled at my response. "I agree with Bishop that you guys are a lot alike."

I put down the rest of my second cheeseburger. "Maybe I should come to Georgia with you two and meet her."

Both Rev and Bishop's mouths dropped open in shock at the same time. "Huh?" Bishop asked.

"Well, apparently I'm not supposed to stay in Texas, although I don't know why not. I sure as hell don't want to go back home, so Georgia sounds good."

Rev took a long gulp of his Coke. As he wiped his hands on his napkin, he appeared to be contemplating just how to respond to me. "Texas is Diablos headquarters. You aren't safe anywhere in the state, but especially not in College Station, where their traffickers do their prospecting."

Just the thought of the Diablos sent a chill prickling over my skin and sent my heart racing with the sudden tension. My bite of cheeseburger felt lodged in my throat, and it took two tries to swallow it. The room dipped and swayed a bit as I heard myself asking, "You think Mendoza is still alive?"

"We haven't received any intel that has confirmed his death."

My stomach twisted into knots at the thought of Mendoza being alive. "Do you think he would come after me?"

"It's a possibility, considering your body won't have been found in the compound."

The thought of ever having to see Mendoza again sent me reeling. My hand flew up to cover my mouth since I knew I was going to be sick. I pushed past Rev to race to the toilet. Over and over I heaved as overwhelming fear held me prisoner. Once I finally finished, I felt a hand at the small of my back.

"I'm sorry, Annabel," Rev said.

I eased past him to go to the sink. After rinsing my mouth, I caught his forlorn expression in the mirror.

"I should have found a better way to tell you that."

"It's okay. I needed the truth."

"You needed some nourishment, and it's my fault you lost that."

"Don't blame yourself." Turning around to face him, I asked, "So now I live the rest of my life in fear?"

He shook his head. "No. You don't. First of all, you're leaving Texas. Second, your father has the resources to protect you." With a grimace, Rev added, "Although it's a horrible prospect, Mendoza will most likely lose interest in you when he rebuilds his camp and another girl catches his eye."

My hand flew to my mouth again as I was sickened anew by the thought of another poor girl having to go through what I did. Leaning back against the sink, I shook my head miserably. "I don't want to go back home." When Rev started to protest, I held up a hand. "Just not yet. I don't think I have the strength to face my parents right now."

Rev didn't respond. Instead, he began to pace around the room. Bishop appeared in the doorway. "You okay?" he asked.

I gave him a weak smile. "As good as I can be."

Bishop nodded before turning his attention back to his brother. "What's his deal?"

Rev abruptly stopped pacing. He turned around and looked at Bishop. "Change of plans. She comes to Georgia with us."

Bishop's eyes widened. "Excuse me?"

"You heard me."

"Yes, but I'm not sure you're hearing yourself. We had a plan, remember? We've played the hero card long enough. After tomorrow, she ain't supposed to be our problem. She has a family to go home to, and it ain't ours."

Despite myself, I gasped at his harsh words while Rev growled and took a step toward Bishop. "You take that back."

"Or what?"

In a flash, Rev had crossed the room and had Bishop pushed against the wall. "Just because we're south of the border doesn't mean I'm not still your president, little brother. I gave you an order."

Bishop's face flooded crimson with anger. With his nostrils flaring and chest heaving, he silently seethed for a few seconds. "Fine. I take it back," he spat.

Gripping Bishop's shirt tighter, Rev said, "Now tell Annabel you're sorry that you were a selfish prick and you would be happy to have her visit us in Georgia."

With his body coiled with rage, Bishop jerked his head in my direction and pinned me with a stare. "I'm sorry I was a selfish prick, and I would be happy to have you visit us in Georgia."

Rev glanced over his shoulder at me. "Annabel, do you accept his apology, or does Bishop need to grovel a little more?"

"I accept it," I squeaked. My legs trembled, and I had to fight to keep myself from falling. It was alarming to witness the brothers at such odds, but it was even more shocking to see Rev, whom I'd only known as so refined and reserved, lose his temper. Especially since it was about me.

Once Rev seemed satisfied with my answer, he released Bishop. He then took a few deep breaths as if to calm himself. "Annabel, will you leave us for a moment?"

"Yes," I whispered and brushed past Bishop.

As the door closed behind me, I heard Rev say, "I'm sorry I had to do that, brother." Although part of me wanted to stand there and eavesdrop, I felt I owed Rev too much for that. Instead, I hurried back to bed and drew the covers over me.

While I didn't want to be the thing that came between Rev and Bishop, I couldn't help being grateful that Rev had taken up for me. I wanted to squeeze him tight to show how thankful I was to not be going home to Virginia. My parents were going to have a conniption fit, but they could get over themselves.

From here on out, I realized, I could rely only on myself. It was going to be all about me.

EIGHT

REV

After Annabel left and I apologized to Bishop, he and I silently stared each other down for a few minutes. I knew what I needed to say to him—what I *had* to say. But while the admission seemed to have flowed so effortlessly from my lips just hours earlier, I found myself tongue-tied, with a mouth full of sawdust.

After clearing my throat several times, I managed to croak, "You want the truth about what happened to me? The truth about what brought me out here?"

He shot me a surprised glance, and I knew that was the last thing he'd expected me to say. "Of course I do."

Leaning back against the tile, I nodded. "Then here it is."

For the second time that day, the bathroom became my confessional. I once again purged myself of the terrible secret I had kept hidden for so many years—and from so many of the people I loved. Telling Bishop was just as frightening as I had imagined it would be. When I finished, I felt as if all the muscles, tendons, and bones in my body had been stripped away, and I stood bare to my very soul in front of him. It was both terrifying and liberating.

Meanwhile I stared Bishop down, waiting for his response. Surprise flooded me at the sight of tears in his eyes. He swayed on his feet, like he wanted to close the distance between us but was unsure of how I might react. "Fuck, man, I don't know what to say."

With a humorless laugh, I said, "That seems to be the consensus when people hear the story."

"And you never told Mama?"

I shook my head. "No one but Preacher Man and Breakneck knew."

"Jesus," he muttered as he scrubbed the tears from his eyes. "I just can't . . . all those years . . ." His breath escaped in a wheeze. "When Preacher Man left, I was just a kid, but I still remember wondering what the fuck could have possibly gone wrong."

"It was because of me."

Bishop's face clouded over, and he jabbed his index finger at me. "Oh hell no, it wasn't. I don't care what kinda guilt shit you've carried around all these years, but I'm not going to fucking stand here and let you blame everything that happened on you. To start with, it was that fucking pervert's fault. And even though I hate to say it, Preacher Man was to blame, too, for letting it get the best of him."

Now it was my turn to fight back the tears. Deep down, I had always feared that if Deacon, and especially Bishop, found out my secret, they would hate me for ruining the family. "Thanks, man. I appreciate you saying that."

"It's the truth. I mean every fucking word. I ain't sugarcoating anything."

I snorted. "You, guilty of sugarcoating? Never."

Bishop grinned. "Damn straight."

Pushing myself off the wall, I moved closer to him. "One reason

I told you my story was because I felt you had a right to finally know. But there's another reason as well."

"What's that?"

"Annabel."

Bishop's brows came together in confusion. "What does she have to do with it?"

"Everything. She's the reason I came out to Texas. At first it seemed like Sarah was the only reason, but after everything that has happened, I understand now. While I might've saved Annabel, she did the same for me by allowing me to finally get rid of the secrets."

"You told her before you told me?" he questioned accusingly.

"Yeah, I did."

Although he appeared angry, I knew Bishop was hurt more than anything. "But I'm your blood, man. I'm your blood and your MC brother."

I placed my hand on his shoulder. "I know that. Just like being in the Raiders bonds us with our brothers, the same thing can be said for me and Annabel and the abuse we suffered."

Bishop rubbed his jaw while eyeing me thoughtfully. "I guess I get what you're saying. But I gotta be honest and say I don't really like it."

"I'm not asking you to like it. I just want you to respect it. And I want you to respect her."

His blue eyes narrowed. "I ain't never disrespected her."

"It's two different things, brother. You need to respect her feelings. There's nothing for her to go back home to besides two self-absorbed assholes for parents. While it might not make any sense and it won't be easy, she should come to Georgia with us if she wants to."

"You talked to Deacon about this?"

I laughed. "Are you suggesting I need to clear my business by him? Last time I checked, I made my own money and owned my row house at the compound."

"It ain't just your business. You're bringing home a former Diablos captive and drug cartel's favorite piece of ass."

My fists coiled in rage at my side, and although I would have hated to do it, I could have totally decked Bishop at that moment, but I managed to hold back. "Do not *ever* refer to Annabel like that again."

Bishop slowly shook his head back and forth. "Jesus, man, what has come over you with this girl?"

I threw my hands up in exasperation. "I already told you—"

"It's more than just that." He eyed me suspiciously. "You're not ready to let her go, either, are you?"

"No, I'm not, but it's not for the reason you think."

"You sure about that?"

"While she's healing, I'll do everything within my power to help her. I don't want Annabel to spend wasted years of her life drowning in useless emotion." Staring straight into his eyes, I said, "I really would like to have you on my side."

Bishop crossed his arms over his chest and grunted. "I should be offended that you even have to question whether I'm on your side." His expression lightened. "You're my brother—I'm always on your side. I might not like the shit you're doing, but I'm with you."

I couldn't contain the smile that spread across my face. "I'm so glad to hear you say that."

"Just remember, though. We never let puss—er, women come between us. Got it?"

"It's a deal."

The next morning began with a flurry of activity. There was a barrage of paperwork to have Annabel released. More money also exchanged hands to protect both Annabel's and our identities. There would be no record of any American girl or American bikers ever being in the hospital's vicinity. It cost a pretty penny to appease the crooked and corrupt police and medical officials, but in the end, it was worth every dime. While Bishop pressed me to ask Annabel's father for reimbursement, I chose to ignore him. We had plenty of dirty money that had been confiscated at Mendoza's compound by some of the other guys. What better way to spend it than on Annabel's freedom?

While Annabel forced down some of the hospital's breakfast, I got into the shower to get ready. I had almost finished when Annabel's bloodcurdling scream had me barreling out the bathroom door, buck naked and ready to take someone out.

With her eyes widened in fear, Annabel cowered on the bed. Her horror came from the three strange bikers standing in the room. Of course, from where I stood, I could see that the back of their cuts plainly read "Raiders." "Wait, it's okay, Annabel. These guys aren't going to hurt you," I said. Quickly, I ducked behind Sidewinder so she didn't have to see me naked.

"Rev?" she pleaded as if she couldn't imagine safety among any bikers other than Bishop and me.

"Yeah. Give me one sec. Okay?"

"Um, okay."

I raced back into the bathroom and threw a towel around my waist. When I came out, Chulo had his hands up as if Annabel was arresting him. I bypassed Snake and Ghost to go to Annabel's side.

Chulo put his hands down and smiled. "We're sorry to have scared you, but we just wanted to stop by and see you before you left."

"You did?" Annabel asked.

He nodded. "I knew you would need something to wear, so I borrowed some things from my girlfriend." When Snake snickered, Chulo smacked him on the back of the head. "They're probably going to be a little big on you because I like my women thick." He then held out the bag to Annabel.

She took it and smiled at him. "Thank you. That was very kind of you. Please thank your girlfriend for me as well."

Chulo grinned sheepishly. "If it's all the same with you, I would prefer not to mention that I was giving some strange woman her clothes."

Ghost nodded. "Lucia would beat his ass if she thought he was cheating."

While I chuckled, Annabel murmured, "Oh." Her face tinged pink. "Well, thank you anyway." When she started off the bed, her face came to eye level with my chest. For a moment, she paused as she stared at my intricate tattoos. She even took the time to read some of the lined verses. The longer she remained pressed against me, the more convoluted my feelings became. I inwardly berated myself for even momentarily enjoying the feel of having her so near to me. What kind of sick asshole would I be if I was remotely thinking of Annabel in an intimate way?

Finally her gaze swept to mine. "I—uh—I'll go get ready now."

"Okay," I replied as I was grateful for her to put some distance between us.

She hurried past me into the bathroom and locked the door behind her.

"Sorry we scared her, Rev," Ghost said apologetically.

"It's okay. I should've mentioned you guys might be coming by."

As the shower turned on, Ghost stared past me to the bathroom. "How's she doin'?"

I shrugged as I reached for a clean shirt. "Good as can be expected, I guess."

"I guess she knows to get the hell out of Texas, right?"

"Yes. She knows." When I pulled my cut on over my shirt, Chulo whistled and shook his head. "What?" I asked.

"Don't be wearing colors at the border. That'll get your shit flagged."

"Oh, okay." I didn't know why I hadn't thought of that myself. As I pulled off my cut, I asked, "You think we're going to have any problems getting out of the country?"

Chulo's dark eyes narrowed. "You doubting our paperwork ability?"

"Of course not. But I'd be lying if I didn't say your comment about the cut spooked me a little."

"Mendoza has no idea who it was who took his girl. *Yet*. You have that in your favor."

"Thanks for the pep talk," I joked as I thumped Chulo on the back.

"Just covering all the bases, man. We're still waiting for any confirmation on whether Mendoza is alive."

The bathroom door cracked open, and Annabel stuck just her head out. "Why is there hair dye in the bag?"

Ghost ran his hand over his beard. "Yeah, uh, about that. I forgot to mention you would need to change up how you look. You know, since your red hair would really stand out at the border check."

Annabel's green eyes widened. "Am I in that much danger?" she asked, her voice wavering in fear.

"It's only a precaution," I assured her while Chulo added, "And we made you a brunette on your passport."

"Wait, how did you get my picture?"

"The less you know, the better," Chulo replied.

While she didn't seem satisfied with his response, smart girl that she was, she didn't question him any further. Instead, she ducked her head back inside the bathroom and shut the door.

After I stuffed my cut into my bag, I turned back to Chulo. "Anything else I need to know about getting across the border?"

"I think everything should be fine. Once you're through the

checkpoint, I would advise burning daylight and not stopping until you get halfway across Texas." He grimaced. "'Course you got a senorita with you who'll probably start bitchin' to stop and take a leak or something."

I chuckled. "I think we'll make it fine. Annabel doesn't impress me as the high-maintenance type."

"For your sake, I hope you're right," Chulo replied.

Ghost threw out his hand. "We gotta be going, brother."

I smacked his palm and then drew him to me for a hug. "Seriously, I can't thank you enough for all your help."

"Sticking it to the Diablos was good fucking fun," he replied.

With a laugh, I pulled away. "We still owe you. Even though we're going legit, we're here for you guys when you need us."

"Glad to hear it. Don't hesitate to call us if you need anything."

"I appreciate it."

After exchanging handshakes and hugs with Chulo and Snake, the El Paso Raiders headed out the door. It was only a few moments later that Annabel emerged from the bathroom. I couldn't stop myself from doing a double take. It wasn't so much the baggy pair of jeans or the oversized, almost fluorescent, orange and lime green shirt. It was more about the fact that she looked completely different as a brunette.

At what must have been my lengthy stare, she brought her hand self-consciously to her hair. "Does it look okay?"

"Yeah. It looks great. No way would anyone recognize you now."

She appeared relieved that a slight alteration would help disguise her identity. "I'm just glad it's the kind that will wash out in a few days." As she gazed down at herself, she said, "I know it's probably a lot to ask, but when we get ready to stop for the night, I would *really* like to find some new clothes."

I smiled. "I think I can handle that."

"Thank you."

"Ready?"

She nodded. "I think I'm all packed," she mused.

I laughed at the forced good humor in her statement. "I do like a woman who can travel light," I replied as I slung my bag over my shoulder. "Let's go."

Even though we were in the relative safety of the hospital, I kept Annabel tucked close to my side. I wasn't taking any chances. When we got outside, we both had to shield our eyes from the glaring sun. We had spent two days under the fluorescent hospital lights.

After peering around the parking lot, Annabel asked, "Where's the car?"

"Bishop and Breakneck are bringing it here."

"It gets its own escort?"

I laughed. "I guess you could say that. The El Paso Raiders wanted to make sure it was kept safe until we needed it."

"Safe from what exactly?" she asked.

"Oh, I don't know. Something along the lines of being rigged with explosives."

Annabel frowned as she lamented, "So many precautions just for me."

"It's not just for you. It's for me as well."

"But you only need protection because you took me from Mendoza."

After shifting my bag on my arm, I shook my head at her. "Even if I had left you to die, I would still be a marked man. I helped storm the home of a Rodriguez cartel lieutenant where not only was his latest batch of girls 'destroyed,' but there was a substantial amount of money taken as well."

"I guess I didn't realize how much risk you had taken on."

Without realizing that she was probably still skittish when it came to being touched by men, I reached over and brushed a strand of dark hair out of her face. Her green eyes widened, but she didn't jerk away. "Sorry I had to rain on your little martyr parade."

She gave a bark of a laugh. "Smart-ass."

It was good to see her being lighthearted. We were interrupted by the roaring sound of incoming bikes. I jerked my head to the left to see Bishop and Breakneck pulling up to the curb. Following close behind them were two cars.

Even before I was told, I knew which one was for us. It looked to be a mid- to late-1980s Oldsmobile. It was the kind of car you didn't have to worry about getting stolen because it was so hideous-looking no one would give it a second glance. But the engine sounded good, so it would do its job by getting us back to Georgia.

"Glad to see you guys. For a minute, I thought you had forgotten us," I said.

Bishop grinned. "Forget your pain in the ass? Never."

"Yeah, yeah," I muttered with a smile. "You guys holding back for an hour or two before heading to the border?"

"Yep. Don't want to draw any unnecessary suspicion," Bishop replied.

When my gaze cut over to Breakneck, I couldn't help feeling a slight pang in my chest at the sight of him on my bike. "You take good care of her, okay?"

Breakneck smiled. "Quit wringing your hands like an old woman. I've been ridin' longer than you've been alive, you little jerk-off, so get it out of your head that I'm going to fuck up your bike."

I punched him playfully in the arm. "Thanks, asshole." Truth be told, I was grateful to see him smiling, period.

"Whatcha think of the car?" Bishop asked Annabel. I knew he was goading her just to get a reaction. He couldn't seem to let go of the fact that she was an "uptown girl," as he jokingly called her. He had thought the same thing about our now sister-in-law, Alexandra, when we first met her, but Annabel and her privileged upbringing put even Alexandra to shame.

Although I'm sure she had never ridden in anything that wasn't brand-new, Annabel smiled sweetly at Bishop. "Looks great. You know, if it's older than twenty years, you can consider it an antique, and I love antiques."

Shaking his head, Bishop grinned. "Oh, I do think I'm going to like having you back with us in Georgia, Uptown Girl."

"High praise indeed," she replied. Of course, she had no idea that when it came to Bishop, it really was the highest of praise.

"Okay, we should get going," I said.

As Annabel started to the car, Breakneck said, "I put a pillow and blanket in the back. The moment you get through border check, you need to lie down."

Annabel whirled around. "I don't think that's necessary."

"I do. And last time I checked, I was the physician here."

I braced myself for an argument, considering Annabel's stubbornness, but instead she merely held up her hands in defeat. "Fine, fine. I'll rest."

"Good. I'm glad to hear it. Another good thing about that car is the wide backseat."

"Lucky me," Annabel muttered as she opened the passenger-side door.

Breakneck reached in the pocket of his cut and pulled out a bottle of pills, which he handed to me. "Those are some painkillers in case she needs them."

"Thanks. I'll make sure she gets them."

"There's enough for both of you in there."

"I'm fine." With a smile, I offered him a joke from *Monty Python and the Holy Grail*. "'Tis just a flesh wound. I'd hardly admit to being shot when I barely got hit."

Breakneck gave me a no-nonsense look. "You still need to take care of yourself. I know you're going to be busting ass to get out of Texas, but you're going to need to stop and stretch your leg some."

"Okay. I will."

Breakneck gave a slight nod before sliding his helmet back on.

"See you guys back home sometime this week," I said.

Bishop nodded. "Be safe, brother. Let us know where you are and how it's going."

"Sure thing." Then I slid into the driver's seat, where I was blinded by the reflection from a set of sequined dice. "Jesus," I muttered before removing them and throwing them in the glove box.

"Not exactly your style?" Annabel questioned teasingly.

"Smart-ass." She smiled at me as I put the car into drive.

We had about a thirty-minute trip to the border. While El Paso and Juárez were separated only by the Paso del Norte bridge over the Rio Grande, both Mendoza's compound and the hospital had been tucked far away from the city.

At first we drove in silence. When Annabel started to fidget in her seat, I asked, "Nervous about the border crossing?"

She nodded. "A little."

By the way she was acting, I could tell her obvious fear was about more than just the border. "Tell me what else is bothering you."

With a grimace, she replied, "It's just little flashbacks of coming over with the Diablos."

"I'm sorry."

She shrugged. "It's okay. Guess it's to be expected."

"Yes, it is." When she continued wringing her hands and crossing and uncrossing her legs, I asked, "Do you want to talk about it?"

"Part of me does and the other part of me is afraid to. Like once I let go a little, I'll just be opening myself up to emotional chaos."

"It's a bad metaphor, but a Pandora's box of sorts?"

Her eyes widened in surprise. "Yes, I suppose you're right."

Cocking her head at me, she said, "I hope this doesn't sound snobby, but it surprises me to hear you speak of metaphors."

"Because I'm supposed to be a dumb biker?"

Her face flushed. "I'm sorry. I hate when people have preconceived notions and end up stereotyping, and here I am doing it myself."

I chuckled. "It's okay, Annabel. Most bikers spout metaphors all the time, but they have no fucking clue what the actual term means. For me, I've always been an intellectual. I've been a reader as far back as when I was a kid, but after the rape, I seemed to enjoy escaping into fictional worlds more and more. Then, as I got a little older, I started wanting to read about history—presidents, soldiers, kings, and emperors. I figured I could learn something from them."

"How fascinating," she replied, with true sincerity.

"Most of my family wouldn't share your praise. They think because I got a two-year degree from community college and can spout off quotes from literature, I'm trying to be above my raising."

"But they're so wrong." She shook her head. "You're truly a Renaissance man. As for me, I don't know anything but math and science."

"That's what you needed to know to be a vet."

She gasped. "How did you know . . . Oh, right, I told you in the hospital, didn't I?"

I nodded. "Actually, I had already found out a lot about you through your missing-persons information."

"Oh, I see," she murmured.

"Don't worry. It was nothing embarrassing."

She laughed. "I would hope not." Turning slightly in her seat to face me, she said, "Quote something for me."

"What?"

"You said you could quote literature. I would love to hear something."

"Seriously?"

Her face brightened. "Yes, please."

"Okay, then. Don't say I didn't warn you." Once again, the sweet peals of her laughter rang in my ear.

"'It was many and many a year ago, / In a kingdom by the sea, / That a maiden there lived whom you may know / By the name of Annabel Lee.'"

Annabel's green eyes widened in delight. "You know Poe's 'Annabel Lee'?"

"I do. I know 'The Raven' as well. Poe's a personal favorite of mine."

"I was named for Annabel Lee."

With a grin, I told her, "I had a hunch."

"My sister is Lenore from 'The Raven.'"

"Your parents must have a love for Poe as well."

"My mother majored in English in college." Annabel rolled her eyes. "Mainly she was there to get the all-important MRS degree, but she managed to snag my father and finish college."

I laughed. "I can't help but wonder how someone like you came from two such horrible people."

She smiled. "That's a good question. It's one I often ask myself as well."

My amusement was short-lived when I saw we had come upon the border checkpoint. Annabel let out a small squeak of alarm as she shot straight up in her seat. "It's going to be fine. We can count on the Raiders to make excellent documents. We'll get right through."

"Okay," she replied softly.

"But try not to look suspicious."

Her eyes widened in horror. "I look suspicious?"

"When you look like you're going to piss your pants."

She giggled, and I was glad to ease the tension in the car. "Okay,

okay. I'll be calm. I'll be the best Mary Jones I can be," she replied, alluding to the name on her passport.

Slowly, the car inched along in the line. When we reached the inspector, I rolled the window down and handed him our passports. He gazed at our pictures and then back at us. Time seemed to tick by agonizingly slowly. Beads of sweat, both from the heat and from my nerves, began to form on the back of my neck.

The officer handed our passports over to another man. He also took his time eyeing us and the documents. Just as I felt the tension threaten to overwhelm Annabel, the man stamped the passports and handed them back to the first officer.

After he shoved them back at me, he waved us on. The moment the car passed through, I exhaled the breath I had been holding. Once we were out of their sight, I gunned the engine, and like Chulo had instructed me, I began to put as much distance as I could between us and the border.

NINE

Manuel Mendoza peered at the blackened desolation of his once-thriving trafficking camp. With his upper lip curled in disgust, he surveyed the construction workers scrambling around the land. It had been one fucking week since those cocksuckers had breached what should have been an impenetrable fortress. His first act after the fires were extinguished was to put a bullet in the head of the man in charge of his security.

Once that was done, he'd had his remaining men search the compound for his Roja. Just picturing her beautiful red hair and creamy white skin sent an ache through his groin. He had beaten her within an inch of her life, but he knew he was justified in his actions. The cunt had called out another man's name when he was fucking her. After everything he had done for her, for her to betray him like that . . . She deserved the violent beating.

When the search of the compound came up empty, he remembered destroying his bedroom in a rage. He had intended for no other man to ever have her—and now she was in the hands of the people who had stormed his compound.

If she'd lived.

He clung to the hope that she hadn't. For if she was alive, the moment he learned where she was he was going after her. She was his, and she would die by his hands like she should have before.

"*Lo siento* for the interruption, boss." It was the sniveling voice of one of his soldiers.

Mendoza jerked his gaze over his shoulder. "Didn't I make it perfectly clear that I was not to be disturbed?" he snarled.

The man's face paled. "Uh, yeah, but, uh, I think this is something you will want to see."

"What is it?" Mendoza hissed.

With a shaky hand, the man thrust out a few black-and-white pictures. "I have some friends at the border. I had asked them to be on the lookout for any American girls who fit Roja's description."

Mendoza snatched the pictures out of his hand.

"I weeded out the ones that couldn't possibly be her. There's a few who have potential. Of course, they're black and white, so that makes it harder to look for her hair."

After staring at two of the photos, he chucked them to the ground. He had every inch of Roja memorized, so he knew when the breasts were too large or small or the face too round.

He grunted with frustration as he came to the last photograph. When he peered down at it, a mixture of hope and anger filled him. Although the image wasn't completely clear, he knew without a shadow of a doubt it was his Roja. But as soon as he had identified her, rage coiled through him at the sight of her with a strange man. Was this the one whose name she had called out? "Find out everything you can about this man."

"But we don't have anything to go on. Not a license plate, and I'm sure if they were fleeing, they used fake passports."

Mendoza narrowed his eyes. "I gave you an order."

The man paled for a second time before he swallowed hard and said, "Yes, sir."

When Mendoza was once again alone, he gathered his scattered thoughts. He loathed unfinished business. First, he would rebuild his camp. Every day that went by without business was money out of his pocket. Taking care of Roja could wait until he was back on his feet.

In the end, she wasn't going anywhere. When he didn't come after her at first, she could have her false sense of security. But then he would track her down.

He would have her tight pussy around his cock one last time before he cut her beating heart from her chest.

Roja. Was. Fucking. His.

TEN

ANNABEL

After the moments of tense scrutiny of our documents at the border, the adrenaline had left me reeling. When Rev instructed me to climb into the backseat, at first I had wanted to argue like a petulant toddler that I wasn't tired. But instead, I had happily eased over the seat and into the back, smiling at the evidence of Breakneck's kindness and concern—the pillow and blanket. Although it was too hot to cover up, I laid the blanket over the worn leather seat and curled up with the pillow. Soon I was lulled into a deep sleep.

I had no idea how many hours had passed when I woke up to Rev gently shaking me. "Time to stop for gas and something to eat, Sleeping Beauty."

With a yawn, I replied, "Not hungry."

"Nope. Don't want to hear anything other than your chewing. You need food to build your strength back up."

I popped one eye open to look at him. "Eesh. You're so bossy."

He grinned down at me. "Come on."

"Perfect," I mumbled as I sat up in the seat. I rubbed my

aching neck with one hand and opened the car door with another. "Where are we?"

"About an hour or two from the Louisiana state line."

I felt my mouth gape open in shock. "I slept the entire way across Texas?"

"Pretty much. 'Course, I was making good time. Cops don't pay much notice to hunk-of-junk cars."

I grinned. "I see." As I gazed around the parking lot at our surroundings, I saw that Rev had stopped at some mom-and-pop greasy-spoon kind of diner. From the eighteen-wheelers lined up in the parking lot, I could tell the place catered to truckers. "We're eating here?" I questioned, trying my best not to openly express my disappointment.

"Are you insinuating this place is a dump?"

My cheeks instantly warmed. "Of course not."

"It's okay, Annabel. I was just teasing you," Rev replied. "This place does look like kind of a dump, but it just so happens to come highly recommended."

"It does?"

He laughed. "Don't sound so surprised. Good food doesn't always have to come on linen tablecloths and on fine china."

"I am well aware of that," I countered. When he ducked his head to rummage around in the trunk, I added, "For the record, I haven't always eaten on fine china with silver. I do know how to be normal."

Rev closed the trunk lid. I saw then he held his leather cut in his hand—the one I hadn't seen him wear since my first night in the hospital. He slid it on, and almost instantly, his appearance changed in front of me. The kind, approachable Rev seemed to fade away and in his place was a tougher, rough-around-the-edges guy. It was more than just a little unnerving.

He had become so in tune to my feelings that he immediately looked at me with scrutiny. "What's wrong?"

"Why did you just put that on?"

While he tried to shrug off the question, I could see his jaw clenching like he was holding back. "It's my cut."

"But why now? I mean, I get you not wearing it at the border where you could be identified." I drew in a deep breath and repeated an earlier question. "Are we in some kind of danger?"

Rev stared at me for a moment before exhaling a loud breath. "Look, Annabel, there's a lot about my world that you don't understand and you don't *need* to understand."

"So you can't explain to me why putting on a piece of leather matters?" I motioned to his cut.

"Just know as long as you're with me, you're not in danger."

"Especially since you're wearing that cut now?"

Rev growled as he shoved his keys in his pocket. "You just can't leave it alone, can you?"

"Being stubborn is part of my being normal, too," I countered.

I was grateful when he finally smiled at me. "I know you can be normal, Annabel. In fact, I don't know if I've ever seen someone able to be so 'normal' in spite of what all she's been through."

"Thank you," I murmured.

"So come on. You need a nutritional meal, and this place is supposed to have really good food—some nutritious shit that you need."

When I realized that was all I was going to get from him, I reluctantly agreed. "Okay."

As we walked across the parking lot, Rev kept his hand at the small of my back. When we walked inside the diner, the bell over the door tinkled, alerting the patrons to our presence. It seemed to me that conversation momentarily halted, but it also could have been just my imagination.

A waitress who reminded me a lot of "Kiss my grits" Flo from the TV show *Alice* came up to us. I'd often watched old reruns on the television set in the kitchen when I was growing up. Our cook had been a big fan of the show. "Two?"

"Yes, please."

She grabbed some menus. "Follow me."

As we passed a row of booths and tables, the hardened-looking truckers took notice of Rev. Then I witnessed an expression of respect pass over their faces. I knew then the reason why he had put on his cut. There was unspoken power in the worn leather, and at the moment, I was grateful for it.

We slid into a booth next to a large glass window. The waitress handed us the menus. "What can I get you to drink?"

"I'll have a Coke," I replied.

"And you?" the waitress asked Rev.

"I'll take a sweet tea and a milk."

The waitress scribbled down our order. "Be right back."

I started to glance over the menu when Rev said, "By the way, the milk is for you."

My gaze snapped to his. "Excuse me?"

"You need the vitamins."

"What if I don't like milk?" I countered.

Rev ran a palm down his face in exasperation. "What if I don't care whether you like it?"

I couldn't believe his sudden audacity. "I have a very controlling father back in Virginia. I don't need another one."

Rev leaned his elbows on the table and shot me a no-nonsense look. "I'm not trying to control you. I'm merely showing concern for your health. You ate like a bird in the hospital, so you're already at a nutritional deficit. I couldn't say for sure, but I would imagine you didn't eat well while you were with Mendoza—"

"Actually, I had all the best food available there since I ate my meals with him." It was the truth. Whereas the girls in the barracks got the bare minimum. Mendoza was too smart to starve them because if they lost too much weight and looked unhealthy, they lost their attractiveness to potential buyers. As for me, I sat up in the main house eating lobster and steak simply because I was Mendoza's favorite of the moment.

Rev held up one of his hands. "I stand corrected. However, with the blood you lost, coupled with your surgery, you're going to have to fight off anemia. After you drink your milk, I would suggest you order a steak, along with some green leafy vegetables like a salad or some spinach."

"Now you're my nutritionist along with my rescuer?" I snapped.

"Annabel," Rev said softly but with conviction.

I sighed. "I'm sorry. You're just trying to be nice, and here I am taking out some shit on you, aren't I?"

"I can understand why."

"You can?"

He nodded. "For the last two months of your life, you were completely under someone else's authority. It's only natural now that you're free that you would fight against anyone trying to exert any control over you."

I blinked at him a few times before I could calm my emotions enough to respond. In the few days I had known him, it never ceased to amaze me how it was possible that Rev could read me so easily. None of my family or even my close friends had ever had such insight.

The waitress returned with our drinks. When she set the milk down in front of Rev, I reached out and slid it over to me. I was rewarded with a genuine smile from him.

"Know whatcha want?"

When he saw I was still uncertain, Rev went ahead with his order. "I'll have the sirloin, well done, a loaded baked potato, and a salad with Italian dressing."

The waitress turned to me. "And you?"

"The same. Except can you make mine a sweet potato?"

"Sure can."

"Thanks." When I caught Rev's eye, I said, "They're full of potassium, which I'm sure I could use."

He grinned. "I'm glad you're taking this more seriously."

Once the waitress left, I began slowly sipping on my milk. I'd never been a big fan of milk outside of a bowl of sugary cereal, but I wanted to do everything I could to help my recovery.

We sat in silence for a few moments, listening to the hum of the conversations around us. Before I met Rev I had always rushed to fill silences with small talk. But there was something about being around him that made silence somehow more tolerable . . . more comforting.

After finishing off my milk, I asked, "So what happens when we get back to Georgia?"

He shrugged. "I haven't thought it out that far. I assumed we could play it by ear, but most of all, I thought I would let you call the shots."

My mouth gaped open in surprise. "Me?"

He nodded. "When it comes to you, I would assume you want to be making the decisions, right?"

"Well, yes, but at the same time, I'll be your guest . . . or the club's guest, or however it is. I would respect that."

Rev appeared thoughtful. "My house is directly behind the club, so I guess you could say the two go hand in hand. But you are my guest, and my brothers will respect that."

"I just don't want to be an inconvenience."

"You won't be. I'll put you to work earning your keep."

I laughed. "Oh, you will, huh?"

Rev grinned. "You said yourself that you didn't want to be an inconvenience."

"I can cook for you."

"You cook?" Rev asked, his voice laced with doubt.

"Yes, I do."

"I'm sorry. It's just you didn't strike me as the type who could cook."

"One of the few decent people in our household was our cook. I hung out with her a lot. You pick up things."

"I see." Rev rubbed his hand over his beard. "So you're willing to cook for me."

"Of course."

"That's going to upset my mama."

"How come?"

He laughed. "She usually cooks for us."

"Oh, well, I could help her, then."

"Actually, I like the idea of having you in my house, cooking just for me."

"Do you now?"

With a wink and a grin, he replied, "Yes, I do."

"Are you flirting with me, Reverend Malloy?" I couldn't resist teasing him, and it felt good to let myself relax a little.

"Just stating facts, Annabel Percy," he replied.

Just then our waitress appeared with our salads. At the sight of the overflowing plate, my stomach growled loudly enough for Rev to hear, which caused him to chuckle.

Once we were alone again, I was suddenly overwhelmed when I realized I had just accused him of flirting. After everything I had gone through, how could I possibly think of teasing a man about flirting? Least of all Rev. Not only did it go against the bond of friendship we had established, but it was probably insulting to a man like him. Considering how good-looking he was, never mind what a sweet side he hid, I was sure he had a constant string of women interested in him, whether he reciprocated the attention or not. He certainly didn't need a physical and emotional mess like me.

"What are you thinking about?"

"Nothing," I lied as I shoved a large bite of salad into my mouth.

Rev's fork stilled on his plate. "Something was bothering you. Your whole expression just darkened, not to mention your brows are all tense."

I swallowed hard. After taking a sip of Coke, I finally looked at him. "I was just wondering what was wrong with me for even mentioning flirting."

"What was so wrong with that? You were just teasing me."

I pushed some of the salad around on my plate. "I have these thoughts about the things I shouldn't say and do after what I experienced in captivity. What I've been through. Things that could be misconstrued as inappropriate and wrong. Maybe they're crazy, maybe they're not."

Rev chewed thoughtfully for a moment before he spoke. "Annabel, there isn't a handbook for people like us. They don't make the 'Dos and Don'ts after You've Been a Sex Slave' manual."

Just the mention of the term "sex slave" caused me to shudder in revulsion. But it was the truth—it was who I was now. A former sex slave. After living through that, I certainly couldn't be squeamish about it now. It didn't have to define who I was, but there was no denying it was a part of me. Somehow that title was also dictating to me how I should feel and act, which in the end felt like another form of enslavement. That would be the prime reason why a man like Rev would *not* be flirting with the likes of me.

While I was lost in my thoughts, Rev reached across the table for my hand. He squeezed it, and that jostled me out of my musings. "You have to do what is best for you, what makes you happy. You can't worry whether it's what someone else in your shoes would do. You are your own person, and you hold the keys to your healing."

Although his words made perfect sense, it was hard to believe them. "I guess you're right."

"Are you afraid someone is going to judge you?"

I nodded as tears filled my eyes. "Like someone would think I was sick and disgusting for even being able to have those kinds of thoughts after what happened to me."

"I don't think anyone would expect you to be a nun for the rest of your life simply because you were raped."

"But to be joking with you like that so soon? Doesn't that mean there's something wrong with me? I should find men repulsive and the thought of sex revolting."

Rev shook his head. "It just means the old you is slowly finding its way back to the new you. Even if the two never totally merge again, you can't be so hard on yourself. We can't help how we feel."

"I guess you're right," I repeated.

"Take death, for example. Everyone grieves differently. Just because someone isn't weeping uncontrollably, it doesn't mean they loved the deceased less than someone who is crying and screaming. We all handle emotions differently. Just like you can't tell someone the right way or wrong way to grieve, you can't tell them how to handle life after sexual abuse."

I tried to digest Rev's words. They seemed so easy to accept, so logical, when they were coming from him. But in my warped frame of mind, I could say the same thing he had and still not believe it. I had hope that one day I would be okay with how I felt, but for now, I knew I had a long, long way to go.

After our waitress brought us our plates, Rev asked, "Are you okay now?" Even though I wasn't, I nodded. "You don't have to lie to me, Annabel."

With a sigh, I picked up my knife and fork and began cutting into my steak. "Fine. I'm not okay. Because I know that even if I stop worrying about it right now, it's going to come up again."

"When it does, just push it away."

"Easier said than done."

"I know it is because I've been there before myself."

"Really?"

He fidgeted in his seat. "Yeah, I have."

"So how did you handle it?"

Rev groaned. "Why do you have to have an example? Can't you just trust me on this one?"

I shrugged. "I guess I just have to have concrete examples. Call it the scientist in me."

"Yeah, well, I'm not sure this one will help," Rev muttered. He momentarily closed his eyes like he was trying to gather his strength. "Okay, fine. Here it is. I thought I was completely sick and twisted whenever I got erections after my attack. I turned twelve a few months later and was a preteen boy who couldn't help what his body was doing. But in my head, I thought it was me being perverted and wanting something I shouldn't."

"Oh," I murmured, trying not to let my mortification reach my cheeks. I then proceeded to try to look anywhere but at Rev.

"You asked for it."

"I know. Trust me, I'm sorry I pressed you for the information."

After a few seconds of embarrassment hung over the table, a laugh came bursting out of me before I could stop myself. When I finally dared to look over at Rev, he was staring wide-eyed at me. I continued laughing, unable to catch my breath. It was like some emotional dam had broken within me, and this was the way everything was getting out. It sure beat crying.

"Annabel?" Rev questioned cautiously once I got hold of myself.

I dabbed my eyes with a napkin. "I'm sorry. I guess it was just the absurdity of the moment. Here I am having a breakdown because I had been thinking we were flirting with each other, not to mention we are two adults who just died a thousand deaths from talking about erections."

When Rev realized I hadn't totally lost my mind, he smiled. "I guess we were being a little uptight."

"Yes, uptight seems to sum up exactly how I've been reacting to my feelings. I'm going to take your advice and push the thoughts away. Most of all, I want to lighten up. Despite what happened to me, I'm lucky to have gotten out of there."

"More than anything, you need to be kind to yourself." After taking a sip of tea, he said, "I know when you asked what the plans were when we get to Georgia, I said it was up to you."

"You did."

"I would make one suggestion. It's one I hope you will take."

He certainly had my interest piqued now. "What is it?"

"I want you to see a therapist as soon as possible."

My stomach churned a little at the prospect. It wasn't that I didn't believe in seeing a therapist. It was just that I didn't want to have to dredge up everything that had happened to me and relive it with a perfect stranger. At the same time, I knew I didn't want to spend the rest of my life dealing with the fallout of emotional issues I tried to bury. So I nodded at Rev. "Yes, I will."

I could tell he was a little surprised at how easily I consented to his suggestion. "My sister-in-law is a teacher. She works closely with a lot of health-care professionals. I can ask her to recommend one without going into your story."

"Thank you, Rev. I would appreciate that."

He smiled. "You're welcome." He then jerked his chin at my plate. "Now eat some more steak."

Despite rolling my eyes, I didn't bother arguing with him. Instead, I chowed down on my steak and sweet potato, which were delicious. I managed to put a lot away until my overloaded stomach began to protest. I set my fork and knife down on the plate and eased back in the booth.

Rev motioned out the window. "Look."

I followed his gaze across the street from the diner where the twinkling, multicolored lights of a small carnival, including a Ferris wheel, stretched high into the sky.

"When we were kids, Bishop and I couldn't wait each year for the fair to come to town. It was set up just down the road from us, and we used to save our money up so we could go every night."

I smiled at him. "Sounds like fun."

His brows shot up. "Did you ever go to a fair as a kid?"

Shaking my head, I replied, "I always wanted to go, but my parents . . ." I grimaced as their words echoed through my head.

"What?"

I twisted my napkin in my lap. "My parents said only low-rent people went to the fair, and I would catch something from them."

Rev barked out a humorless laugh. "Well, I'm pretty sure they were right about my family's low-rent status, but we never spread any diseases."

I stared down at my plate, wishing I had answered him differently. In that moment, I hated my parents even more. I hated their hypocrisy of acting like they cared for the poor by having thousand-dollar-a-plate fund-raisers, but at the same time staring down their noses at anyone who wasn't in their social class.

Even though it wasn't the sufficient apology he deserved, I whispered, "I'm sorry."

"You have nothing to be sorry about."

"But—"

Rev shook his head. "You're not your parents, Annabel."

"I know."

"Good." He reached around to get his wallet out of his pants. After tossing out some bills, he grinned at me. "I think it's time you went to your first carnival."

"Seriously?"

"Sure."

"But since I'm still healing, I can't ride anything."

"We can still walk around and take in the sights."

I had to admit the prospect definitely excited me. "Are you sure we have time?"

Rev smiled. "We'll make time."

I laughed. "Okay, let's do it!"

We made our way out of the diner, looked both ways before hurrying across the highway, and then inched our way up the line to the ticket booth.

Once we got inside, I was momentarily overwhelmed by the crowd. So many strangers. *So many strange men.* In spite of the heat, a chill passed over my skin.

As if he could sense my apprehension, Rev drew me close against him. "Anytime you want to leave, you just tell me."

Although part of me would have preferred to turn around then, I knew I owed it to Rev—and to myself—to try to stay. I was safe with him. No one could hurt me as long as Rev was around. And in some small way, if I did stay, it would be a victory of overcoming my fears. "I will," I replied.

As we walked around, I battled the sensory overload I found myself in—the noisy chatter, the smells of popcorn and funnel cakes, the screams from people on the roller coasters and other rides. Each time I would meet the eyes of a strange man, I would burrow closer to Rev. Thankfully, he didn't seem to mind.

"What was your favorite part of the fair growing up?" I gazed up and tried to focus on him rather than the crowd around us.

"That's a tough one. Even though they're kinda cheesy now, I really loved the rides. The bigger the adrenaline rush, the better time I had. But I also liked playing the games." He smiled down at me. "As I got older, I would try to win something to give to a girl."

"Aw, that's so sweet."

He laughed. "Yeah, that was my idea of being a suave Casanova. I had a lot to learn."

My gaze caught the glittering lights of the Ferris wheel. "I can wait here if you want to go on some of the rides," I offered. Secretly, I would die a thousand deaths until he returned, but I was willing to do it for him.

Rev immediately shook his head. "I'm fine."

"Well, the least you can do is play some games. You know, for old times' sake and all."

With a smile, Rev said, "Yeah, I guess I could." He then led me over to one of the booths. The game was set up so you won if you could hit the bull's-eye on the target.

The guy behind the counter eyed Rev's cut before handing him the toy gun. I could tell by his expression he didn't much care for Rev playing the game—as if wearing the cut gave him an unfair advantage or something. If Rev noticed it, he didn't let on.

Instead, he focused on the target in front of him. His first shot pinged against the center of the bull's-eye, knocking it down. "Great shot!" I exclaimed.

"What prize?" the man asked.

"It's the lady's choice," Rev replied.

I laughed. "Really?"

"Of course."

"Hmm," I murmured as I gazed up at the stuffed animals on display. A cute brown and white dog caught my eye. "I'll take that one," I said, pointing to it. The man took it down and then handed it to me. "Thank you."

"Come on. Let's try some other ones," Rev said.

"Ah, I've created a monster, huh?" I teased.

"Yes and no. I fully intend to have you play some as well."

"Me?" My voice squeaked.

He grinned. "Why not?"

"Rev, I wouldn't even begin to know how to shoot," I protested.

"We'll find you one that doesn't involve shooting."

"One thing I haven't told you is I'm not very athletic."

"I'm not sure I'm too surprised to hear that."

I smacked him playfully on the arm. "Hey now."

"Here. Let's try this one." He motioned to a booth where smaller children were picking up floating ducks to match prizes.

"I don't think I'm so bad that we have to start at a kiddie booth."

Rev laughed. "Okay, okay. You pick one."

I gazed around at my choices. "How about that one?" Across from us was a booth that boasted milk jugs. To win you had to toss a ring over the top of a jug. I figured it couldn't be that hard.

"Looks good to me."

After we walked over, Rev paid the man for some tickets. I was handed three rings. My first attempt didn't even make it to the milk jug. The next smacked against the bottom. And after I put some oomph into the third, it went flying behind the jug. When I dared to look at Rev, he gave me an innocent look. "Want to try again?"

"Sure. Why not?"

Once again he paid and I was handed the rings. Once again I managed to get them nowhere near where they were supposed to be. "Again?" Rev asked.

I shook my head as I fought the embarrassment I was sure was tinging my cheeks. "No, I want to find the nearest concession stand. I plan to drown my inadequacies at carnival games in some cotton candy."

Rev laughed. "Sounds like a plan."

It wasn't too hard locating the food. We simply had to follow the delicious smells wafting through the air. I decided on a corn dog and fresh lemonade along with my cotton candy. Rev ordered a funnel cake and a beer.

When he once again got out his wallet, I sighed. "What's wrong?" he asked.

I frowned. "I just hate you're having to pay so much for me. I'll be glad when I can find a local branch of my bank and have some money of my own."

"I don't mind paying."

"I know you don't. It's me who minds."

"If it will make you feel better, I can start you a tab."

"Smart-ass."

While we ate our food, we walked around the other side of the fair, taking in the rides and various booths. As dusk started to fall, I became a little apprehensive. There was something more menacing in being around strangers in the dark versus the daylight. Every little noise from the rides made me jump.

When a man who had clearly had too much to drink bumped into me, a scream burst from my lips before I could think better of it. Rev rushed forward, grabbing the man by the throat and pinning him to the side of one of the booths. "What the fuck are you doing hitting her like that?" Rev demanded as his broad chest rose and fell with harsh pants.

The man's blue eyes widened in fear as he took in both Rev's imposing size and the menacing expression on his face. "N-Nothing. I swear."

Feeling ashamed at my overreaction, I tentatively reached out to touch Rev's arm. "It's okay. Rev, he didn't mean anything by it," I said softly, trying to calm him down. This hair-trigger-temper side of him wasn't something I was used to seeing, and if I was honest with myself, it was a little alarming.

Whether it was because of my touch or my reassurances that I was fine, I didn't know, but Rev calmed down enough to release the man. He apologized repeatedly as he stumbled away from us. For a few seconds Rev refused to look at me. When he finally did, his features had returned to normal. "I'm sorry about that."

"It's okay."

He shook his head. "No, it isn't. I scared you, which is the last thing I wanted to do."

I closed the gap between us. "I would be lying if I said that scene just now didn't alarm me." Staring up into his apologetic blue eyes, I added, "You just seemed so different."

"In my world, I have to be violent to get things done."

Although there was regret on his face, his tone was matter-of-fact. I realized then that there was so much more to Rev than I had originally imagined, and I wasn't sure if I really wanted to know everything.

"Guess we better head out," Rev said, breaking the tense silence between us.

"Okay," I murmured. As I clutched the dog he had won me tightly against my chest, I let him start leading us out of the fair.

Just before we got to the exit, Rev abruptly stopped. "Can I have just a few more minutes?" he asked.

"Of course."

He took my hand and led me over to one of the few booths that were close to the exit. I watched as he handed over some tickets and then started to play. It wasn't a shooting game, but Rev still managed to master it.

When the guy asked what prize, I half expected Rev to turn to me. Instead, he pointed to a green alligator wearing a pink tutu and ballet slippers. When he turned back to me, he wore an accomplished smile.

"Just who is that alligator for, Casanova?"

He laughed. "It's for my niece, Willow. She's a ballerina."

I stared at him in surprise at that; he had never mentioned

having a niece. From his tone when he spoke about her, coupled with the fact that he had gone to the trouble to win something for her, it was obvious he loved her very much.

"How old is she?"

"Six going on sixteen."

I smiled at his summation. "I bet she's crazy about you."

"What makes you say that?"

"If you're as kind and devoted with her as you are with me, then she would have no reason not to be crazy about you."

With a grin, Rev replied, "I can't speak for her, but I do know I'm crazy about her. She's been such a blessing to my family since she came to live with us a year ago." At what must've been my surprised expression, Rev proceeded to tell me all about his niece's tragic early years with a drug-addicted mother, her mother's murder, and how she came to live with his older brother, Deacon.

"Poor thing," I murmured as we started out of the exit.

"She's the most amazing little girl. Smart, funny, and sweet. Resilient as hell. You'd never know by seeing her now that she'd ever been through such hard times." He cut his gaze over to mine. "I can't wait for you to meet her."

His words sent a surge of warmth through my chest. I couldn't help feeling grateful he wanted me to meet the niece he adored. Suddenly it felt like we were as connected as we had been during most of this trip, and the discomfort I'd felt when he confronted the guy back at the carnival disappeared. Now our bond seemed even stronger.

"I can't wait to meet her, either." I motioned to the alligator. "And to see her reaction to her present."

"It's not much, but I know she would be pissed if I was gone and didn't bring her back anything."

"She'll adore it."

Rev stared down at the alligator. "I just hope I have a kid like her one day."

I sucked in a harsh breath—hearing him state his desire to have children felt the same as if someone had punched me in the gut. In truth, it was more like someone drove a dagger into my chest. I had once spoken with the same conviction about children as Rev had. I guess it wasn't too surprising he wanted a family—the vast majority of people did. It was more about the way he had said the words, the desire that resonated in his tone. There was not a doubt in my mind that he would make a wonderful father.

While I could hear Breakneck's words that it wasn't impossible for me to be a mother, it did little to make me feel better.

Thankfully, we arrived at the car then, and if Rev realized how his words had stung me, he didn't let on. I was glad he hadn't. I'd always hated having someone's pity, especially Rev's.

After Rev started the engine, the physical and emotional exertions of the day caught up with me, and I nodded off. I awoke to Rev pulling me to him. "Come on, Annabel." Before I could protest to give me a few minutes to wake up so I could walk, he was lifting me into his arms.

Panic overcame me when I felt myself floating. My eyelids snapped open, and I furiously took in my surroundings. My chest rose and fell in painful, panicked breaths. It took everything within me not to scream as a flashback overcame me.

Sensing my distress, Rev began murmuring softly to me. "It's okay. It's just you and me. No ghosts of the past allowed."

Tears stung my eyes at the kindness of his words and the fact that he was carrying me into the motel room so that I didn't have to exert myself. I curled my fist tighter into his shirt. Somehow his strength was enough to ward off the flashbacks. I wasn't back at the motel with the Diablos. Instead, it was Rev, and only Rev, with me.

After he kicked the door closed, Rev asked, "Do you want to change?"

Since I could barely keep my eyes open, I replied, "Just sleep."

"Okay." He eased me down onto one of the beds and pulled the cover from the other side over to wrap me up. "Sweet dreams, Annabel."

"Same to you," I murmured before sleep once again overtook me.

*N*aked after his last attack, I lay on my side with him pressed against me. As his fingers skimmed over my back, I prayed that even though it was early in the evening, he would fall asleep.

He had been gone most of the day. Business meetings of some sort. He had returned, finely dressed in one of his thousand-dollar suits and reeking of alcohol.

"Go put on my dress shirt," he commanded.

Since I always did just as he asked, I slipped out of bed and padded silently across the cool marble floor as I went over to the chair where he had tossed his shirt. Quickly, I slid it on and buttoned it up. Because of his height, it reached my knees.

With a flick of his wrist, he beckoned me to him. "Come here."

I drew in a breath of trepidation, but immediately went back over to the bed.

Mendoza stared up at me, drinking in my appearance from head to toe. "Mmm, you look sexy in my clothes." He shoved his hands into my hair and jerked my head closer to his. Within seconds, his lips were moving frantically against mine.

In another time and place, far from here, I might have considered his dark, chiseled features handsome. But because of the monster I knew him to be, I never looked at him without thinly veiled repulsion. His ego was so enlarged that he expected me to enjoy his rapes. At first, I had wept inconsolably during each attack, and in return I got beaten. I had learned very quickly to use my imagination. Instead of Mendoza, I pretended it was Brad Pitt or Henry Cavill in the bed with me—anything to endure it.

He pulled me down onto the bed beside him. After rolling on top of me, he shoved up the dress shirt. "Roja," he murmured against my lips.

I disconnected the moment he slammed into me. Instead of Mendoza's black, soulless eyes looming over me, it was the gentle, caring eyes of Dr. Josh Jenkins. What I imagined with him wasn't even sexual. It was more about the kindness he had shown me, the dimples that appeared when he smiled, his tender bedside manner with his four-legged patients.

Because I missed him, the animals at the clinic, and most of all my former life, I found myself murmuring, "Oh, Josh."

Mendoza's pounding in and out of me immediately ceased. When I finally dared to open my eyes, his menacing gaze made me shudder, even though I knew better than to show any reaction to him. "What did you say, bitch?"

"Nothing," I whispered as I shrank away from him.

His fingers came to curl around my neck. "I'll kill you for letting another man's name come off your lips."

When his other fist blasted into my cheek, I began to scream.

My eyelids fluttered as I tiptoed along the line between consciousness and unconsciousness. Someone was shouting my name. "Roja!" "Annabel!"

I focused all my strength on the one who called my real name. When I dared to open my eyes, I found myself staring into the kind, concerned face of Rev. I exhaled a breath of relief. It had been a dream. Just a dream. I wasn't back at Mendoza's.

"Are you okay?"

Since I couldn't speak, I merely nodded. My body shivered and shook like a newborn colt taking its first steps. No matter how hard I tried, I couldn't seem to stop the tremors.

Without saying a word, Rev's strong arms reached out to draw me against him. "Shh, it's all right. You're safe," he murmured against my ear.

My trembling arms came up to wrap around him. I burrowed deeper into his chest, into his warmth. Closing my eyes, I pressed my face against his skin, searching out the sound of his beating heart. I marveled at the thought that a relative stranger could provide the comfort I so desperately needed. "You want to talk about it?" Rev asked.

Only with him would I allow myself to go there. I swallowed hard. "It was about that last night with Mendoza . . . how he wanted to kill me." The tremors ricocheted through me again like I was being shaken by someone.

Placing his hands on each side of my face, Rev pushed my head back so I could look into his eyes. "Believe me when I say that you never have to worry about Mendoza hurting you ever again."

"How can you be so sure?" I whispered.

"Because I will put a bullet between his eyes before he ever has the chance."

My heartbeat skipped erratically, as if it were playing a manic game of hopscotch. For a moment, my instinct was to recoil from him with disgust by what he had just suggested. I couldn't fathom how the compassionate and caring Rev could also be a coldhearted killer.

Rev stared down at his hands. "I'm sorry if I disappoint you, but that's who I am. I will protect what's important to me. You need to understand that." From the look of determination that was etched across his handsome features, I knew he spoke the absolute truth.

I shook my head. "Regardless of what you say you are, I could never let you do that. If you got caught, you would go to jail because of me."

"It would be worth it to end the life of such an odious creature. Mendoza doesn't deserve to live."

Although I wanted Mendoza dead even more than Rev did, it was still hard hearing him say the words. Anxiety ricocheted through me, and before I could stop myself, I blurted, "But if you went to jail, then I wouldn't get to be with you anymore!"

Rev's smile once again sent my heart skipping, and it amazed me how quickly he could shift from intimidating to sweet and tender. "I'm not going anywhere."

"But if you—"

"I won't get caught."

"How can you possibly believe that?"

"Just trust me."

"Rev—"

"Because I've done it before."

My brows furrowed in confusion.

He shook his head slowly back and forth as if he were trying to get me to see the light. "I've killed before, and I'll kill again."

A shudder ran through me at his words. My savior couldn't be so soulless. He saved lives; he didn't take them. He dried my tears and comforted me, which wasn't part of a killer's profile. With my stomach roiling in revulsion, I argued, "No . . . no, you're not like that."

"But I am." He exhaled a breath that sounded tormented. "Right now, in your current frame of mind, it's easy for you to think of me as only a knight in shining armor. But that's just make-believe. When my club, my brothers, have been threatened or are in danger, I have fought with them. And I have killed with them."

I sat in a dumbfounded stupor as the veil of my ignorance concerning Rev and his brothers was stripped away. Besides my time with Mendoza, I had never been in the presence of a murderer before. When I was a little girl, I had seen the faces of death row inmates on signs when groups of protestors were petitioning my grandfather for clemency. They had scared me then, and they scared the old Annabel of a few months ago.

But if I was truly honest with myself, the new Annabel was only slightly alarmed. Maybe it was because I had been through enough to see that things weren't completely black and white in the world. There was a gray area, which many unsuspecting people were pushed into against their will. Maybe they were defending themselves against violence and it got out of hand, or maybe they were avenging those they loved. Who was I to pass judgment?

Rev must've misread my silence, because now he was the one putting distance between us as he rose from the bed. "I'm sorry if I've scared you. I don't want you to think badly of me. But I want you to be able to say I was always honest with you."

"I appreciate that."

"I'm not so sure you do right now, but I think you'll come to appreciate it in the next few days. I think it will make it easier to get on a plane to Virginia once we get back to Georgia."

"I'm not going back to Virginia."

"Did you not just hear what I said?"

"Every word."

"Then what is your problem?" he demanded.

A borderline-hysterical laugh burst from my lips. "My problem? I'm pretty sure I have more than just one problem, and at the moment, your past is the least of them."

"You're not thinking clearly."

"Have you ever just walked up to someone and shot them for the hell of it?"

He narrowed his eyes at me. "Of course I haven't. Who the fuck do you think I am?"

"So, if you've reached that point of violence, basically you've killed when you had to—when you or your brothers were threatened or when an innocent girl was being held against her will?"

"Yeah, that's right."

"Then I'm thinking perfectly clearly when I tell you nothing you have said would induce me to want to leave."

Rev stared wide-eyed at me. "How can you, of all people, condone what I have done? Maybe you think it's okay, but if you knew all the things I've done, if you really stopped and thought about it, I'm not sure you would feel the same way."

"It's not for me to judge you."

"Bullshit."

"Excuse me?"

"Anyone with a moral compass has the right to judge me."

I rose and crossed the room to stand closer to him. "Do you regret what you've done in the past?"

Rev stopped his manic pacing. After running his hand over his beard, he replied, "Yes. Yes, of course I do." His eyes, which were somewhat cloudy, met mine. "Regardless of what type of person they were, I took their life. I took away someone's son, someone's father, someone's husband."

"But you are sorry for it," I said softly.

He closed his eyes. "Yes, I am."

"You know what a wise man once said? That by showing true repentance for what you have done, you can find redemption. All one has to do is ask for forgiveness to whatever higher power or being you believe in."

"As long as I keep doing it, then I'm not truly repentant, am I?"

More than anything I wanted to make him feel better, but at the same time, I knew I had to be honest with him. "No, I suppose not."

"Our club was supposed to be going legit. It was something my new sister-in-law demanded before she married my brother."

"Why did you stop trying?"

He exhaled a harsh breath before sitting back down on the bed. "I guess you could say it's my fault for what I did in Mexico."

My heart skipped a beat at his words. "Oh no. Please tell me I'm not the reason."

Rev shook his head. "It's because I went after Sarah. Mendoza is tied to the Diablos—one of the toughest clubs around. Like I told you before, I was a marked man the minute I entered that compound, regardless of what happened to you."

"And you were willing to risk all that for Sarah?"

He nodded. "Because of what I'd been through and because of what Breakneck had done for me."

At that point I felt my heart might burst with the magnitude of respect and admiration I felt for him. Maybe even some form of love. I realized then I could go the rest of my life, and I would never meet another man like Rev.

I walked over to stand in front of him. "Rev Malloy, I think someone would have to try very, very hard to find a man with as pure a heart and as kind a soul as yours."

He gave me a weak smile. "I think you're just being nice."

"No. I'm not. You just keep trying to make your club legit. All the pieces will fall together."

"I really want to believe that."

As I surveyed his face, I realized something. "You know, I don't think I know your real name."

He winced. "It's Nathaniel."

"That's a beautiful name."

"I'm glad you think so. The only person who gets away with calling me that, though, is my mother."

"It makes sense that it's a biblical name since your father was a minister."

"You think I look like a Nathaniel?"

I smiled. "I think you look like a Rev to me."

Rev laughed. "I'm glad to hear it." He glanced at the clock on the desk. "Think you can sleep now?"

The prospect of being in the dark, alone, and facing my nightmare again caused my stomach to churn. "Would you lie down with me?" At Rev's slight hesitation, I added, "Just until I go to sleep."

"Sure. Of course."

After I walked around the side of the bed, I pulled back the covers so we could both get under them. Rev turned out the light on the nightstand. I moved as close to Rev as I could. Although I was probably making him uncomfortable, I was more than happy to be selfish in the moment and think only of myself.

As we lay in the dark, a thought came to me. "The other day when you recited from 'Annabel Lee,' was that all you knew?"

He chuckled. "Why do I get the feeling if I say I know more I'm going to end up being forced to perform?"

"I'd love to hear it all."

"I've got to learn to tell you no," he muttered. Then, after drawing in a deep breath, he began to recite the poem. I closed my eyes and burrowed against him. The deep, rich timbre of his voice relaxed me. And although the poem's content was rather depressing, I focused more on a man whose love for his Annabel Lee could not be stopped even by death.

ELEVEN

REV

As I started to wake up, something tickled across my nose. When my hand reached up to swipe it away, I realized it was a long strand of hair. A woman's hair. Oh fuck, it was Annabel's hair. I had fallen asleep with Annabel in my arms.

Opening my eyes, I peered down to see if she was awake. One side of her face was pressed against my chest as if she were trying to listen to my heartbeat. From the soft rise and fall of her chest, I could tell she was still sleeping peacefully. I debated whether to move, since I really shouldn't have been in bed with her. Sunlight had yet to streak through the curtains, so I knew we didn't have to get on the road yet. A glance at the clock on the nightstand told me it was a little after five. More than anything, I hated to wake Annabel when she was resting so comfortably.

Even though she had asked me to sleep with her, I knew it wasn't a good idea. But I had taken her into my arms and then slept beside her. I hadn't slept with a woman in years. Sure, I'd had sex with several girls since my girlfriend had broken my heart. There was never a shortage of sweet butts who wanted to ease my pain. But whenever I took those women up on their offers, they never stayed the night. To my way of thinking, sharing a bed or sleeping beside someone was almost more intimate than the act of sex itself.

I stared up at the ceiling. How in the hell had I gotten myself into this situation? I was completely in over my head. A week ago I had left to save Sarah, and somehow my whole life had changed. But as twisted as it sounds, it had changed for the better. The truth was I enjoyed spending time with Annabel. I loved her laugh, her smile, and the way she felt comfortable teasing me. I may have saved her from Mendoza, but in a way it felt like she had saved me.

No matter how much I was enjoying being with Annabel, though, I couldn't turn off the voice of doubt in my head. Part of me wondered if I was tripping on the high of a hero complex, where being the savior of a beautiful girl gave me some kind of sick pleasure. After all, I thought, if she hadn't been abused at Mendoza's hands, she would have never given a guy like me a second glance.

I hated those thoughts.

Most of all, I was afraid of doing anything that would hurt Annabel. I didn't want to be the cause of screwing up her recovery. Like I had told her at dinner last night, there was no handbook on the right or wrong way to heal. In another time and place, Annabel would have been the type of woman I pursued. Beautiful, sweet, innocent, and a little bit sassy. As crazy as it sounded, I almost wished I had rescued a less attractive girl, or a girl who had a boyfriend or husband waiting on her at home. Anything but a girl who would catch my interest.

Instead, fate could be a cruel bitch.

Of course, I had to wonder what kind of sick fucker I was to even be thinking about Annabel in a sexual way. Last night, I'd tried to put her at ease about her feelings while at the same time I struggled with my own needs. After all, I'd known the girl a week—one part of which was spent rescuing her from sexual slavery and watching her heal. I mean, for fuck's sake, there had to be something wrong with me. Annabel had been through mental and physical hell and had every right to be confused by her feelings for me. Me, I had no excuse whatsoever.

Annabel shifted and stretched in my arms. When I looked at her again, her eyes were open and she was taking in her surroundings. "Morning," I said softly.

She jerked out of my arms. "Um, morning."

"Sorry if I scared you."

Annabel shook her head. "No, it's nothing like that. I'm just a little embarrassed about how I acted last night."

"Annabel, you have nothing to be embarrassed about. Nightmares and flashbacks are horrific. I know that as well as you do."

"I hope you were able to sleep, considering I was lying all over you."

Even in the short time I had known her, it was clear to me that she always worried too much. "I actually slept through the night. I just woke up a little before you did."

"Guess we better get on the road, huh?"

I nodded. "If we haul it, we could make it to Georgia by tonight."

"Really?"

"It's about twelve hours when you don't have a lead foot like mine. Of course, I know I owe you a quick shopping stop."

She laughed. "Yes, you do. I promise to be quick."

With a smirk, I replied, "A woman who shops fast? I'll believe it when I see it."

"Then I'll be happy to prove it to you."

Annabel was true to her word, and after a stop at Walmart, we were on the road by six thirty. We ate both breakfast and lunch in the car. I made sure she did lie down in the back for several long stretches. The rest of the time she was up front in the passenger seat beside me. As for me and my wound, I managed to keep my leg pain under control with some Advil.

We learned a lot more about each other on the drive home. It's amazing what you can talk about when you're trying to pass the time on a long stretch of road. Of course, I learned new things about her, but they didn't change what I already knew. It just made me appreciate who she was even more.

When we crossed the Georgia state line, I called Bishop to let him know where we were. Since bikes made better time, he had gotten home early that morning. I wondered if he and Breakneck had even stopped to sleep much—they had probably crashed along the way at one of the Mississippi or Alabama Raiders' clubhouses. He informed me that the guys were anxious to have me back.

I didn't know just how anxious until we got home. As I pulled into the roadhouse parking lot, both in- and out-of-town Raiders swarmed the car. Cheers and whistles went up in the group, while others pounded their fists on the hood and trunk. Ordinarily I would have appreciated the show of support, but I knew the ruckus was the last thing Annabel needed.

Her agonized whimper drew my attention away from my brothers and over to her. She had drawn her legs up and tucked her chin to her knees. Her arms were wrapped tight around her body like she was trying to keep herself together and not lose her shit.

"I'm sorry. I didn't know they were going to do this."

She didn't respond. Instead, I watched as her body began trembling on the seat. "Fuck," I muttered under my breath. Throwing the gearshift into reverse, I started slowly backing away from the crowd. My brothers' elation quickly turned to confusion and then anger. I could hear the shouts outside the car grow in volume.

Just as I rolled the window down to try to explain, the voice of

Kim, the widow of Case, our former president, interrupted me. "Are you all fucking insane? After everything that poor girl has been through, you think mobbing her is a fucking good idea?"

Leave it to Kim to say exactly what was on my mind but what I wouldn't dare say. Thankfully, the guys got the message and hustled out of the way. Once I backed out, I pulled around the roadhouse and started down the gravel path to my own house, which happened to be across the street from Mama Beth's.

After I put the car in park and turned off the ignition, I tentatively placed my hand on Annabel's shoulder. "Hey," I said softly. She turned her head slowly to look at me. "I'm so sorry about that."

"It's okay."

"No. It's not. I can tell how freaked out you are."

She sighed as she eased her legs down. "You're right that seeing all those men—all those *bikers*—did a number on me. But you can't blame yourself, and you can't blame them. It's something I have to deal with. They were just happy to see you."

"While I know Kim has chewed them out by now, I'll make sure to tell them to give you some breathing room."

"That's sweet. Thank you. I really appreciate you letting me come here."

"You're welcome." Motioning to the house through the windshield, I said, "Come on. Let's get you settled inside." I opened my door and started to haul ass around the front of the car to Annabel's side so I could help her, but then my leg reminded me that I'd been shot ten days ago.

Annabel was already out of the car when I reached her. "Rev, you don't have to be a gentleman every time. I can manage my own door, you know."

"But I want to." At her frustrated huff of breath, I added, "Even though I know you're capable and you're a strong, independent woman."

She laughed. "Fine. I guess I'll be better about you helping me." She gazed up at the house. "So this is your place?"

Kicking a few gravel pieces with my boot, I replied, "Yeah. It's not much. I'm sure you're used to places that are a lot finer."

"Rev," Annabel chided softly. When I looked at her, she shook her head at me. With her eyes, she conveyed the message that I shouldn't be ashamed of what I had. "I like it. It looks very cozy."

"You may change your mind when you see inside."

"Are you saying I might be shocked at what a bachelor's house looks like?"

"A bachelor biker's is probably even worse."

"Hmm," she mused.

"Nathaniel," Mama Beth called from behind us.

Annabel whirled around and widened her eyes at the sight of my mother. "Hey, Mama," I said, hurrying down the driveway to her side.

I hugged her tight before pulling away to kiss her cheek. Her bottom lip trembled slightly, and I could tell she was fighting back her tears. "I've been so worried."

"I'm fine."

She gave a slight shake of her head. "Don't do that to me again. And don't ever leave in the middle of the night to do something so very dangerous." She brought her hand to her chest. "My heart just can't take it."

With just a few words, she had the ability to cut me down and make me feel three feet tall. I rubbed her shoulders. "I'm sorry, Mama. I truly am. But you don't have to worry anymore. I'm home safe and sound."

"I'm a mother—my worry never ends. Especially when I have three such headstrong sons."

"If it makes you feel better, I did miss you."

She chuckled. "You missed me? Or my cooking?"

I appreciated her effort to lighten the heavy mood. With a smile, I replied, "A little of both."

Mama Beth then turned her attention away from me. Glancing over my shoulder, she said, "Hello there."

It was then I realized that Annabel had come across the driveway to stand quietly behind me. Taking her arm, I drew her up beside me. "We have company," I said.

"Hello," Annabel said softly.

Extending her hand, Mama Beth said, "I'm Elizabeth, Nathaniel's mother." Mama Beth gave Annabel a kind smile, but she didn't make a move to hug her. In her infinite wisdom, she could sense Annabel's apprehension and was giving her the space she felt she needed.

"I'm Annabel."

"Won't you both come to my house? Supper should be ready soon. I decided to cook a little later when you told me you were coming home today." Before I could say yes or no, Mama Beth frowned. "Or maybe you'd rather rest. I'm sure that was a tiring drive." Mama Beth was rambling a bit. I had slightly unnerved her by showing up with Annabel. I was sure she would have a million questions for me the moment we were alone.

Before Annabel could answer, Willow came bounding off Mama Beth's porch with her almost-grown puppy, Walter, yipping after her. "Uncle Rev!" she shrieked.

She dove into my arms the moment she reached me. "Hey, rug rat, you miss me?"

"Mmm-hmm." She gave me a smacking kiss on the cheek. "You and Uncle B were so mean to leave at the same time Mommy and Daddy did. I've only had Grandma Beth and Walter to play with."

Mama Beth wagged an accusatory finger at Willow. "Now you know that isn't true. You've had Jenny over to play almost every day."

Jenny was the youngest of Case's children. With the loss of her father, I was sure she needed the playtime just as much as Willow did.

"But she doesn't do everything I say like Uncle Rev and Uncle B do."

I grinned. "So you've met your bossy little match in Jenny, huh?"

"I guess so." Her dark eyes, which were her father's, peered into mine. "Did you bring me anything?"

I laughed. "Was I supposed to?"

Willow's lips turned down in a pout. "Mommy and Daddy brought me back some presents from their trip."

My brows rose in surprise. "Deacon and Alexandra are back?"

Mama Beth nodded. "Got back this afternoon just in time for Alexandra's doctor's appointment."

The word "doctor" got my attention. "Everything okay?"

"Yes, worrywart. Just the usual appointments for pregnant women."

"Good."

Placing her hands on my cheeks, Willow turned my face to look at hers. "What about the present?"

"Willow, where are your manners?" Mama Beth chided, but I only chuckled.

"I just might have something for you in my suitcase."

"Really?" she asked, her eyes lighting up.

"I'll give it to you after dinner."

Although she didn't look too thrilled at the prospect of waiting, Willow managed to nod. Once she got the topic of a present out of the way, her attention was drawn elsewhere, right to Annabel. "Hi," she said brightly.

"Hello," Annabel replied with a smile.

Bending over closer to my ear, Willow whispered, "Did you bring home your girlfriend?"

While Annabel's cheeks tinged pink, I couldn't help laughing. "You're a nosy little shit."

"Well, it's about time you had a girlfriend," Willow answered in a matter-of-fact tone.

Now it was Annabel's turn to laugh. "I'm sorry to disappoint you, but your uncle and I are just friends."

Willow appeared genuinely let down at the news. "But you might grow to like each other. My mommy and daddy didn't like each other at first, but then they grew to love each other."

I shook my head at her. "You're too much, you know that?"

She giggled. "Daddy says that all the time."

"Come on. Let's get inside and get washed up for dinner," Mama Beth suggested.

I gazed over Willow's head at Annabel to gauge her reaction to the invitation. When she nodded, I knew she was fine with having dinner with Mama Beth.

I eased Willow down to the ground, and she bounded straight over to Annabel. "What's your name?"

"It's Annabel."

"Does anyone ever call you Belle like in *Beauty and the Beast*?"

Annabel laughed. "No. Not really."

"I think that's what I'll call you."

"That's okay with me."

At the sight of Willow slipping her hand into Annabel's, I held my breath that the touch would be okay. While I knew she was still gun-shy about men, I didn't know how she felt about strangers in general.

But Annabel didn't shrink away. Instead, she squeezed Willow's hand tight. The small gesture made my heart swell. Glancing back at us, Willow said, "I'll show Belle where to wash up."

"That would be very nice of you."

"That way you'll have time to get my present out of the car," she replied sweetly.

I groaned but obediently nodded my head. As the women disappeared up Mama Beth's walk, I went back to the car and got out the ballerina alligator. I would worry about our luggage later.

When I got into the house, Willow was chattering incessantly to Annabel about ballet. Annabel was nodding as she tried to keep up with Willow's fast-paced conversation. As soon as she saw I had returned, Willow abandoned Annabel in midsentence and came galloping over to me. I knew there was not a chance in hell I could wait until after dinner to give her the stuffed animal. So I merely thrust it at her instead. "Here you go, rug rat."

She grabbed the alligator and squealed with delight. "Ooh, it's a ballerina just like me." She then wrapped her arms around my waist and hugged me tight. "Thank you, Uncle Rev."

"You're welcome, sweetheart."

"All right, it's time to wash up," Mama Beth instructed.

"Yes, ma'am," Willow replied. She once again grabbed Annabel's hand. "I'll show you where the bathroom is, Belle."

"Thank you. I would appreciate that," Annabel replied.

"And I'll show you my old room. I get a whole new room at my mommy and daddy's house."

After Annabel and Willow disappeared down the hall, I walked over to the sink. As I lathered the soap up to my elbows, I could feel Mama Beth's eyes boring into my back.

"What is it, Mama?" I questioned without turning around.

"Bishop told me not to be too surprised when you showed up with a girl."

"Did he?" I held my tongue about saying any more.

"Yes, he did. I'm surprised you didn't tell me as much when I spoke to you the other day."

"I figured it could wait. Besides, she was with me when I was talking to you."

"Is Annabel in some sort of trouble?" she asked. When I threw a glance at her over my shoulder, she pursed her lips at me. "Is that why you brought her here?"

"Yes, she was in trouble."

"Is she the reason you left?"

"No. She isn't." I turned off the water and grabbed a hand towel. I realized then that no one had told her about Breakneck and Sarah. Since I didn't know how long Willow would keep Annabel occupied, I gave Mama Beth a condensed version of the story.

When I finished speaking, her kind eyes were filled with tears. "I had no idea."

"It hasn't been made well known because it's his story to tell. I'm sure Breakneck will be letting the rest of his brothers know soon."

Mama Beth chewed her bottom lip like she wanted to say more—it was a trait Bishop had inherited. I was sure I was exasperating her with my short responses.

Finally, she couldn't keep it in any longer. "She isn't like us."

"Excuse me?"

"What I mean is unlike Sarah, Annabel isn't from an MC family, is she?"

"No, I guess you could say she's about as far away from us as is humanly possible."

"Is that why you're keeping her at arm's length?"

Tossing the towel back on the counter, I replied, "What is it with all the questions?"

"I watched you two out there. The way you look at her, the way she looks at you. You care about her very deeply."

"Yes, I do care about her, but it's not what you think."

"Are you sure about that?"

"I've known her less than a week, Mama. And there's been nothing intimate between us. Not after what she's been through," I countered.

Her blue eyes flashed defiantly at me. "And I knew I wanted to marry your father after three days when we hadn't even kissed. What's your point?"

I closed my eyes and tried to control my temper. I'd never imagined my mother would think Annabel and I had feelings for each other that ran any deeper than friendship. "Would you listen to yourself? I just walked through the door, and you're giving me the fifth degree about a girl I barely know and one you've just met. A girl who has been through hell and back."

"You left in the middle of your brother's wedding reception and told no one where you were going or why. Then when you do show back up, it's with a strange girl! A beautiful one, I might add, but one who looks two steps above even Alexandra. Considering all that, I think I deserve to give you a little grief."

"Not when that girl is just down the hall."

"Then you will tell me everything later?"

I nodded. The truth was, I had so much to tell her, more than she could probably imagine. Once I had told Bishop, I realized I should be honest with Mama Beth and Deacon, and I would do that just as soon as I could get a moment alone with them.

Our conversation was thankfully interrupted by the back door blowing open. "Over my dead body are we naming our son Diesel or Axel," Alexandra huffed as she stepped into the kitchen.

"Just what the hell is so wrong with those names?"

Alexandra didn't respond. Instead, she just threw him a death glare. Deacon's eyes lit up at the sight of me. He crossed the room in two long strides to meet me. "When the hell did you get back?"

"About an hour ago."

Deacon gave me a tight hug. "Glad you're home."

I thumped his back, appreciating his show of emotion. "Thanks. It's good to be back."

Once Deacon released me, Alexandra quickly replaced him. When she pulled away, she tenderly kissed my cheek. "I'm so glad you're safe."

I could see the concern for me in her eyes, and I hated that I had been the cause of it. "I'm sorry for worrying you."

"It's okay. Just don't do it again," she replied with a smile.

"I'll do my best."

She smacked my arm playfully. "You'd better."

"So what's this I hear about a boy?" I glanced between her and Deacon. "You two have some news for us?"

Alexandra shook her head. "Not yet. But we did get to see the baby at today's appointment." She thrust a grainy black-and-white image in front of my face. Once her hand steadied, I surveyed the picture of my future niece or nephew. My heart swelled with pride at the sight of the new life.

"Looks strong and healthy."

Beaming with happiness, Alexandra replied, "The doctor said everything looks great. The baby is even measuring a few days ahead of its due date."

I smiled at her. "I'm glad to hear that."

"Tell him about the heartbeat," Deacon urged.

With a slight roll of her eyes, Alexandra huffed, "Just because the ultrasound technician commented it might be a boy because of the heart rate, Deacon has it in his head it's one hundred percent a boy."

Deacon grinned as he placed a hand on Alexandra's stomach. "I'm telling ya, that's my son in there."

Jutting her chin out, Alexandra countered, "It could just as easily be a girl."

Deacon grunted. "We already have a girl. We need a boy—a son to carry on the Malloy name."

"You're impossible," she muttered.

"But you love me anyway," he countered. He then wrapped his arm around her waist and drew her closer to him.

She grinned up at him. "Yes, I do."

It was at that moment Willow came into the kitchen leading Annabel by the hand. From Annabel's lighthearted expression, I could tell she enjoyed being around Willow. That wasn't surprising to me. Despite all the horrible shit she had been through in life, Willow possessed a carefree nature that was infectious.

At the sight of Annabel, both Deacon's and Alexandra's brows rose in surprise. Then they both looked from Annabel over to me.

Swinging Annabel's arm back and forth, Willow said, "This is my mommy and daddy. This is Belle."

"Actually, that's Annabel," I corrected her.

Both Deacon and Alexandra continued to stare at Annabel and me. Finally, Alexandra shook her head slightly like she was shaking herself awake or out of a stupor. "Hello," she said as she took a step forward.

She offered her hand to Annabel. After Annabel shook it, Deacon came over. "I'm Rev's brother, Deacon."

Annabel smiled. "I've heard a lot about you."

Deacon's lips curved in his signature smirk. "I hope it was all good."

"Yes. It was. Your daughter is delightful. She's been so sweet to show me around."

Like the proud father he was, Deacon beamed at Annabel's praise of Willow. "I see she was showing you her good side."

"Daddy!" Willow protested with a pout.

He reached over and ruffled her hair affectionately. "Just teasing you."

"Why don't we all sit down?" Mama Beth suggested.

"Bishop not coming?" I asked as I steered Annabel over to the table.

"Nah, he's getting shitfaced up at the roadhouse," Deacon replied.

"David, honestly," Mama Beth chided.

Unlike with the rest of us, he didn't dare argue with Mama Beth. Instead, he took a seat next to Alexandra. After we had all gathered around the table, Mama Beth asked Deacon to say the blessing. During dinner, the conversation remained light. Deacon and Alexandra told us about their honeymoon in Hawaii—or at least they shared the G-rated details with us. Willow filled us in on all we had missed while we were gone. Luckily, no one pressed Annabel with any questions that were too personal.

When we finished dinner, Deacon and I went outside for him to have a smoke. I could tell there was something he wanted to say to me in private. I figured it had to do with potential blowback from what had happened with Mendoza. Of course, I should have known Deacon would never cease to surprise me.

"What do you say we go up to the roadhouse and see the boys?" Deacon asked.

"I would, but I really need to get Annabel settled in."

"My phone was blowing up during dinner with texts. They're itching to see you, Prez. You've been gone almost ten days," Deacon argued.

I snorted. "You act like the brothers have been pining away for me like some lovesick teenagers."

He laughed. "They have been deprived of the Malloy brothers all at the same time for the first time ever."

"What a tragedy."

"Come on, man." He glanced over his shoulder back into the house where we had left the girls. "Not that I would want her to know, but I've missed being with the guys while I was off honeymooning."

"Your reputation as the ultimate lover is waning in my opinion if you were missing the guys while with a beautiful and sexy woman on your honeymoon."

"Cocksucker," he muttered as he smacked my arm. "Spending all that time just with Alexandra has made me miss having beers and shooting the shit with the guys."

"I really don't think it's a good idea for me to leave Annabel tonight. She's in a new place with a bunch of strangers."

"I think I'll survive a few hours for you to go just up the hill," Annabel said.

I whirled around to see her propped against the doorframe. "You weren't supposed to hear that."

"And according to your mother, you boys weren't supposed to duck out on drying the dishes," she replied with a smile.

Deacon grunted. "I'm a grown fucking man who is still being bossed around by his mother."

"And now by your wife," Alexandra said from the doorway as she crooked her finger at him.

"Fuck me," he muttered before he went into the house.

Annabel came out on the deck to join me.

"Would you really be all right staying here for an hour or two?"

"Of course I would."

"You're not just saying that, are you? I know how women will say one thing when they totally mean another."

Annabel laughed. "Rev, I'm a politician's daughter. I've been raised to work a crowd of strangers. Regardless of what I've recently been through, I think I can handle a few hours with the girls."

"Don't speak too soon. Willow can wear anyone out in a matter of minutes."

At the mention of Willow, Annabel's eyes lit up. "She's adorable, and I love how she has all the men around here wrapped around her little finger."

"Yes, I can see where you would find it amusing that three hardened bikers are totally owned by a little six-year-old girl."

"Exactly."

Deacon appeared in the doorway. "I did your part, too, brother. So are we on?"

Annabel threw a look at Deacon over her shoulder. "Yes, he's on." Before I could argue with her, she added, "Make sure he has a good time. He deserves to unwind and cut loose."

Deacon grinned at Annabel. "It will be my pleasure." He came over and grabbed my arm. "Come on."

Although I was still a little reluctant, I allowed Deacon to drag me off the porch. As I got to the bottom of the steps, I glanced back at Annabel. She smiled and waved.

Our boots crunched along the gravel road. Deacon lit up a cigarette, and when he offered one to me, I decided to take one. I needed to settle my nerves a bit for what I was about to do.

We passed by Case's place, which had been rebuilt in the six months since his death. Kim and her kids still resided there, even though there wasn't a patch member in the house. Part of the Raiders creed was to care for our old ladies, and until she remarried, Kim was still an old lady.

I realized then an overwhelming sense of irony that the house had burned down. Before it had been Case's, it had been Miss Mae's. The physical dwelling where I had lost my innocence in such a brutal way no longer existed. By telling first Annabel and then Bishop, I had begun to demolish my own house of secrets.

When we reached the back door of the roadhouse, I stepped in front of Deacon. "You got a minute before we go inside?"

He took a long drag on his cigarette. "Yeah, sure. What's up?"

I flicked the ashes off mine before I spoke. "There's something I need to tell you—something I should have told you sixteen years ago."

Deacon's expression darkened in confusion. "What are you talking about?"

"It's the reason why Breakneck called me, out of all the guys, when Sarah was in trouble."

"I'm listening."

My chest tightened as I braced to once again unburden myself. Maybe the third time was the charm—it seemed to go a little easier this time. When I finished, I didn't have the quickening, anxious breaths or the erratic heartbeat that I'd had before.

I took another drag on my cigarette and waited for Deacon to respond. What he did next shocked the hell out of me. With all the strength he had, he shoved me against the back door. "What the fuck?" I demanded.

His dark eyes narrowed on me. "Why? Why the hell didn't you tell me?"

"I didn't tell anyone. Not even Mama Beth knows. Once I told Annabel, I realized my brothers and my mother had a right to know."

"Jesus, Rev," Deacon muttered through gritted teeth.

"This wasn't exactly the reaction I expected you to have."

He released my shirt and took a step back. After jerking a hand through his hair, he shook his head. "I'm not mad at you, brother. I'm mad at myself."

"But why?"

"I'm just so fucking angry that I couldn't protect you from being hurt."

Tears burned my eyes at his words of remorse. "You were just a kid yourself."

"I was a fighter before Preacher Man got me. I could have taken that fucking pervert out."

I shook my head. "No one could have done anything to stop it from happening. Thankfully, Preacher Man ended it."

Deacon threw down his cigarette and stubbed out the glowing embers. "More than anything, I hate that you thought you couldn't tell me. That I would think differently of you or something."

"I'm sorry. Preacher Man thought it best not to tell anyone."

With a snort, Deacon replied, "I think the old man's greatest fault was his fucking secrets. It was one thing for him to keep them, but he shouldn't have imposed them on his kids."

My brows furrowed with confusion. Was Deacon hiding a secret of his own?

He reached in his cut and lit up another cigarette. I fought the urge to tell him he needed to cut the shit out now he had a kid and one on the way. "When I was fifteen, Preacher Man found where my real father was. He offered to let me be the one to put a bullet in him." Deacon stared at me straight on. "So I did."

"Jesus," I muttered. I'd had no idea anything like that had ever happened. I just knew Deacon's biological father disappeared after he killed Deacon's mother.

"Guess you could say I started early with my body count."

"You had every right to take that motherfucker to ground, Deacon. Just like Preacher Man had every right to kill Kurt."

Deacon exhaled a puff of smoke and then grinned. "Don't think I've spent one single night wishing I hadn't killed my old man."

"I didn't think you had. It's just a lot for a fifteen-year-old kid to have to deal with."

"You can say that again." Then, in a totally uncharacteristically Deacon move, he pulled me to him for a hug. "I love you, brother. Always have and always will."

It took me a moment to process his words. Deacon and Bishop hadn't told me they loved me over the years, but then again, they hadn't needed to. I just knew. But knowing now that both my brothers would have defended me, would have killed Kurt for me, branded me with a different strength. Solidarity within family as well as within the Raiders. I did, however, fear how Mama would react. This would break her heart.

I smacked his back and squeezed him tight. "I love you, too."

As he pulled away, I thought for a second I saw a tear in his eye, but I quickly dispelled that thought. Nothing made Deacon cry. He jerked his head at the door. "Enough of the emotional bullshit. Let's go in there and get shitfaced."

I laughed. "Sounds like a plan."

With a wink, he said, "First round's on me."

TWELVE

ANNABEL

The next morning once again found me in a strange room and a strange bed. When the familiar feeling of panic began to creep over me, I closed my eyes and tried to focus on the fact that it wasn't completely foreign, since it was Rev's room and Rev's bed. Even though I had protested that he shouldn't sleep on the couch, he had refused to hear me out. I felt dwarfed as I stretched in the massive king-sized bed. When the comforter brushed across my face, I instantly smelled Rev's masculine scent, and I finally felt safe, protected . . . cared for.

A knock at the door had me shooting up in bed. "Yes?"

Rev poked his head in. "I just wanted to see if you were awake."

I offered him a smile. "I woke up a few minutes ago, but I'm lying here being lazy."

"I wouldn't call it being lazy. It's more like you need the rest."

"Yes, Dr. Malloy."

"Anyway, I came in to see if you wanted some breakfast."

"Yes, but I can fix it. I don't want you to wait on me."

A sheepish expression came over his face. "Actually, Mama Beth cooked. She called earlier to see if we wanted to come over."

"I would love to. I'll be ready in five minutes."

"Okay," he replied before closing the door.

I threw back the covers and hurried into the bathroom. Rev had informed me last night how he and his brothers had worked on remodeling the old duplexes into one house. Next door to us was Deacon and Alexandra's house, and on the other side of them was Bishop. Apparently some of the other club officers lived in the other houses.

While he might've been worried about what I would think of his house, I found it gorgeous. If you had walked inside not knowing the occupant was the member of an MC club, your first impression would have been that someone highly intellectual lived there. Like me, Rev seemed to love anything old, so the furniture could have fit in among the contents of any antiques store. I couldn't wait to explore the wall-to-wall bookshelves in the living room.

After I brushed my teeth, splashed some water on my face, and threw my hair, which was about one wash from being back to its natural color, into a ponytail, I came out of the bathroom and slipped into the clothes I had worn the day before. I was hoping in the next few days to find a local branch of my bank. I didn't want Rev to continue paying for food and clothes. I already owed him far too much.

When I came out of the bedroom, I found him in a pair of jeans and a T-shirt. It was when he turned around to face me that I did a double take. "Your beard," I gasped.

He ran his hand over his smooth, hairless face. "Yeah, I don't usually wear one. The guys gave me some shit last night about it, so I figured it was time to get rid of it."

It was surprising how different he looked—younger, softer, and maybe more approachable. As I continued staring at him, he ran a hand over his face. "Do I look that bad?"

I shook my head furiously. "No, no, it's not that at all. It's just I've never seen you without a beard."

"From your expression, it looks like you prefer me with one."

"Actually, I think I like you without one just as much as with one."

"You do?"

"Yeah, I do."

He grinned. "Then you'd be one of the few who does like me with a beard. The guys were calling me Professor Malloy last night, like I was trying to be some pompous ass instead of a hard-ass."

I waved my hand dismissively. "Don't listen to them. Grow it back if you want."

"I'll take it under consideration." He crossed the room to open the door. "Ready?"

"I am."

We made the quick walk across the street to Rev's mother's house. Even after spending the evening with her, I still found it hard to call her Beth, as she had requested. "Mrs. Malloy" seemed to come off my tongue easier.

I wasn't too surprised to find the table laden with food and occupants. Deacon was fixing Willow a plate while Alexandra helped Beth get the food on the table. A sleepy-eyed Bishop lounged in a chair, dressed in nothing but boxer shorts.

At the sight of his brother's half-naked form, Rev cleared his throat. Bishop stopped rubbing his eyes to question, "What?"

"I think you can afford our guest a little more decency," Rev replied through gritted teeth. I knew he was worried that seeing a half-naked man might be a trigger for me. The truth was a stranger might have bothered me, but I knew Bishop well enough to know he wasn't a threat.

"Seriously?" Bishop questioned.

"Dead serious."

As Bishop started to argue with him, Deacon smacked him on the back of the head. "I'm with Rev. You need to have a little more respect for the women."

"I thought we were all family here," Bishop argued.

Alexandra set down a plate of bacon. Then she patted Bishop's shoulder. "Your brothers are just worried that they might look bad in front of us after we've seen your magnificent form."

Her lighthearted response was just what the room needed to ease the tension. Bishop immediately hopped out of his chair. "When you put it like that, I'm more than happy to cover up so these douchebags can save face."

I laughed and Alexandra smiled, while Rev and Deacon only shook their heads at their brother's antics. "What's a douchebag?" Willow asked innocently.

Deacon groaned. "It's not a nice word, and your Uncle B should get in trouble for saying it."

When I noticed that Willow had the alligator Rev had given her in the crook of her arm, I nudged him. "Looks like someone really likes her present."

Rev grinned. He then went over and bestowed a kiss on Willow's cheek. "You like that ugly old alligator, huh?"

Willow nodded and then craned her neck to stare up at Rev. "You cut off your beard."

"I did. Do you like it?"

"Oh yes. It tickled too much when you kissed me."

Rev laughed. "Then I'm glad I shaved it off."

Once Bishop returned in a shirt and jeans, Beth asked Rev to say grace. When he finished, I happily dug in. Beth had made pancakes, which were a favorite of mine. I had to wonder if Rev had somehow managed to tell her.

As I sat around the table with them, listening to their conversation and laughter, I tried to imagine myself a part of their world. While everything felt comfortable and familiar between them, I couldn't help wondering how they handled the danger that came with being a part of the biker world. As unsure as I was about my future, I didn't know how I could ever fit in here. After all, I'd experienced enough danger and violence in the last two months to last a lifetime. I craved peace and safety more than anything in the world.

When I was so full I thought I might pop, I placed my napkin on the table. "Did you get enough to eat, Annabel?" Beth asked.

"Oh yes. More than enough. Everything was delicious."

Beth beamed at my compliment. "I'm so glad you enjoyed it."

"Do you feel up for a walk?" Rev asked.

"Sure. What did you have in mind?"

"There's somewhere I'd really like to show you," he replied, with a shy smile.

I returned his smile. "Okay."

Like the true gentleman he was, Rev held out his hand for me. I slipped mine into his and let him pull me up from my chair. "Wait, shouldn't we help clean up?" I asked.

Beth shook her head. "You two go on. The fresh air will be good for you, and there's a storm supposed to move in later today."

"Okay. If you're sure."

"I'm positive," Beth replied with a smile.

With a nod to his brothers and mother, Rev and I walked out the back door. We headed down the porch steps and then into the thick woods.

Rev pushed slightly ahead me, and a rush of warmth flooded my chest when I realized it was so he could keep branches from hitting me. I fought the urge to reach out and pinch him to see if he was real. He was certainly unlike any man I had ever known, and that included the ones in my family.

"Where is this place you want to show me?" I asked, breaking the silence between us.

Glancing at me over his shoulder, he replied, "About a mile into the woods. Give or take."

"We're going hiking?" Since I was supposed to be taking it easy and Rev was still healing from his gunshot wound, I certainly hoped we weren't about to do anything intense.

"No. Not really."

"Then what is it that's hidden away a mile into these woods?"

He cut his gaze over to mine. "It's a surprise."

I cocked my brows at him. "Seriously?"

"What? Don't you like surprises?"

With a shrug, I replied, "I guess so. It's just . . ."

"Just what?" he implored.

"You don't impress me as the kind of guy who does surprises."

He teasingly swept a hand to his chest. "I take offense to that."

"I'm sorry. I didn't mean it in a bad way."

"In my line of work, it doesn't pay to be impulsive and care-free. I guess that bleeds over to my personal life."

"You shouldn't be anyone other than who you are."

"Obviously I should, since I'm being categorized as boring."

"That is not what I said." Crossing my arms over my chest, I countered, "If that's the truth, then you should call me boring, too, because there's no one I would rather be with than you."

The look that flashed in Rev's eyes almost made me regret my words. It was a mixture of both acknowledgment and longing. My chest rose and fell with harsh breaths as I rode the waves of my inner turmoil. Did I want Rev to feel something deep for me? Did I want to feel something deep for him? He was so very different from any man I'd ever known, least of all dated. But regardless of the differences, I was attracted to him—both physically and emotionally. With his good looks, gentle soul, and protective streak, who wouldn't be?

But surely I was jumping to conclusions and letting my imagination get the best of me. Both in and out of his world, Rev was a catch. He couldn't want someone like me. It was impossible for me to forget how the experience with Mendoza had tarnished me. And even if he did feel like I did, he deserved better.

In an effort to change the subject, Rev motioned around us. "Two hundred years ago, all this land belonged to the Cherokees. Within the acres and acres of land, there was a sought-after place where tribe members from all over the Southeast often made a pilgrimage."

"What was so special about it?" I asked as we ducked under some low tree limbs.

"It was said to be a place of healing waters."

My brows shot up in surprise. "There's a lake out here?"

He opened his mouth and then closed it. Then with a sheepish grin, he replied, "You'll have to wait and see."

I couldn't help laughing. "You're terrible."

"I'm pretty terrible at surprises. I've practically given it all away." With a teasing wink, he added, "Of course, you do seem to be a very gifted manipulator."

"Hey now," I said before playfully jabbing him in the ribs. As we started up a slight hill, Rev reached out and took my arm to help guide me. "How do you know so much about the Cherokees?" I asked him.

"My great-grandmother was full-blooded Cherokee. She and her parents hid out in the mountains to escape removal by the government. She passed her knowledge on to my grandmother."

After studying his profile, I said, "I can tell you have some Native American in you."

"Seriously?"

I nodded. Reaching out, I ran my thumb across one of his cheek-bones. "These are high, which is one of the characteristic traits."

"Is that so?" he questioned in a low voice.

"Yes." Breaking his stare, I gazed down his body. "Of course, your height certainly departs from the similarities."

When my eyes lingered on his body, Rev cleared his throat almost painfully. "Come on. We're almost there."

Unable to speak, I merely nodded and followed him. I silently berated myself for staring at his body like I had. What was I thinking? What had he thought I was thinking? Once again, I was totally clueless on how to think and act in this new life I found myself in.

After reaching a tight thicket of trees, we pushed on through to step out into a wide clearing. Waist-high green grass swayed back and forth like ocean waves. It ran almost as far as the eye could see until it ended at the banks of a stream.

"They called this place *tohi a-ma*."

"What does it mean?"

"'Healing waters.'"

Shielding my eyes with my hand, I took in the landscape before me. "It's beautiful."

"Wait until you see it up close." Once again, Rev offered me his hand, and I gladly accepted his touch. We then started wading through the tall grass to get to the water's edge. A gentle breeze rippled our clothes, making the heat a little less oppressive.

Closer to the shore, I could see that the water lapping against the bank was so crystal clear you could see through to the bottom. "In the Cherokee language, the word *tohi* is the word for 'peace.' They believed that bathing or swimming in these waters helped to cure illnesses of the body and the mind. It was a way to purify themselves."

"They seriously thought just a dip in the water could cure something?" I asked skeptically.

"Yes, they did."

"Hmm, seems a little far-fetched to me."

"Maybe I can make a believer out of you."

My brows rose in surprise. "You mean you've been in there?" I asked, motioning to the water.

"Would you be surprised if I said yes?"

"Most definitely."

"When I was kid, my brothers and I explored almost every inch of these woods. But in all those years, we never came across this place. It wasn't until I was raped and my father brought me out here that I discovered it existed."

"Did he think it would help you to come here?"

Rev nodded. "At first, I thought he was crazy. Like I was going to go submerge myself in some allegedly blessed water. But then he surprised the hell out of me by stripping down to his boxers and wading in. I just stood there, staring at him. And then he glanced at me over his shoulder. 'You think this is all for you, boy?' he questioned. He dipped his hands into the water and brought them back up to the surface. 'I'm here for me, too. To wash my hands clean of the vengeance I took.'"

He glanced from the water back to me. "I think after he joined back up with the Raiders, he came out here a lot. It was his way of atoning for his sins. He knew what he was doing was wrong, but it still didn't stop him. He became more about *act first and ask forgiveness later*."

"So then you followed him into the water?"

"Yeah, I sure as hell did. I figured if my old man believed in the shit, then I might as well try it."

"How did it feel?"

A slight blush tinged his high cheekbones. "It'll sound a little crazy."

"No, I'm sure it won't." He remained quiet, shifting on his feet. "Please," I implored.

He drew in a ragged breath and then exhaled in a long sigh. With a slight shake of his head, he replied, "It was strange, like I was being anointed with liquid peace from the top of my head down to my feet. And when I finally walked out onto the shore, it felt like all the pain and all the suffering I had been dragging around was being washed away from me."

My breath caught in my chest. Suddenly the very hokey myth seemed believable. More than anything in the world, I wanted to experience what Rev had. I wanted to be able to bury what had happened to me and to move forward. To be able to experience life as a survivor, not as a victim. Could it all be so easy as taking a dip in alleged healing waters? Regardless of how crazy it sounded, I wanted to believe it.

Misjudging my silence, Rev ducked his head and jammed his hands into his jeans pockets. "I'm sorry. . . . I thought this might be something that would make you feel better."

I couldn't respond. In truth, I didn't even know how to begin to respond. Here was a man who was trying in every single way possible to help me find peace and healing. A man who had connected with me because he had been through his own hell. A week ago, he would've been a stranger to me, and now I couldn't imagine a world for myself where he wasn't a part of it.

When I finally found the strength to look up at him, I knew deep within me that in some way everything was forever changed between us. Deep down, I imagined I could fall in love with Rev Malloy with all of my heart and soul, regardless of the length of time that had passed or the circumstances that had brought us together. That revelation caused tears to well in my eyes.

Rev's eyes widened. "Oh shit. I've really fucked up, haven't I?"

I shook my head vigorously and hurried to tell him, "No, no. You've done everything right. I swear."

"I have?" he asked, the surprise evident in his voice.

Unable to hold back anymore, I threw myself at him. As the sobs racked my body, I clung to Rev—my lifeline, my protector. His strong arms came up to wrap around me and I leaned into his embrace. "Please don't cry, Annabel. Bringing you here wasn't supposed to be about making you cry."

"It's okay. I'm not crying about that."

"You're not?"

Pulling away, I gazed up at him. "I'm crying because of how sweet you are."

His shocked expression was almost comical. "You're crying because of me?"

"Yes. I've never met anyone who is as caring and selfless as you are. You barely know me, yet you're willing to do anything and everything to help me heal. It's truly noble."

His cheeks flushed pink at my compliments. "Well, I don't know about all that."

"It's the truth. Believe me." Turning my head, I peered out at the water. "I'm grateful that you brought me here, and I want to give it a try."

"You do?"

"Yeah, I do."

A relieved look flashed in his eyes. "I'm glad to hear it." Motioning to the water, he asked, "Ready?"

"I don't have to get undressed?"

Rev smiled. "You don't have to do anything you're not comfortable with."

The thought was very comforting, but at the same time, I couldn't manage to bring my foot up and start into the water. For a few agonizing seconds, I stood frozen, unsure of what to do.

"I can understand if you want to do this alone. I can head back into the woods to give you some privacy."

Nibbling my bottom lip, I debated his offer. My pain was very personal and very private. Although Rev had been a witness to a lot of it, I wasn't sure if I wanted him with me. I wondered if I needed to be alone to fully purge myself of the horror I had endured. To not have to worry about him seeing me become hysterical yet again. The idea was very freeing. "I think I would like to go in alone."

"That's totally understandable. I won't go far. Call for me if you need me."

I nodded. "Thanks."

He turned and walked back through the high grass and into the woods. Once he was out of sight, I reached down to take off my shoes. I then took a tentative step into the water, quickly drawing back and sucking in a breath at how cold it was. My feet sank into the cool mud of the bank. But when it came time to take another step, I suddenly froze. It wasn't that I couldn't do it alone—it's just that I didn't want to. Whirling around, I saw that Rev had made his way halfway across the grass. "Rev!" I cried out.

He momentarily froze with his back to me before turning around. Silent and unmoving, he waited to hear the words from me. "I need you!" I shouted. The moment the words left my lips, he began quickly making his way back across the clearing.

When he reached me, he stared intently at me, searching my face. "I don't want to do it alone."

"I understand." He bent down to take off his shoes. Once he was barefoot, he stepped in front of me to where he would go in the water first. He held out his hand. "Come on. I won't let anything happen to you." And as I slipped my hand into his, I knew without a shadow of a doubt that he wouldn't let anything ever hurt me— not today and not a year from now.

As we went deeper into the water, the cold temperature took my breath. I knew it would take a few minutes for me to get used to it. When we were waist-deep, Rev let go. "It's up to you now," he said.

I completely understood his meaning. He couldn't keep leading me—I had to do it on my own. As determination surged through me, I kept on walking until the water was up to my shoulders. Then I closed my eyes, held my breath, and took the next step into the unknown.

Immediately I became enveloped in what I imagined was a watery grave. After all, I was looking to be changed, so what better way to do it than through death and rebirth. I stayed submerged until my lungs ached and burned from holding my breath. Finally when I thought I couldn't take it one more second, I kicked my legs and reached the surface.

But when the bright rays of the sun hit my face, I didn't feel its warmth. Instead, I felt like my past was an anchor that would drag me down under the water until I drowned. Where was the peace Rev had spoken of? Sure, I had felt something when I was submerged, but it had all left me when I reached the surface again.

"Annabel?" Rev asked.

When I turned toward him, his face fell. My expression must've told him what I couldn't. The next thing I knew, he was coming to me. When he reached for me, I thought it was to comfort me. I never could have imagined he would have grabbed the top of my head and dunked me.

I was submerged for only a second before I came back up, sputtering and hacking. Swiping the hair out of my face, I became enraged at the sound of Rev's laughter. "Are you kidding me? You think what you just did was funny?"

Nodding his head, he replied, "I wish you could have seen your face."

I huffed out an indignant breath. "You . . . asshole!" Then with a complete lack of maturity, I splashed water in his face.

"Easy now. Don't get so riled," Rev cautioned with a grin.

"You ruined my moment. Why would you do that?"

The amusement on Rev's face slowly faded. He stared at me so intently that I almost took a step back from him. "I could see in your eyes that you were overcome with too much sadness and negativity. I wanted to show you that even in the middle of all that, things can change, life can be made better. There can be levity amid the desolation—a reason to double over laughing, rather than curling up and crying."

My mouth gaped at his words. "Are you for real?"

He blinked at me. "What do you mean?" he questioned in a low voice.

With a tentative hand, I reached out to cup his cheek. His skin felt so warm under my fingers. "After everything I've been through, sometimes it's hard for me to wrap my mind around the fact that a man like you even exists. One who is caring, compassionate, sensitive, but at the same time was willing to risk his life to save me."

His expression seemed guarded. Whereas I freely spewed my emotions when I probably should have tempered them, Rev seemed to be trying to find just the right words to respond to me. "When it comes to me, I think your sweet nature is far too complimentary," he replied. "You give me too much credit. I just did what I thought was right. I would do it again, for you or anyone else who needed me."

"And you're too modest," I countered. I knew he had grown up in a rough, masculine world where feelings were squelched for fear of seeming unmanly. But at the same time, he had a wonderful bond with a mother who had taught him compassion and kindness above everything else.

Rev drew in a ragged breath. "I just want you to see the real me. Regardless of what you say, I still think you're looking at me through rose-colored glasses."

I shook my head. "The truth is the truth. More than anything, I wish you could see the real you, so you would believe me." As I swept the wet strands of hair out of his face, I smiled. "Maybe I was meant to save you."

"Excuse me?"

"I believe in my heart of hearts that you were meant to save me. So maybe in turn, I'm meant to help you by showing you what a wonderful person you are, regardless of what the negative voices in your head tell you."

Rev smiled. "I'll happily let you wear the hero hat if it gets you off my back."

Once again, I splashed water at him. "You're impossible, Rev Malloy."

"I would say the same thing about you, Annabel Percy." He held out his hand. "Come on. We should head back. Breakneck will have my hide for bringing you here when you're supposed to be recuperating."

As I slipped my hand into his, I smiled. "Thank you so much for bringing me here."

"You're welcome. Anytime you want to come back, I'll bring you."

Although it defied reason, my heart did a funny little flip-flop that was usually reserved for my latest crush. Instead of exploring that line of thought any further, I pushed it out of my mind as I walked out of the water.

THIRTEEN

REV

As we started our journey back through the woods, Annabel remained quiet and contemplative. Of course, there was already a noticeable difference in her—a peace that she hadn't shown before she had gone into the water. I was sure she was trying to sort through her feelings. Even as a kid, I remember being overwhelmed by what I had experienced. Children seemed to be able to appreciate the unexplainable better than adults. I was sure that as a person of science Annabel was struggling very hard to find a rational explanation for what she was feeling.

Out of nowhere, a keening animal's cry broke through the silence. It came from somewhere to the left of us. "What is that?" Annabel whispered.

"Sounds like a fawn."

"Why would it cry like that?"

"It's probably trying to find its mother."

When the pitiful cry continued, Annabel shook her head and then started tramping through the brush toward the sound.

"Annabel, wait!" I called after her quickly disappearing form. While I wanted to argue with her that she shouldn't be running, there was also another pressing matter. "The mother won't come around as long as we're close to it."

My decision to follow her was made when she ignored me and kept running. But I soon caught up with her. She stopped so abruptly that I didn't have time to anticipate her movements, and I ended up running into her. "Sorry." It was then that a smell invaded my nose—the sickeningly sweet smell of rotting flesh.

My gaze went to the same spot where Annabel's eyes were drawn. About a foot from us was the badly mauled body of a doe. A coyote or other animal had attacked and killed her. "Poor thing," Annabel murmured.

The cry came again, louder now that we were closer. "It must be her baby," Annabel reasoned as she started toward the cries. I fell in step behind her. When Annabel gasped, I knew she had found it.

Like all does are prone to do when they give birth, the mother had concealed her baby in the brush. Annabel turned back to me. "We can't leave it alone to die out here or get eaten by predators."

Crossing my arms over my chest, I asked, "You want to take it back with us?"

She nodded. "I've taken care of motherless kittens before. It can't be much different."

"But this is a wild animal, not a domesticated cat," I reasoned.

"Just what would you suggest, then?" When I didn't immediately reply, she snapped, "Why don't you go get your gun and shoot it? Then at least it'll be out of its misery quicker than having to starve to death or be mauled."

I knew then there was no way in hell we were leaving the woods without that deer. "Okay. Let me get it, though. You don't need to be carrying anything."

Her eyes, which had been narrowed at me, brightened. "Thank you! I promise I'll do all the work. You won't even realize it's there."

I snorted. "I think a baby deer living in my house will be hard not to notice." With slow steps, I approached the bush where the fawn was hidden. I didn't want to do anything to scare it and make it run away. I reached inside the foliage and gently picked it up, which caused the animal to frantically start kicking its legs. Its screams of panic almost deafened me until out of nowhere it stopped.

With all the noise from the deer, I hadn't noticed that Annabel had come over next to me. She had the tiny fawn's head in her hands, and she was staring straight into its dark eyes. Something about her presence had calmed the deer. "What did you just do?" I asked, in awe of the sudden silence.

She smiled. "I have this weird thing with frightened animals. Back at my old job, I was always able to calm them down." She stroked the top of the fawn's tiny head. "I'm just so thankful I haven't lost my touch."

I was thankful, too. Not only because I didn't think I could have taken having to hear the fawn's screams all the way home, but because after all she had lost at the hands of Mendoza, he hadn't managed to take that from her.

"Come on. Let's get home before you catch a chill and I get kicked to death by this crazy thing," I suggested.

With an almost girlish giggle, Annabel released the deer, and we started walking side by side out of the woods. From time to time, she would glance over at me cradling the deer and smile. It was the most beautiful and genuine smile I had ever seen. And I realized then that she was finding real happiness again. She might've saved the fawn, but it was certainly going to save her as well.

I had hoped we could make it to my house without getting ambushed by anyone asking questions. I wasn't so lucky. Deacon, Alexandra, and Willow were leaving Mama Beth's when we stepped out of the woods. They all three stopped to stare at us as if we had suddenly grown two or three heads.

"How on earth did you two get wet?" Alexandra asked.

"Is that a baby deer?" Willow questioned excitedly as she bounded over to us.

I stared pointedly at Deacon and Alexandra. "We went swimming at *tohi a-ma*."

"Oh," they both murmured at the same time. I knew that Deacon often visited the waters, and after Alexandra had gone through such a horrible time after killing one of the Raiders' rivals, and the man who killed her parents, Deacon had taken her there as well.

"This fawn is orphaned, so we're going to take care of it."

Deacon glanced from me to Annabel and back. "You are?" he questioned rather skeptically.

I rolled my eyes. "Yes, we are. Apparently Annabel knows what to do."

Once again, she giggled infectiously. "I think Rev is having second thoughts about taking me into the woods. But some of my veterinary training dealt with livestock and wild animals. It'll be good to be back in the swing of things after these last few months." She looked at Willow. "Of course, I'm going to need some help. Would you want to help me?"

I don't know why Annabel bothered to ask. Willow loved animals, so helping out with a baby deer was right up her alley. "Yes, I would."

"Is that okay with you two?" Annabel asked Deacon and Alexandra.

Deacon smiled. "Yeah, it's okay. It'll get her out of our hair for a while."

We all laughed at the perturbed scowl that crossed Willow's face at her father's remark. She peered up at the deer in my arms. "What are you going to name it?"

Annabel pursed her lips thoughtfully. "Actually, we hadn't gotten that far yet."

Bringing her hands to her hips, Willow said, "Well, it needs a name."

"Probably something unisex since we don't know what it is," I mused.

Annabel cocked her head. "How about Poe?"

"Like 'Poe a deer' instead of 'Doe a deer'?" I questioned with a teasing smile.

"I'm not even going to ask how you know a song from *The Sound of Music*."

I laughed and jerked my chin at Willow. "Ask Miss Show Tunes over there."

"I meant for Edgar Allen Poe."

With a wink, I said, "I figured as much."

"So it's Poe?" Willow asked.

I glanced down at the deer. "Yep, Mr. or Miss Poe."

"A very distinguished name," Alexandra said with a grin.

"Now that Poe has a name, we need to work on getting some food into him or her." Annabel turned to me. "I'm going to need some things from a pet store. I can make you a list."

"I'll be happy to go get them for you. Especially a pen."

"Oh, but I planned on letting it sleep with me," Annabel teased.

"Think again."

Her smile once again reached her eyes, and in that moment, I would've let the damn deer sleep with her if I could see that much happiness on her face again. I had thought she was beautiful before, but when she truly smiled, she was breathtaking. And while I welcomed her newfound joy, I also knew I was in deep, deep trouble.

FOURTEEN

REV

ONE MONTH LATER

I had thought initially that having Annabel living with me would mean that my life would drastically change. But once we learned the pattern of each other's days and nights, everything fell into place. She rose before I had to leave for work and made coffee and cooked breakfast. She even brought me a home-cooked lunch at my job at the Raiders-owned pawnshop next to the clubhouse. She hadn't been exaggerating when she'd said she knew how to cook. I had already gained five pounds since she had come to live with me. Thankfully, she had regained some of the weight she'd lost as well.

While I was at work, she sometimes went over to Mama Beth's and helped her cook dinner. The two were growing very attached to each other. I could tell Mama Beth was everything in a mother that Annabel had never had yet had longed for. In turn, Mama Beth had always wanted daughters, especially those who wanted to help her with the things she loved, like cooking. While I loved that they got along so well, I knew it was only going to cause pain in the long run for both of them when Annabel left. But I kept my mouth shut.

Physically, she seemed to heal almost overnight. You could attribute it to her age and her resiliency to overcome what she had been through. Breakneck would come by often to check on her. As he had directed, she spent a lot of time off her feet and resting.

It was her emotional state that worried me. She still refused to let her parents know her location. She did call them once she got to my house, and once again she used a disposable phone. Although I didn't totally agree with it, I didn't press her about it. It did slightly alarm me when she started researching the veterinary program at the University of Georgia. She seemed hell-bent on never returning to Virginia, and I wasn't sure how I felt about that.

She grew more and more dependent on me. After I had spent several nights on the lumpy couch, she finally talked me into sleeping in my bed with her. It wasn't uncharted territory, since we had spent the night in the same bed before. But at the same time, there was an illicit feeling about it. I felt like a teenager sneaking off to do something I shouldn't, which was not something I had felt for a very long time. While I didn't want to think about Annabel in any sexual way, it was hard not to when she came to bed in pajama shorts that revealed her legs or thin tops that showed off her cleavage. I knew better than to say anything to her about it, lest I'd look like some pervert who had been getting off on her.

There was also the fact that waking up with a beautiful woman wrapped around me did nothing to stop my morning wood. If Annabel ever noticed, she didn't say anything. I also hoped she didn't notice my longer-than-normal *cold* showers to eradicate said morning wood. Again, if she knew, she never said anything. I could have easily taken out my frustrations with one of the club whores. Even though I had come home with a woman, it hadn't deterred some of them from their interest in me. Before, just a flash of a pair of tits would have had me hard as a rock and raring to fuck whatever was closest to me. But after Annabel, it didn't have the same allure. It seemed my dick had allegiance to only one woman, and painfully, it was the one who was off-limits.

Of course, any inappropriate thoughts easily fled when she woke up, screaming and thrashing, from nightmares at least two to three times a week. Since I was no stranger to those types of wake-up calls, I would merely reach through the sheets to bring her body closer to mine. "It's okay, Annabel. You're okay," was usually all I would have to say. She would spend a few minutes steadying her breathing in the dark, as if she was trying to believe that she was really with me in Georgia and not back in Mexico with Mendoza. Finally, after a small eternity, she would calm down and go back to sleep. I wondered what it would be like for her if I weren't in bed beside her. Would she be able to calm down, or would she suffer a lot of sleepless nights like I had in the past?

While I was helping Annabel, it didn't escape my mind how much I enjoyed her presence, either. I wanted her to be well, and to not need me, but her presence was a comfort, too. One I expected I would miss when she left.

But at the same time, I was beginning to feel like the human equivalent of a child's safety blanket. While I wanted to be there for her, I was still so frightened that I was impeding her healing. That as long as I allowed her to use me, she would never be well on her own. However, she never mentioned her therapist's voicing these concerns. With Alexandra's help, she had managed to find one she liked, and had started twice-a-week appointments.

The true bright spot in her life, and if I let myself admit it, in mine as well, was Poe. Who knew a little deer could bring so much love and enjoyment to our lives? Through Annabel's care, he— we'd discovered we had a boy—was thriving. I was amazed at how much knowledge she possessed to care for him. The whole routine of stimulating him to pee or poop with warm cotton balls blew my mind. When I had said as much, Annabel only giggled. "Well, his mother would do that in the wild to protect him from predators."

"But how . . ."

"With her tongue," she replied.

"Disgusting," I muttered.

Poe had moved from a small crate in my bedroom to a larger crate on the back porch. He was soon going to be big enough to use an old dog run we had on the property. Annabel never had to do his feedings alone. Willow often came to help give Poe his bottle, but the most amusing scene was when Deacon or Bishop would come by and gather the blanket-wrapped deer up like a baby to give him his bottle.

Friday night found me finishing up a feeding with Poe. I had insisted that Annabel take it easy after she helped Mama Beth cook a big meal for a family who had a sick relative. When I sniffed my shirt and got a strong whiff of animal, I knew I needed to grab a quick shower before heading up to the roadhouse.

After I showered and shaved, I came out of the bedroom to find Annabel reading on the couch. At the sight of me, she lowered her e-reader, and then narrowed her eyes suspiciously. "Going somewhere?"

"Uh, yeah, actually I am. I have to go up to the roadhouse. One of our prospects is getting patched in."

Her face took on a bewildered expression. "Patched in? What does that mean?"

I laughed. "It means he's a full member of the club now. He doesn't have to run around doing errands. He's proven he's worthy of us."

"That all comes in the form of a patch?"

"Before, he had to wear a prospect's patch, which is like a sign saying you're everyone's bitch. Now he gets the real deal."

"Sounds interesting."

"I don't know about that. Of course, Crazy Ace, the guy we're patching in, could make anything interesting."

"Oh really?"

"If you want, I can walk you over to Mama Beth's on the way," I suggested as I grabbed my keys.

"Do women ever go to these things?"

I turned around to stare at her in surprise. In the entire month since she had been with me, she had never once set foot inside the roadhouse. One by one, the Raiders had come down to meet her. She seemed to do well with a few of us at a time. "Um, yeah, they do."

"Then can I come? I mean, I hate to invite myself, but I'd like to get out for a while. And I've never seen the roadhouse."

I fiddled with the keys in my hand. "Are you sure you're up to it?" While I knew my brothers would be on their best behavior around Annabel, I was more concerned about how she would react to them. Strange men in cuts could inevitably lead to a flashback of her time with the Diablos.

She rose off the couch with a determined expression. "I think I'd like to try."

"Then I'd like to have you join me."

Glancing down at her clothes, she asked, "Am I dressed okay?"

I laughed. "Compared to what some of the women will be wearing, you're overdressed."

"Should I go change into something more revealing?" she teased.

"No," I replied a little too quickly. Annabel ducked her head, but I thought I saw the hint of a smile on her lips. "Come on. We'd better be going."

When we got to the back door of the roadhouse, I stopped her. "What is it?" she asked.

"If at any time you don't feel comfortable, you just let me know. Even if I'm taking part in the patching, you can come and get me. Okay?"

"Thank you, Rev," she replied. She then proceeded to shock the hell out of me by reaching up and tenderly kissing my cheek. "You're so good to me."

Feeling like I had been knocked on my ass, I threw open the back door and ushered her inside. Live music blared from the house band that played on special occasions. The steady roar of conversation came from all around us. At the far end of the roadhouse, the women had set up a long table filled with home-cooked food. Kim and Alexandra, along with some of the other wives, were helping the men through the line.

"Hungry?" I asked Annabel.

"Not right now. But don't let me stop you."

I glanced from the table back to her. "Kim's chili is fucking amazing."

Annabel smiled. "Then let's get you some before it's all gone."

Placing my hand on the small of her back, I started to guide her through the crowd. At Annabel's sudden intake of breath, I quickly demanded, "What's wrong?"

She motioned to Willow, across the room. "I was just surprised to see her here."

"Since it's a patching ceremony, wives, girlfriends, and families are invited. The first part of the night is pretty calm with the celebrating." I grinned at her. "It'll be around midnight, after the kids are put to bed, when things get really crazy."

When she caught sight of us, Willow made a beeline to our sides. After giving us both hugs, she asked, "How's Poe?"

"I just gave him his bottle right before we left."

"Did you remember to poop and pee him?"

"Yes, Miss Priss, I did. I think I know how to care for Poe."

"Just checking."

Annabel grinned. "We were going to get Uncle Rev some chili. Do you want some?"

"Sure." She slipped her hand into Annabel's, and they started walking together slightly ahead of me. I figured Annabel was just as safe with Willow as she was with me. After all, the guys knew if one hair on Willow's head was harmed, Deacon would have their asses.

We got in line behind Archer, who was talking to Alexandra. The two shared a bond over joining forces to save Deacon's life. After he leaned over to give her a hug, he caught my eye. "Prez! Good to see you, man." He threw out his hand, and I happily shook his.

Turning to Annabel, I said, "You remember Archer? He came by the house a few times."

She smiled and offered her hand, which surprised me. "It's nice to see you again."

"He just got patched a few months ago," I told her.

Archer chuckled. "Yeah, I was saying to Alexandra it feels like I was just at my patch ceremony."

"Hard to believe it's been four months, huh?"

He nodded. Archer had just taken a long pull of beer when Willow said to Annabel, "Archer is my favorite. I'm going to marry him someday."

Archer's beer spewed out of his mouth all over the plastic plates and forks. After he wiped his mouth, he shook his head. "Jesus, kid. You want your old man to kill me?"

Willow's dark brows scrunched together in confusion. "Why would my daddy kill you for marrying me?"

I chuckled. "Because daddies are very particular about who their little girls marry."

Willow waved her hand dismissively. "But Daddy likes Archer. After all, he helped save Mommy's life."

Archer sat his beer down on the table. Alexandra was managing to stay out of the conversation by cleaning up Archer's beer mess. Archer crouched down to where he could be on eye level with Willow. "I like you a lot, kid. You know that, right?" She nodded. "But I can never be your boyfriend."

"Why not?"

"For starters, there ain't no way in hell your daddy is ever going to let you date one of his brothers. But the most important reason is I'm too old for you."

"Just how old are you?"

"Twenty."

Willow cocked her head and gazed up at the ceiling like she was concentrating hard. "But one day I'll be twenty, and you'll be thirty-four."

"And I'll still be too old for you."

Her lips turned down in a pout. "Don't you want to be my boyfriend?"

Archer jerked his head up and gave me a pleading look.

"Willow, it's fine to pretend that Archer is your boyfriend for now. But it'll just have to be pretend, okay?"

"I guess so," she replied glumly.

Both Archer and I froze at her sniffle. Without a word, Annabel put her arm around Willow's shoulder. "Come on, sweetheart. Let's have a woman-to-woman talk about boyfriends." She then took Willow behind the table where the women were gathered, which I knew would feel safe to both her and Willow.

Archer let out a low whistle. "Son of a bitch. She's gonna be the death of me at six years old."

I laughed. "Deacon isn't going to put you to ground just because his daughter has a little crush."

With a shudder, Archer replied, "I just don't want anyone thinking anything pervy about me. Like I was encouraging her or something."

Now it was my turn to do the comforting. I put my arm around the kid's shoulder. Even though he was just seven years younger than me, he was new to the club, and it aged you like dog years. "You just keep acting the same way to Willow as you always have. Next week she'll have moved on to someone else."

"I sure as hell hope so."

I smacked his back. "Come on. Let's get some chili."

Whatever Annabel said to Willow worked like a charm, and she was back to her sunny self within minutes. When they rejoined me, I leaned over to whisper into Annabel's ear, "Thanks for doing that."

"I was glad to help." She cocked her head at me. "No matter what the age, it always hurts to be rejected," she said knowingly.

I dropped my gaze to my bowl of chili, since it seemed a hell of a lot safer than looking at Annabel at that moment. Her words were as loaded as if I were looking down the barrel of a shotgun. The last thing I wanted to do was press the matter of the underlying tension between us.

Thankfully, I was saved by Deacon coming up to get me for the ceremony. "I have to go to the front now. Why don't you go back with Alexandra and Kim?"

She smiled. "Okay. I'll be fine. Don't worry."

I watched her move around the side of the table and go stand between Alexandra and Kim. I was so thankful they all got along so well. It was almost a test of how well your girl would fare in the long run if she could get along with the other old ladies. I shook my head, as I sure as hell shouldn't have been thinking of Annabel in those terms. *Don't even go there. She isn't your girl or your old lady, and she never will be.*

After I motioned to the band, the music stopped. All the patch-holding guys came forward to form a circle. "Tonight we bring another brother into our ranks. Over the last year, he's proven himself to be worthy of wearing a Raiders patch." I signaled to Archer, who went out the back door to get Crazy Ace. As per tradition, he had been forced to wait away from the party until he was called for.

Although his usual persona was cocky as hell, he came in with his head down. His usual pimp walk was gone. I could tell he took this as seriously as he was supposed to. The room was so quiet you could have heard a pin drop. Even the babies in some of the women's arms were subdued. When he approached me, I turned to Deacon, who handed me the new patch. "Crazy Ace, do you wish to patch in as a full member to the Georgia chapter of the Hells Raiders?"

"I do."

"Do you swear to uphold the principles of the club while always having your brothers' backs, even if it means sacrificing your own?"

"I do."

I smiled and slapped him on the back. "Then welcome to the club." I passed the patch over to him and then reached in to hug him.

After the hugging and backslapping had died down, I went over to join Annabel. "So, what did you think?" I asked when she handed me a beer.

"It was interesting." She jerked her chin to where Crazy Ace now sat at a table alone, sewing his patch onto his cut. "Does he need some help with that?" When I chuckled, she narrowed her eyes at me. "What's so funny?"

"Nothing. It's just that no one but Crazy Ace can sew his patch on. It's too sacred."

"But what if he doesn't know how to sew?"

"Then he learns real fast."

She grinned. "It's kind of funny seeing a tattooed guy covered in piercings with a needle and thread in his hands."

"You're always responsible for your cut. You never let an old lady take care of it. It's your job to treat the leather and make sure the patches aren't falling off."

"Sounds pretty serious."

I nodded. "During the rest of the night, some of the guys will try to take Crazy Ace's cut as a way to test his loyalty. He would be in deep shit if it ever got out of his sight. First night I had my patch, I slept with my cut on so some smart-ass couldn't take it."

Alexandra nudged Annabel with a laugh. "It's really like a sorority when you think about it. All the rules and procedures."

"Not quite," I shot back, with a smile to soften my words.

Just as the band was about to start back up, Deacon jumped up onstage. At the sight of him, whistles and catcalls went up around the room. "I know this is Crazy Ace's big night, but my old lady and I got some pretty kick-ass news today that I have to share."

"Deacon," Alexandra said, laughing at his description.

He smiled down at her with love that I had never imagined he could possess for a woman. "So raise a glass in honor of my son!"

My gaze went from Deacon to Alexandra, who was beaming. A boy. I was going to have a nephew—another male to carry on the Malloy family name. I couldn't have been happier in that moment if the news had been my own.

The elation I felt was short-lived, for when I turned to smile at Annabel I saw that her expression was one of extreme anguish. I knew in that moment that what she had been denied was coming front and center to torment her. At any second, I expected her to burst into tears. Instead, she seemed to be getting her game face on right before my eyes. She straightened her shoulders and walked over to Alexandra. She gave her a hug. When Alexandra whispered something in Annabel's ear, her composure momentarily faltered, and her entire body shuddered like she was in physical pain.

Once again I held my breath in concern that she was about to fall apart. But instead, she pulled away from Alexandra with a smile. Without a word to me, she then made her way through the crowd to the bar. I quickly caught up to her. "You okay?"

"Fine. Just wanted a drink."

Since Alexandra had demanded that Deacon's ex, Cheyenne, be banned from the club, we hadn't found a new bartender. Instead, it became the job of the prospects, and it was the reason why you never ordered any mixed drinks.

"What can I get you?" our newest prospect, Jolting Joe, asked.

"A shot of Crown Royal," Annabel requested.

Jolting Joe's expression showed his confusion. "Is that some sorta mixed drink?"

I laughed. "Honey, we don't have anything that expensive here."

"Then what's a good whiskey that will get me drunk?" she asked in a matter-of-fact voice.

I eyed her cautiously. "You think that's a good idea?"

"I need to get drunk. I haven't been drunk in months. In fact, I haven't been truly rip-roaring drunk but maybe three times in my life." Sweeping a hand to her hip, she asked determinedly, "So what's gonna get me drunk?"

"Tequila's good," Jolting Joe suggested.

Annabel grimaced. "No tequila," she whispered. I knew she had probably been exposed to Mendoza's drunken rages after he'd partaken of too much tequila.

"Give her some Jack and Coke."

"Don't sugarcoat it for me," Annabel protested.

Deacon joined us at the bar. "Give the girl a bottle of Jack and a glass, brother."

Annabel turned to smile sweetly at Deacon. "Thank you."

I shook my head. "I don't think this is any of your business."

He grinned. "Actually, it kinda reminds me of the time you didn't think anything was wrong with Alex drunkenly dancing on the bar." His comment earned him a smack from Alexandra.

"I can't believe you just brought that up."

"You were so sexy that night," Deacon mused, his gaze becoming hooded.

Alexandra rolled her eyes. "On that note, I'm taking Willow and going home." When she started past him, he grabbed her and pulled her to him, molding her body against his own.

"I won't be long." He kissed her hungrily. When he pulled away, Alexandra appeared to have forgiven him. She took Willow's hand and waved good-bye.

Turning back on his barstool, he took a longneck from Jolting Joe. "Anyway, as I see it, payback's a bitch."

"Asshole," I muttered under my breath. "Fine. A bottle of Jack and a glass."

"Yes, sir," Jolting Joe replied. After he retrieved the whiskey and thankfully just a shot-sized glass, rather than a regular-sized one, he placed it in front of Annabel. She unscrewed the lid and poured the dark liquid almost to the brim.

After cutting her eyes in my direction, she asked, "Aren't you drinking?"

"Someone needs to stay sober to keep an eye on you."

"Oh, Rev, you're actually sounding like an old fart."

She knew just how to goad me. "Fine. I'll take some Jack, too."

Once I had a glass as full as hers, she clinked the two together. "Bottoms up." I'd barely had a chance to bring the glass to my lips before she had knocked hers back. Her eyes pinched shut as a shudder ran through her body. When she opened them, she grinned. "That was intense."

I shook my head in disbelief. "I can't believe you just downed that."

She grinned. "Let's just say I learned a lot during extracurricular activities my freshman year."

"I see." When I swallowed my Jack, Annabel poured us another drink, but this time she sipped at it more cautiously. When Jolting Joe left us, we were alone again. "You want to talk about earlier?" I asked.

"No," she replied, then took another sip. She cut her eyes from watching the couples on the dance floor back to me. "I'm sorry I freaked out like that," she said softly.

"You didn't freak out, and you don't need to apologize."

She sighed. "I feel so selfish being jealous of Alexandra. I mean, it's not like I'm ready to have a baby right now. Maybe it's something stubborn in me that only wants what it can't have."

I shook my head. "I think you have every right to be upset. A part of your future was taken away. It doesn't matter if you wanted a child today or if you'd never wanted one."

Annabel gave me a sad smile. "You always say just the right thing."

"Once again, I think you're flattering me."

"Guess I haven't worked my magic on you in the last month," she mused.

"What's that supposed to mean?"

"I told you that day at *tohi a-ma* that I wanted you to be able to see how wonderful you are. Being modest is admirable, but it doesn't mean you always have to discredit your strengths and talents."

Just like Annabel, I remembered that day. What she had said to me had stayed with me this past month. Part of me was flattered by her compliments, while another part of me doubted their authenticity. As much as I hated to admit it, everything seemed to have changed between us. No matter how hard I'd tried to stop or fight it.

With most of the wives and families clearing out, the band had cranked up even louder. Some of the unattached men were enjoying the scantily clad sweet butts or club whores who came around on party nights. When clothes started coming off, I turned to Annabel. "Maybe it's time we got out of here."

She giggled. "Oh, Rev, that"—she motioned with her glass to the half-naked women gyrating against the men—"doesn't bother me. I might as well be back at a sorority party."

Although she said it didn't bother her, I didn't want her to be around anything that could trigger a backlash of emotions for her. "I would feel better if we went back to my room."

"Your room?" she questioned in surprise.

"Yeah, the officers in the club have rooms in the back so we can crash here. Tonight some of the other guys will be using them."

"For indecent purposes?" she teased.

I laughed. "Yes. I'm sure for that."

"I don't think I've had so much Jack that I can't make it back to the house. I might not be able to walk a straight line, but I'm pretty sure I can walk."

"I'm sure you can. As president, I need to hang around a while. I'll feel better knowing you're close."

She smiled. "Well, when you say it like that, how can I refuse?" She hopped down from her stool and staggered a bit. "Hmm, maybe I have had a little too much."

"I think anything after the first shot was too much."

Slinging my arm around Annabel's shoulder, I drew her closer to me as I led her to the back. "I don't know how easy it's going to be for you to go to sleep with the music going."

"I'll be fine. I can always read."

"Did you bring your e-reader thing with you?"

With a grin, she replied, "No, but I figured your room would have some books."

My chest tightened at the fact that she knew me so well and could even remember it in her slightly inebriated state. I opened the door for her, and she stepped inside. Turning around in a circle, she took in the room. She pointed at my bookcase. "Told ya."

I laughed. "Okay, okay. You know me too well."

Annabel tossed her purse onto the bed and then walked over to the bookcase. "The complete works of Shakespeare." Making a *tsk*ing noise, she added, "You are hard-core."

"I like the tragedies."

"Why doesn't that surprise me?"

Even through the walls and the closed door, the beat of the music was audible in the room. When the band changed over to a slow song, Annabel began to sway back and forth on her feet. "Are you all right?" I asked.

Glancing at me over her shoulder, she said, "Dance with me."

My heartbeat skipped and seemed to pop erratically like an old vinyl record. "What?" I managed to ask when I recovered.

"Dance with me."

"Here?"

"Why not?" Turning around, she walked over to me. Although in my warped mind, it was more like she stalked over to me like a cat. "Don't tell me you can't slow-dance."

"I can slow-dance just fine."

As my arms went around her waist, I drew her flush against me. The contact of our bodies caused us both to suck in a breath. Sliding her arms up my chest, Annabel then brought them around my neck. When her fingers glided through the strands of my hair, I fought to keep my composure. Call me a pussy, but there was something that turned me on about a woman playing with my hair, tugging on it wildly as she rode out an orgasm.

I lowered my head to rest it on Annabel's shoulder. Closing my eyes, I allowed my mind to wander. Like the dirty bastard I was, I envisioned having Annabel on the bed, legs spread wide, my head between them, and her clutching and clawing my hair and scalp as she came on my tongue. Just the thought sent a shiver of need down my spine and caused my whole body to tremble with desire.

"Are you cold?" Annabel asked.

"I'm fine," I croaked.

She tightened her hold on me while pressing her body tighter against mine. It was a sweet gesture of compassion to warm me up that had the opposite effect than what she had intended. "Rev?"

"Hmm?"

"Look at me."

When I pulled my head off her shoulder, I stared into her green eyes. The look in them told me everything I needed to know about what was going on in Annabel's head. Motherfucker. I was a dead man.

I knew right then and there I needed to extricate myself from the situation and get the hell out of there. But instead, I remained frozen in place. I didn't even jerk back when Annabel brought her lips to mine.

Oh damn. Those lips. Those soft, soft lips. Warm, inviting, and full. I imagined them moving all over my body, especially on my dick. As her mouth worked against mine, those fingers began to work their magic in my hair.

Grabbing my shirt, she pulled me down onto the bed. While our arms and legs tangled together, our mouths never parted. When she thrust her warm tongue into my mouth, I groaned and gripped her tighter. It was all so wrong and so right at the same time.

When I started to get up, she tried to pull me closer. "Where are you going?"

"I need to check on the guys. Make sure everybody gets out."

"Oh. Okay." A pleading look entered her eyes. "But you'll come back to me. Won't you?"

"Sure. Just let me take care of some things. I'll also lock the door."

She gave me a drowsy smile as her head lay back on the pillow. Her eyes closed in contentment, and she sighed. "You're always so good to me. No wonder I'm falling in love with you."

Her words had the same effect on me as standing in a field during a lightning storm. Electricity zapped the top of my head and ran through my body. Without a word to her, I backed quickly away from the bed and disappeared from the bedroom. I had been fearing something like this in the last month—the way she looked at me, the way she talked to me, the way she'd wrapped herself around me in the night. I'd been a selfish bastard and enjoyed it too much to put a stop to it. Now I'd somehow managed to lead her on. I was the sickest type of fucker out there. I'd preyed on an abuse victim.

As I walked up the hallway to the tune of my self-deprecating tirade, another voice broke through. Forceful and unrelenting, it was one I battled daily. It liked to call itself the voice of reason, but it was more like the voice of lunacy to me.

Man up. That beautiful girl in there loves you, and you love her, too. You've probably loved her since the night she called for you in the hospital. You're just too fucking scared to admit it. You want to try to say she doesn't know what she's saying or doing because of what she went through with Mendoza. But the truth is you're afraid you're not good enough for her. After all, you're just a biker with a two-year degree, and she's political royalty from a privileged upbringing.

"Go fuck yourself," I muttered to the voice.

"Excuse me, Prez?" Jolting Joe asked. He had a trash bag in one hand and was tossing beer bottles in with the other. As a prospect, he wouldn't be getting any ass tonight like some of his brothers were. He would be on cleanup duty, and from the looks of it, he was going to be busy for hours.

"Sorry, Joe. I wasn't talking to you."

"You okay, Prez? You look a little pale. Need me to make you a hangover drink?"

I shook my head. "No. I'm good. Thanks." When I started to the back door, I stopped. "Hey, Joe?"

"Yeah, Prez?"

"Take five on the cleanup and go stand outside my room. Annabel's sleeping in there. If she wakes up or screams or something, call me on my cell."

"You got it."

I wouldn't be gone long. I had promised Annabel to come back to her, and I would never let her down. Not intentionally at least. When I reached my house, I grabbed a beer out of the fridge and then sat down on the couch. There was a phone call I dreaded to make, but it had to be done. I knew I would hate myself in the morning, but in the long run, it was what was best for all of us.

FIFTEEN

Annabel

When I woke up in the morning and surveyed my strange surroundings, I bolted straight up in bed and screamed. The door flew open and a bleary-looking prospect, whom I had met last night, tumbled in. At the sight of him, I drew the covers tighter around me.

The guy held up his hands. "I ain't here to hurt you or anything. Prez put me on post in case you woke up."

"Where is Rev?"

"He's having breakfast."

I nodded. "Thanks for letting me know." When I sat up straighter in bed, I winced at the pain that shot through my head.

"Regretting the Jack from last night, huh?" he asked with a smile.

It was then that I remembered he had been the bartender. "Jumping Joe?" I questioned.

He laughed. "Jolting Joe. Got my soon-to-be road name from Joe DiMaggio."

"You were a baseball player, huh?"

His jovial expression turned sheepish. "Uh, it's more for the way I can swing a bat and knock someone out."

I didn't know if I should be amused or horrified. "Well, thanks for letting me know where Rev is."

"No problem."

Once Joe closed the door, I threw back the covers. Gazing down at myself, I realized I didn't have any reason to be modest since I was still in my clothes from last night. When I rose from the bed, my entire body ached. It had been so long since I'd had anything alcoholic to drink. For the life of me, I couldn't remember what had possessed me to have so much last night.

Then it hit me. Hearing Deacon and Alexandra's announcement about their baby boy had sent me spinning. Like an idiot, I thought alcohol would fix things—like some sort of liquid bandage for my broken soul. But in the sober light of day, I still had to face the fact that it would take nothing short of a miracle for me to become a mother.

Rubbing my shirt above my bruised heart, I gazed around the room. Memories from Rev bringing me in last night came flooding back to me. We had danced. And then I had kissed him. Just when I wanted to feel extreme remorse for what I had done, I remembered he had kissed me back. He was a good kisser, too, from what I remembered.

But then I couldn't ignore the fact that he had pushed me away before things had gone too far. Of course, it appeared to be under the pretense of him having to take care of business. I wondered if he had ever returned, but then I peered down at the bed and saw the indentation of his body.

I wondered what was going through his mind this morning. He was noble to a fault, so I imagined he would be feeling the remorse that I probably should be. Although only a month had passed since the Raiders had freed me from my captivity, I was ready to move on. My therapist encouraged me to try to move forward in all aspects of my life, from school to my ability to trust men. During our sessions, the mantra that not all men were evil and were going to hurt me was something we frequently repeated. It was hard to overcome my knee-jerk reaction to feeling threatened in a strange man's presence. While we had yet to work through how a future love life might work for me, I couldn't help being confused as to why my love life seemed to still need blocking with yellow caution tape like the police did at crime scenes.

At the end of the day, Mendoza would haunt me until I was able to give myself emotionally and physically to another man. I had to wonder if the longer I waited, the more I was allowing emotional scar tissue to build up, making it harder and harder to be intimate with someone. Many victims of trafficking and rape were in relationships or married, so it wasn't like they put on a habit and went to their local nunnery. They had to work through the emotional landmines to reconnect physically with their partners.

I felt I had spent the last month getting to know Rev on such a deep level that I was ready to risk a relationship that went further than friendship. I just didn't know how to convince him that his steadfast image of me as a cracked china doll wasn't who I was.

After running a brush through my hair and improvising without a toothbrush, I decided to go in search of Rev and some strong coffee. When I got to the end of the long hallway, I faltered at the sight of all the strangers milling around the front room. Closing my eyes, I inwardly chanted, *You can do this. These people are Rev's family. They won't hurt you.*

My eyes flew open at the sound of a familiar voice. "Morning, Uptown Girl," Bishop said with a wave. His warm grin instantly put me at ease.

"Morning, Bishop."

"You hungry?" he asked as he came to meet me.

"A little. More than anything, I'd love some coffee."

"Come on. I'll take you to Rev."

I smiled. "Thanks, Bishop."

Whenever I met the eye of one of the Raiders or their old ladies, which was still a hard term for me to get used to, I received a nod of the head or a friendly smile. I didn't know if they were being kind because of what I had gone through or because I was with Rev, so to speak.

When Rev caught sight of me, a range of emotions flashed across his face. After settling on the one that looked like he was glad to see me, he came forward and gave me a hug. "Good morning."

"Morning," I replied as I squeezed him tight. His usual manly smell was mixed with coffee and bacon, which made me feel both comfort and longing.

When I pulled away, he appeared apologetic. "Sorry I left you this morning, but you were sleeping so peacefully I hated to wake you up."

"It's okay." With a sheepish grin, I added, "I definitely needed to sleep off the alcohol."

He laughed before turning to pour me a cup of steaming coffee. "Have some of this while I fix you a plate."

Leaning back against the counter, I blew tiny rivulets in the black liquid to cool it off. At the same time, I kept an eye on Rev as he went about getting my food. I thought that when he was around a large group of his brothers, he might shy away from openly taking care of me, like somehow it would be seen as him being pussy-whipped. But the one thing I most loved about Rev was how he never put people's opinions of him above being his kind, caring self. It was truly endearing.

When he came back with a plate heaped with bacon, eggs, and hash browns, my eyes widened. "You can't be serious."

"You need some good, greasy food after all that alcohol."

Glancing down at the plate, I said, "But I couldn't eat all of this even if I didn't have a weak stomach from drinking."

Rev winked. "Just eat what you can."

"Okay."

He placed a hand on my back and guided me out into the main room. We sat down at a table with Deacon, Alexandra, and Bishop. "What did you think of last night?" Alexandra asked.

"It was interesting."

Bishop snorted. "Interesting how?"

I chewed thoughtfully on a piece of bacon as I tried to put into words what I had experienced.

Misjudging my silence, Deacon said, "It's okay if you didn't like it, Annabel. This life ain't for everyone."

Shaking my head, I replied, "No, no, it isn't like that. I enjoyed watching the patching ceremony and seeing the way everyone acted like family." I looked pointedly at Deacon. "It showed me how someone would want to be a part of this life."

My response seemed to please the Malloy brothers. Deacon even gave Rev a knowing look, which Rev responded to by ducking his head.

After finishing what I could of my meal, I noticed an old upright piano across from us. I stood up and went over to it. "Does anyone ever play this?" My fingers were already tinkling lightly over the keys.

"Not since Jim Beam died," Rev replied as he came to my side.

"Excuse me?" I asked.

Rev laughed. "Jim Beam was the oldest member of the club. He literally lived and died with a bottle of Jim Beam in his hand. He could even ride one-handed and drink."

"I guess that's how he got his road name, huh?"

"Yes. It is." He nudged me closer to the bench. "Why don't you play something?"

I widened my eyes as I shook my head wildly. "Oh no, I'm out of practice."

"I'm sure you're just being modest."

"Ah, hell, Rev, don't encourage her," Bishop said behind us. When I turned around, he winked. "She'll just end up torturing us with some of that fruity classical shit."

Crossing my arms over my chest, I countered, "Is that all you think I can play?"

"Like you know any hard rock or blues. That's what Jim Beam always played. You'd swear sometimes you were listening to Jerry Lee Lewis."

"Impressive. Did he also play the piano while holding a whiskey bottle?"

Bishop grinned. "Hell yeah."

"Well, I'm afraid ol' Jim Beam beats me on that one. But . . ." I pushed the piano bench aside and sat down. "Maybe I can find something that would impress even Bishop's musical taste."

"Bring it on," Bishop challenged.

I hadn't lied when I told Rev I was out of practice. It had been months since I had touched a piano. In fact, it was even before my captivity with Mendoza. But I was never one to shy away from a challenge.

My hands momentarily hovered over the keys as I closed my eyes and mentally went over the opening of the song. Within seconds, it all came flooding back to me. My fingers hit the ivories and I began pounding out the opening of "Great Balls of Fire." It was actually a song I had wanted to learn back in the day, especially since my parents hated me to do anything that wasn't classical or tasteful. Regardless of the fact that he was a musical genius, it would be hard to argue that Jerry Lee himself was very tasteful.

As soon as the guys recognized what I was playing, a roar went up among them. I was treated to catcalls and whistles, which fueled me to play even harder. A pleasant warmth ran through me as I was mentally able to slide another piece into the puzzle that made up my former self.

I finished the song in a flourish. Strong applause rang through my ears, sending a flush to my cheeks of both embarrassment and pride.

When I dared to look over my shoulder at Bishop, I found him grinning like the Cheshire cat. "Damn, Uptown Girl. I'm sure as hell glad I didn't put money on that. You would have owned my ass."

I laughed at his summation. "Once again, I think I have to do a song just for you."

Sweeping a hand to his chest, Bishop replied, "I'm touched."

Although I would have loved to play "Uptown Girl" for him, I didn't know it, so I had to settle for another Billy Joel classic, "Piano Man." When he recognized the tune, Bishop clapped his hands in appreciation. "I need to get my lighter!" he shouted over the music.

As I laughed, I couldn't help feeling more alive than I had in a long, long time. It was something about my converging worlds. If I was honest with myself, I probably felt more alive among Rev and his brothers than I ever had back in my old world.

"Annabel."

At the sound of that voice, my fingers froze on the keys. No. This couldn't be happening. Before panic could set in, I whirled around on the bench. Seeing him caused my chest to clench in agony.

"F-Father?"

He forced a smile to his face—one that didn't reach his eyes. "You look well," he said, as if he was surprised to find me in one piece or not covered in tattoos and piercings.

"I am well. Thank you." I fought the urge to add, *I've told you as much on the phone.* But I didn't.

His hands fidgeted with his gold cuff links. "Your mother is outside in the car. She wanted to wait to make sure you were all right before she came in."

I fought the urge to roll my eyes at that statement. Of course she had refused to come inside. She probably thought she would get some disease simply from being around some of the Raiders.

It was then I knew I had to ask the question that was weighing heavily on my mind. "How did you find out where I was?"

My father didn't answer. Instead, he glanced behind me at Rev. I pinched my eyes shut as the sudden horrible realization crashed down on me. It couldn't be true. Rev wouldn't do that. He respected my feelings on the subject of my parents. More than anything, he knew how much that would hurt me, how it would ruin every perfect thing between us.

Slowly, I turned around to face him. His ashen expression told me everything before he said, "I did. I called him."

As his betrayal washed over me, I literally staggered back, my legs bumping into the piano bench. When Rev reached out to steady me, I slapped his hands away. "Don't you dare touch me!" I hissed.

"Annabel, please."

My mind spun with questions. What had Rev been thinking, calling my parents? How could he possibly not know how much I didn't want to return to Virginia and my parents? After our time together, was it possible I had completely misjudged who he was? After taking several deep breaths and letting the initial shakes run through me, I regained my composure. There was no way in hell I would break down in front of all these people, nor would I go off on Rev in front of his brothers. Although I felt he had disrespected me in the worst way, I wouldn't do the same to him.

Instead, I walked on trembling legs over to my father. "I'll go get my things and meet you at the car."

Relief flooded his face. I'm sure in his mind he had prepared himself for some kind of showdown in which he would have to resort to taking me kicking and screaming back to Virginia. But after what Rev had done, there was nothing left for me here, and certainly no reason to stay.

As I started for the back door, Alexandra came to my side. "Would you like some help?" she asked softly.

"No. I can get it myself." When I looked over at her, I saw tears in her eyes.

"I don't mind."

I shook my head and reached over and hugged her. "Take care of yourself and the little man."

She sniffled. "I will." She pulled back to stare intently at me. "I don't care what Rev did or how you feel about him. You do not have to go back with them. You would always have a home here."

Her words touched me deeply because I knew they were sincere. Regardless of what Deacon or Rev might say, she would insist on having me stay. It was the truest example of a female friendship I had ever experienced. "I wish I could. But I can't."

After gently placing a hand on her belly, I kissed Alexandra's cheek and walked out the door. The tremors that ricocheted through my body made it difficult to walk. I stumbled several times. I hadn't made it halfway down the street before Rev chased me down. "Would you just stop for one minute to let me explain?"

"There's nothing to say. You went behind my back when you explicitly knew I didn't want my parents to know my location. How the hell can that possibly have a reasonable explanation?" I didn't wait for his reply. Instead, I stomped up the front stairs and then growled in frustration when I had to wait on Rev to bring the key.

"I didn't call them to come and get you. I just thought they had a right to know where you were. I thought they might come down for a visit or something. I didn't think it was good for you to be away from them. It never crossed my mind that they were going to come down here right after I talked to them last night."

I froze. "What did you say?"

He jerked a hand through his hair. "I said I called them last night."

I momentarily fought to breathe. I didn't know how things could get worse, but I was learning otherwise. "Last night after we kissed?"

Rev stared down at the rug. "I guess."

Streaks of red-hot anger blurred my vision. "You fucking coward! You got so freaked out by kissing me that instead of acknowledging your potential feelings for me, you decided to get rid of me."

Gone was the hard-core biker and my tough-as-nails rescuer. In his place was a broken man. When he still didn't look up, I placed my hands on his chest and shoved him with all my might. "Dammit, at least have the nerve to look me in the face!" I demanded.

When he finally looked up, his eyes were haunted. "I thought it was for the best."

"No, you only thought of what was best for you. I mean, God forbid you actually admit that you have feelings for me."

"That's not true."

I rolled my eyes. "Oh, please, Rev, like you could actually acknowledge the crazy, broken sex slave as your old lady. What would your brothers say?"

His expression darkened. "I don't give a damn what they might have to say. That's not what this is about."

"Then please enlighten me. Because I find it extremely ironic that after being with you for a month, you just happen to call my parents on the night we kissed."

"What I did last night was not fair to you with all you've been through."

"Excuse me?"

"You're still recovering. I should've never made a move on you."

I snatched up a pair of my shoes from the floor and spat, "In case you missed it, *I* was the one who made a move on *you*."

Rev exhaled an agonized sigh. "Because you're confused and mixed up. For Christ's sake, Annabel, a month ago you were imprisoned and enslaved by a fucking maniac. You don't get over that shit so quickly. You've been through too much to know what you really want."

Anger and hurt flickered and flashed through me like lightning slicing across a troubled sky. Although I'd been raised to always temper my emotions, I couldn't hold myself back. With all the strength I had within me, I threw one of the shoes at him.

Rev ducked just in time, and it narrowly missed his head. Closing the gap between us, I demanded, "How dare you tell me what I feel? I'm not crazy when it comes to how I feel about you!"

"I never said you were crazy," Rev argued softly.

"You're implying it, which is just as bad."

"I didn't want to do anything to hurt you."

"Too. Fucking. Late," I spat before I rushed past him and slammed the bedroom door. Hot tears streaked down my cheeks as I went to the closet and grabbed the small suitcase Rev had bought me on the way home from Texas. As I threw my clothes and toiletries inside, I expected him to come into the room and continue our argument.

But he didn't.

It was like he had raised the white flag of defeat when it came to us. He wasn't going to fight. He was going to do what he thought was the honorable thing and just let me go.

Once I finished packing, I threw open the bedroom door to find Rev standing in front of me. His mouth opened, but then he quickly closed it. When he reached for my suitcase, I jerked it away from him. "Please, Annabel. You're still recuperating from surgery. You shouldn't be carrying that."

Angrily, I slammed it down at his feet. "Fine, then. Since you seem to still have concern for my physical state, you take it. I want to say good-bye to Poe."

Without another word to him, I turned and fled to the back porch. At the sound of the back door opening, Poe was already standing up and waiting for me in his pen. I stepped off the porch and walked around to him. It was amazing how much he had grown since he had moved from the crate to an old dog run that had belonged to one of Rev's MC brothers.

"Hey, sweet boy," I said as I unlocked the latch on his pen. He came out tentatively like he always did, cautiously surveying his surroundings. Tears filled my eyes as I stroked his head. I could never regret my time here with Rev because it meant saving Poe's life. He had given me a focus and shown me once again there was nothing else on earth I wanted more than to be a veterinarian.

I kissed the top of his nose. "Be a good boy. You'll be leaving soon. You'll be big and strong enough to go back to the woods. I know you're going to do just fine."

I think I was saying the words more for me than for Poe. In a way, I had just had my own release back into the wild. More than anything, I needed reassurance that everything was going to be all right.

At the sound of Rev approaching behind me, I asked, "You remember what to do for him when it's time to release him?"

"Yes, I do," he murmured.

"Good."

"Annabel, don't leave like this," Rev pleaded, his voice thick with anguish.

"You ask me not to leave like this, yet you haven't once told me to stay." I glanced over my shoulder at him. "Considering all of that, how else would you presume I left? You've told me I don't know what I feel, but more than anything, you've made me feel that my feelings for you are based on some sort of reverse Stockholm syndrome, like kidnapping victims experience for their captors." I shook my head. "I just wish you could see what's truly in my heart."

With a resigned sigh, I eased Poe back into his pen. As much as I hated to leave him, I knew without a doubt that Rev would take good care of him, even after he was released into the wild. I stood up and breezed past Rev to the porch steps. After making one last sweep inside the house for anything of mine, I went out the front door onto the porch.

As I started down Rev's front steps, I saw that my parents' limousine had pulled around to the cul-de-sac. I started walking to the car, but a small voice behind me caused me to stop.

When I turned around, Willow was staring up at me with her big brown eyes. "Belle, are you leaving?"

Fighting back tears, I nodded. "I wish I could stay longer, but I really have to go back home now."

Willow's lips turned down in a pout. "But I'm going to miss you so much. Will you come to visit?"

Although I knew the answer to her question was no, it broke my heart to disappoint her. "Maybe one day." I bent down to her level. "Will you help Uncle Rev with Poe? It won't be much longer before he's ready to be released."

"Yes, I will. I promise."

I pulled her into my arms. "Be a good girl for your mommy and daddy. I know you're going to be a wonderful sister to your brother."

"I will."

I kissed the top of Willow's head and then slowly pulled away. Beth stood behind us, a stricken look on her face. I don't know if it was because of Willow or because of the weight of the emotions, but neither of us spoke. Instead, our eyes conveyed everything we needed to say. Beth wanted me to know that Rev was struggling with his feelings. But the tears in my eyes let her know he had made his intentions clear. He wasn't fighting for me . . . for us. So there was nothing left but to go.

She put her arms around me and hugged me tight. I clung to her, realizing how close I had grown to her in the last month. She was the mother I wished I had—the kind which, if fairy tales were true, I would have wished for. But this was real life.

In fairy tales, this would be the moment when Rev swooped to my side and told me everything I wanted to hear. He would hoist me into his arms and carry me back into the house, and we would live happily ever after.

But this was real life. And I had already learned how much real life could hurt you.

When I pulled away from Beth, I let the sobs overtake me as I hurried to the waiting limousine. I slid inside without looking back for him. At the sight of my tear-streaked face and my chest heaving with sobs, my mother recoiled in her seat. "Annabel, honestly," she chided. I knew she was at a loss to understand how I could be so bereft at leaving such people.

She would never understand that within the walls of Rev's small house and among the salt-of-the-earth people who were his family, I had learned how to truly live for the first time.

SIXTEEN

REV

Sometimes we find ourselves damned to hell by outside forces. But then sometimes we are the very ones who damn ourselves. The burden of suffering I had taken on after Annabel left was of my own doing, and I had no one else to blame but myself. Doing what I had assumed was the right thing had never been so wrong.

Since I had never been one who couldn't admit his mistakes, I tried calling Annabel several times. Each call went unanswered until the number was changed altogether. My wounded male pride then overrode any other overtures I should have made to make things right between us. Instead, I did the immature thing and drowned my sorrows in Jack Daniel's.

My days and nights became a boozy haze. I slept until noon, and I didn't show up for work at the pawnshop. I basically became one of the walking dead or, I guess more aptly, a dead man walking. The only time I took life seriously was when it came to the club and club business.

No one could reach me. Deacon and Bishop talked, yelled, and cursed until they were blue in the face. Even Alexandra tried using her feminine approach to get through, but I was a hopeless case. No one was more frustrated by my behavior than I was. But each day, as I poured another glass of Jack, I reasoned that what I had done was for the best for both Annabel and me. She'd had one traumatic life experience, so she sure as hell didn't need to end up with me. I could only imagine her waking up one day and looking at me with a regret that would have broken my heart even more than letting her go had.

Mama Beth was the only one who didn't try talking to me. I think she was so disgusted by what I had done concerning Annabel and what my life had become that she was for once washing her hands of me. Of course, her disappointment wounded me deeply. One day, three months after Annabel had left, I lashed out at her in a way I never would have believed myself capable of. After talking it over with Deacon and Bishop, we had all decided it was best not to tell Mama Beth about my rape. As sensitive as she was, it would be too horrific and painful for her to have to endure.

But in my drunken, self-loathing phase, I forgot all about that. Since I was surviving on a liquid diet, she had brought lunch to my house. I never intended to let her in, but she had a key of her own. Being her stubborn self, she had come on in and promptly poured a pitcher of cold water on my ass to get me awake. To get her off my back, I had finally come out to the kitchen.

When I peered down at the table, a simple piece of her chocolate cake set me off. "What the fuck is that?" I demanded.

Mama Beth's blue eyes popped wide at my language and tone. "Why, it's chocolate cake. Your favorite."

Once upon a time, it had been my favorite. After my attack, I could barely stomach it. But to keep the secret and the peace, I would smile and eat it, only to excuse myself and throw it up moments later. Too much had happened for me to do the same thing now. Lunging forward, I grabbed the cake and took it straight to the trash. I slammed it down into the trash can so hard that the plate popped up before falling down.

"Nathaniel, what are you doing?" Mama Beth asked in her most concerned voice.

"You know what happened to me because of chocolate cake?" Mama Beth shook her head. "You're out-of-your-head drunk and not making any sense. Please eat something. I made all of your favorites."

"Always trying to make things right with food, aren't you, Mama?" I snapped.

"Nathaniel, I do not like your tone or your attitude. I know things have been strained between us since Annabel left, so I came down here to try to make things right."

"So you brought me some good ol' chocolate cake." I laughed a little maniacally. "One baked cake never cost me so much . . . or us so much." I staggered toward her. "Do you remember years and years ago when you asked me to take a cake down to Miss Mae's?"

"Yes," she murmured, her forehead creasing in confusion.

"Miss Mae wasn't home. Instead, a vagrant named Kurt was there. He drugged me and dragged me into her bedroom, where he raped me!"

Mama Beth gasped in horror, her eyes widening to the size of dinner plates.

"The reason Preacher Man left his church and left us? It's because he blew Kurt's head off after seeing him violating me."

As long as I live, I will never forget the look on her face. It was an agonizing expression of shock, disbelief, and pain. Her hand flew to her mouth as she swayed on her feet. "Why didn't you ever tell me? Why didn't he tell me?"

"I don't know. We thought it was best to keep it a secret."

As she stared at me almost like I was a stranger, I felt like the biggest bastard to have ever walked the earth. "Mama Beth, I'm sorry," I murmured. I wanted her to scream at me. To slap my face for telling her in such a horrible way. To hate me for ruining her marriage and, in a way, her life.

Instead, tears streamed down her cheeks. "No, I'm the one who is sorry, Nathaniel. I'm so, so sorry."

"Don't apologize to me. I'm an asshole for telling you like that."

She brought her hand up to cup my cheek. "You've been under a tremendous strain these last three months. While I should be angry at you for the way you told me, I can't be. You're my son, and I love you. More than anything, my heart breaks for you. How I wish I could turn back time to be there for you when you were suffering."

"You were. You just didn't know the why."

Shaking her head, she said, "I wish your father was alive, so I could give him a good talking-to for keeping it from me."

I laughed. "Knowing him, it probably wouldn't have done any good."

"It would have made me feel better." She wiped her eyes. "He should have known keeping secrets never does any good. Maybe things could have been different if he had only been honest." She glanced up at me. "Maybe you'll learn from his mistakes."

"What do you mean?"

"With Annabel."

"I don't want to talk about it."

"I'm not asking you to. I'm just telling you that keeping the truth from me hurt me far worse in the long run." She then opened her arms. "Now come let your mother hug you and try to make it better."

Although I was a grown man, I allowed my mother to comfort me like the scared eleven-year-old boy wished he had been comforted.

That had been a month ago, and while I wished I could say that her talk had made me see the light, I once again was too stubborn. I retreated back into drinking, although I did manage to make it to church meetings with the club and returned to my job at the pawn-shop. Of course, I wasn't sober for any of it, but at least I was phys-ically present.

The next afternoon found me walking home from the pawn-shop. The December chill had me reaching inside my cut for my flask. After sucking back some liquid warmth, I put the flask back. Just as I started up the stairs, I remembered I needed to feed Poe. It had been two months since he had been released into the wild. Even though he was doing fine on his own, I still gave him his favor-ite treat of dried corn. It helped to bring him back around. Even though he was a constant reminder of Annabel, I still wanted to see him.

As I lurched around the side of the house, I heard Willow talking in a singsong voice to Poe. She giggled at the loud way he crunched on the corn she was feeding him.

"Whatcha doin', rug rat?" I asked.

After glancing at me over her shoulder, she gave me a disap-proving look. It had a greater effect than she could have ever imag-ined. I had never felt so cut down to size by anyone, not even after Mama Beth's talk. "Feeding Poe," she finally replied.

"That's nice of you, but I'm the one who does that."

"You don't do much of anything but drink lately," she mur-mured softly.

Fuck me. She might as well have knifed me in the chest. I didn't know what to say to her. Finally, I settled on, "I'm sorry, rug rat."

After tossing the rest of Poe's corn to the ground, she turned to face me. "My first mommy used to tell me she was sorry. But then she would go right back to drinking." She stomped her pink-sneakered foot dramatically, and then swept her hands to her hips. "I don't want you to be like her, Uncle Rev. I don't want you to hurt people like she did. . . . I don't want you to hurt me."

While I had expected her to be the one crying, I was the one whose eyes became moist. Christ, where had I gone so wrong? I had once been a hero in Willow's eyes. Now she was disgusted and disappointed by me. She was just another woman whom I had loved and had alienated myself from.

"Do you want to know why Poe comes back for the corn?"

Swiping my eyes with the back of my hands, I muttered, "Because he's a spoiled brat."

Willow shook her head. "He comes back because he knows we want to take care of him. He could survive out there with his deer friends, and maybe he would be better off, but he still wants to see us. We show him we still love him by leaving him the corn."

I blinked at her. I wasn't sure, but I suspected that she was trying to make some strange correlation between Annabel and Poe. She didn't give me a knowing look like Mama Beth might, or Alexandra. She just appeared to be talking from her heart.

And it was time for me to start talking from mine.

SEVENTEEN

ANNABEL

Four months, three days, and nineteen hours. That's how long it had been since I had seen or even spoken to Rev Malloy. While he had tried to reach me by phone, I had refused his calls. He had wounded me too deeply at a time when I was at my most vulnerable. After what I had been through with Mendoza, I couldn't have imagined ever going through something worse. But I was wrong. Having the man you care deeply for question your feelings for him and allude to your being crazy was just as bad. Maybe it was even worse because of the additional element of being kicked when you were already down.

The rational part of me understood why Rev had done what he did. Deep down, I had questioned the root of my feelings for him. Did I want to be with him because of who he truly was or because he was my savior? Was he just the safe choice after what I had been through? Was it some weird reversal of Stockholm syndrome? Of course, Rev could never be compared to a monster like Mendoza. He might've been a tough biker who had made some choices I might not understand, but I knew that at his core he had a heart of gold.

But regardless of the time, distance, personal reflection, and therapy I allowed myself, the answer remained the same. While it defied all reason and made no sense, I had fallen in love with Nathaniel "Reverend" Malloy.

"Annabel? Are you up here?" My mother's voice broke through my clouded thoughts.

"Yes. I am."

She appeared in my doorway, bedecked in the finest of couture gowns along with some of our family jewels. She then bestowed upon me her usual disapproving look—the one strictly reserved for me. "What are you doing still up here? You should be downstairs greeting guests."

I rose from my vanity chair as best I could in my formal gown. "I'm sorry. I was just finishing with my makeup. I'll be right down."

"I should expect so." She turned and flounced out into the hallway. With a resigned sigh, I started across my bedroom. It had been my refuge in the months since returning home. Moving back in with my parents was practically a fate worse than death, but my parents insisted on it. Allegedly, it was the best way for my father's hired protection to keep an eye on me. I think it was more about getting his money's worth from the security detail—and what better way to do that than to have them stationed at the house?

A bodyguard followed me wherever I went, which these days consisted of home and my job at the veterinarian's office I had worked at during my undergraduate program. I would be returning to vet school at the University of Virginia in January. Between my captivity and my time with Rev, I had missed the beginning of the semester.

These days I rarely went out socially. While my friends had reached out to me after my return, I found spending any time with them to be awkward. The fact I had been a sex slave was always a dark specter hanging over any lunchtime gathering or movie night. There was also the fact that I wasn't the same girl I had been six months ago, and in many ways I had outgrown some of them. The sorority-sister hijinks I had once reveled in now seemed childish.

As I made my way to the top of the massive, winding staircase adorned with Christmas garland, the sounds of the party threatened to overwhelm me. The mindless chatter coupled with the jazzy Christmas carols from the band grated on my nerves. It took everything within me to will my Christian Louboutin heels forward. Every fiber of my being wanted to run back to the safety of my bedroom. Of course, if I had my way, I would have preferred being at the Raiders compound with Rev, Mama Beth, Alexandra, and Willow.

Even in the past, I had never been a fan of my parents' stuffy annual Christmas party. It was less about goodwill toward men and more about how my father's votes could be influenced, or dare I say bought. All the finest local society families would be there, each trying to outdo the others with expensive overseas trips or glittering diamonds. To prove that we were the picture-perfect all-American family, my older sister, Lenore, and I, in our glittering party dresses, would be prevailed upon to perform for the guests. Although we had usually practiced for weeks, we would pretend to be totally caught off guard when the request came through. I would take my seat at the piano to play while Lenore's operatic voice would regale the guests.

And after my kidnapping, I dreaded the party even more. I didn't like crowds, least of all crowds filled with men, most of whom were strangers. At each unfamiliar face, it was as if, for a split second, I could see my captors looming over me. The only time I had felt safe and like my old self in a crowd was when I had been with Rev and his brothers.

Just the thought of Rev caused my chest to tighten with the

familiar grief-stricken pain. Lifting the hem of my emerald green dress, I began making my way down the stairs. When I got to the bottom, I drew in several deep breaths, trying to calm my nerves. Slowly, I began to advance through the crowd.

Men tipped their heads at me while ladies gave me forced smiles. No one bothered to cease their conversations to speak to me formally or engage me in a discussion, for which I was relieved. I would make my obligatory rounds so my mother would get off my back, and then I would disappear back upstairs.

As a waiter went past me in his white tails, I grabbed a champagne flute off his tray. After taking a sip, I turned around to see a woman staring expectantly at me. "Hello," I said.

"Hello. You're one of the Percy girls, aren't you?"

I forced a smile to my face. "Yes, I am."

The woman wore a curious expression. "Are you the lawyer or the one who got kidnapped into sex slavery?"

Both stunned and appalled by the audacity of her question, I merely opened and closed my mouth like a fish out of water, gasping for air. The sounds of the party ground to a halt, and I could hear the drumbeat of my heart pounding in my ears. I had to get away. "Excuse me," I muttered as I brushed past her.

As I rushed through the crowd, the world around me became a colorful blur. Unable to get through the crowd to the stairway, I made a beeline for the veranda instead. Heedless of the cold, I threw open the doors and rushed outside. I stalked to the iron porch railing, gripping the metal between my hands to steady me. My breath came in rushed pants.

"Annabel?"

The sound of the voice caused my heart to shudder to a stop. I gripped the railing even harder; otherwise my knees would have buckled, sending me crashing to the marble floor. For a moment I feared I had finally cracked, lost my mind. After all, that seemed to be the only explanation for why I was hearing *his* voice. He couldn't possibly be here.

Slowly, I turned around. When I saw him standing before me, I once again grew weak in the knees. My hands flew to cover my mouth to muffle the shocked scream. Over the last few months I had envisioned what seeing him again might be like, what I would feel. But nothing I had imagined or fantasized could quite live up to the reality of seeing Reverend Malloy standing before me.

His shoulder-length hair was swept back into a neat ponytail, his handsome face was still clean-shaven, but the most arresting detail of his appearance was the close-fitting black tux he wore. He radiated the air of a distinguished gentleman. Only I knew that beneath the fine lines of the tux were the intricate lines of his tattoos.

Shaking my head, I tried to extract myself from my stupor. Without even a hello, I demanded, "What are you doing . . . ? How did you . . . ?"

"I made a last-minute donation to your father's reelection campaign." He took a few tentative steps toward me. With a twinkle in his blue eyes, he added, "They really should be a little more careful about who they let in here."

"I can't believe you're here," I murmured.

"Part of me feels the exact same way." He glanced down at his tux. "This is actually my first time in a monkey suit."

"Really?"

He nodded.

"Well, no one would ever know by the way you're wearing it." I smiled ever so slightly. "You look good. You really do."

His wonderfully reverent gaze held mine. "I could say the same about you." His eyes then raked the length of my body. "You look so beautiful tonight."

I laughed. "I do clean up nicely from time to time."

Rev shook his head, a determined expression on his face. "You're always beautiful, but tonight . . . in that dress with your hair pulled back"—he sighed—"you take my breath away."

His words sent tingling sparks down my spine and throughout my limbs. "Thank you," I replied breathlessly.

An awkwardness I'd never faced with him before hung heavy between us. To ease the tension, I asked, "How's Poe?"

A genuine smile filled Rev's face. "He's great. He's grown like a weed, and he took to the woods like second nature. Of course, Deacon likes to call him a pussy because he comes back every day to get the corn we leave for him."

I giggled at Deacon's summation. Reaching into his suit pocket, Rev pulled out his phone. "I have some pictures of him."

"You do?"

Pink tinged Rev's cheeks as he came even closer to me—so close I could smell his delicious scent. The one that used to bring me such comfort. When he held out his phone, my shaky hands reached for it.

As I gazed at the image, tears blurred my eyes. The dam I had so carefully constructed to hold back my emotions broke with the weight of seeing him. Before I could stop myself, I was sobbing. When Rev's arms started to come around me, I pushed him away. I couldn't stand his pitying comfort, nor could I afford to allow myself to be held by him. The safety and protection of his arms had once meant the world to me. "Why? Why did you come here? Damn you! I'd only just begun to put myself halfway back together again."

Rev wore an anguished expression. "I had to come, Annabel. I had to tell you I was sorry for what happened."

I shook my head furiously. "I don't want your fucking apology. Your words mean nothing to me. I will never be able to forgive you for turning me away."

"Even if I came here to make it right?"

After swiping the tears from my eyes, I stared suspiciously at him. "What do you mean?"

"The last four months have been the worst months of my life. I've spent most of them drunk off my ass, trying everything in the world to forget you." Tentatively, he reached out to cup my cheek. Although I should have jerked away from him, I couldn't bring myself to. "But you're unforgettable, Annabel."

Unforgettable. He thought of me as unforgettable.

His words caused the tears to come harder and faster. Rev reached out and drew me against him. My hands fisted the front of his tux as I clung desperately to him. "Please don't cry. You break my heart when you cry, especially when I'm the one at fault," he murmured, his words warm against my cheek.

"I can't help it. You're not the only one whose last four months have been miserable. No matter how hard I tried, I couldn't forget you, either."

Rev kissed the top of my head. "I'm so sorry. I never wanted to do anything to hurt you, but all my fucking good intentions just got in the way. I've never been so wrong about trying to do what I thought was the right thing." Easing back from me, Rev stared into my eyes. "You were right that I freaked out about kissing you that night at the roadhouse. But what you didn't remember was you also told me you were falling in love with me."

I heard myself gasp. "I did?"

"Yes, you did. Although part of me was glad to hear you say it, I was afraid that you were just mixed up in the way you felt about me because of what you had gone through. But more than anything, I didn't feel I deserved you."

"How can you think such a thing?"

"How can I not? You're this beautiful and intelligent woman who is unattainable to someone like me. Your grandfather was the fucking governor, while mine worked in a cotton mill."

"You know that none of that matters to me—pedigrees, blood-lines, all that bullshit. You always knew how I felt about my parents and their world." I motioned to all the grandeur inside. "This has never been and never will be my world."

"But you deserve to have the finest things that life has to offer, and I can't give you that."

Shaking my head, I countered, "I don't want any of that. None of that is important to me. I just want what you can give me."

With a scowl, he said, "All I can give you is a sixty-year-old house and stakes in a pawnshop and a gym."

"You can give me what none of the richest men at this party can."

"And what's that?"

"Your love."

Rev's blue eyes shone with a fierce intensity. "I do love you, Annabel. I fought it for a long time, but I know now without a shadow of a doubt that you're the only woman in the world for me."

My heart skipped a beat at his declaration. "You really mean that?"

He nodded. "Do you think that even after the way I acted you could love me again?"

I smiled as I brought my hand up to his cheek. I brushed the back of it over his smoothly shaven skin. I couldn't seem to keep my hands off him. "I never stopped loving you. No matter how hard I tried, no matter how hard I wanted to."

Rev's response to my words was to bring his lips to mine. Every molecule in my body seemed to come alive as our lips pressed together. His mouth worked tenderly against mine, almost timidly, as if he didn't want to spook me. But then I also realized it was the type of kiss you gave someone who you loved.

I pulled away to stare up at him. "Take me away from here."

"Are you sure?"

"There's nothing that I want more than to be with you. Your home, your family, and your club are in Georgia." I smiled. "That's where I want to be."

Rev returned my smile. "You don't know how thankful I am to hear you say that."

Taking him by the hand, I started to lead him to the stairs. When he tugged on my hand, I stopped. "What?"

"Don't you need to go pack?"

I shook my head. "I don't want to waste another minute here when I could be with you. I can send for my things later." The truth was I didn't want to ruin this perfect moment by having a verbal altercation with my parents.

Rev laughed. "Whatever you say." We then hurried down the veranda steps and around the side of the house.

"Annabel? Annabel, where are you going?" my bodyguard, Bradley, called out after me. He was breathing a little harder, as if he had broken into a run to catch up with us.

"I'm going home."

Bradley's blond brows furrowed in confusion. "I'm sorry?"

I smiled at Rev, then glanced back at Bradley. "You are relieved of your duties. Should my parents ask, you can tell them I left willingly with the biker I'm in love with."

When Bradley started to protest, Rev stepped between us. "Don't even bother trying to stop us. It won't end well for you," he practically growled. A shiver went through me at seeing his protective side again. Even outfitted in a tux, he still harbored the rough, bad-boy-biker side I'd fallen in love with.

I guess Bradley realized Rev wasn't worth fighting because he held up his hands and backed slowly away. "You know I'll have to tell your parents immediately," he said.

"I understand."

Glancing between me and Rev, he said, "Be careful."

"Trust me when I say that no one can protect Annabel better than I can," Rev said.

With a tentative smile, Bradley replied, "I don't doubt that for a minute."

Rev took my hand and tugged me forward. When he breezed past the valet, I began to wonder where he had parked. And then I saw a motorcycle down the street. "You rode all the way from Georgia to here?" I asked as my breath hitched and all the excitement I had possessed dissipated.

"I hadn't been on a long haul in a while. I thought I could use the time to think." His chewed his bottom lip and he stopped walking. "Fuck. I didn't even think if you would be okay with it. I mean, I didn't imagine you wanting to talk to me, least of all wanting to come with me."

"It's okay."

The truth was that I hadn't been on a motorcycle since that fateful night with Johnny. When I was with Rev in Georgia, I had been around them, but I had never ridden one. I had been too afraid it might trigger some of my old memories.

And I had been right. Although Rev squeezed my hand reassuringly, I fought an inner battle against the heart-racing, chest-heaving anxiety and fear that threatened to overtake me all because of a motorcycle. Searching my mind, I recalled the words my therapist had given me to use when I came in contact with an emotional trigger. *You have a choice. You are safe. You are not in danger. You always have a choice.*

At what he must have realized was my emotional turmoil, Rev said, "Look. You do *not* have to get on my bike. I can get us a cab to the hotel."

I was touched and maybe a little tempted by his offer. But considering that the man I loved was a biker, I knew this was something I *had* to conquer. "I'll be fine."

Always the gentleman, Rev took off his coat jacket and handed it to me. "Are you sure you want to do this? I wish you had at least stopped for a coat. It's cold now, but it's going to be hell once we get started."

"I'm sure I'll survive."

Rev handed me his helmet, and I slid it on. I then tried hiking up the hem of my ball gown as best I could. When Rev chuckled, I wagged a finger at him. "I'd love to see you try to maneuver in this thing."

"If it's any consolation, I don't think I've ever seen you more beautiful than you are in that dress."

I momentarily stopped fidgeting to look up at him and smile. "Thank you." Yet again, Rev showed his caring side with just a small compliment to put me at ease.

Once I had gotten the dress up as best I could, I eased onto the seat of the bike. After I was in place, Rev got on. I brought my hands around his waist and snuggled against his back. It felt so good to get to hold him again. I had missed the feel of him over the last few months.

While it had been unseasonably warm for December, it might as well have been subzero given how cold I was once we got started. When we got to the first red light, Rev turned around to see how I was doing. I guess my shivering and teeth chattering told him all he needed to know. "My hotel isn't far. Hang in there. Okay?"

"I-I'll t-try," I stuttered.

Thankfully, it wasn't too much farther. I was also grateful that Rev had chosen a hotel with rooms inside, rather than a motel like I had been taken to that night with Johnny. When the bike came to a stop, I didn't want to pry myself away from the small amount of warmth I was getting from Rev.

I whimpered when he got off. After he took my hand, he frowned. "Jesus, Annabel, you're like a block of ice. Let's get you inside and warm you up."

He wasn't going to get any protests from me. After tucking me to his side, he hurried us into the lobby and onto an elevator. When the elevator dinged on the fifth floor, he dug his key card out of his pants pocket and led me out into the hallway. He unlocked the third door on the right and ushered me inside.

Instead of letting me go, he continued on through the bathroom. After flipping the toilet seat down, he eased me onto it.

"What are you doing?"

"Getting you into the shower." At what must've been my skeptical expression, he added, "It's the fastest way to get you warm."

"I see," I murmured.

He made quick work of turning on the water and testing it with his fingers. When it seemed to his satisfaction, he turned back to me. I still sat on the toilet, shivering and trembling.

We stared at each other for a moment. Rev jerked a hand through his hair. "Yeah, uh, I guess I better let you get in now."

When he started to go, I grabbed his arm. "Wait. I need help getting out of this dress."

His eyes flared at my request. It wasn't a come-on in disguise. I had needed the help of one of our maids earlier that night to get it zipped.

Instead of asking me to stand up, Rev bent over my back, bringing his hands to the zipper. Slowly, he tugged it down. As the front gaped open, I didn't bother trying to cover myself.

Rev's hands momentarily faltered, and when I looked up, I met his gaze, which was fixed on my bare breasts. I hadn't needed to wear a bra because of the tight-fitting bodice. He cleared his throat several times, then tugged the zipper the rest of the way down.

There was not a doubt in my mind, heart, or body about how much I wanted him. I knew he expected me to want to take things slow in the sex department, but that's not how I felt. Regardless of the ghosts of the past, I wanted him more than I had ever wanted any man. I wanted him to be the one who proved to me that sex was physically and emotionally safe. That it could be a loving act between two consenting people.

But with the roller coaster of feelings rocketing through me, it was more about an all-consuming lust and desire.

When Rev stepped back from me, I rose to my feet. The dress slid down my body and pooled at my feet, leaving me in only my panties. Both empowerment and vulnerability raced through me.

"Rev, I want you to look at me." He shook his head and kept his gaze on the floor. "I said I want you to look at me," I repeated.

"That's not what this is about. It's about you getting warm before you catch pneumonia," he countered.

"I could care less about getting sick. Right now what I care about is seeing the man I love want me sexually. To look at me like he wants to devour me."

His eyes, which burned with lust and unfilled desire, snapped to mine. "How can you ever doubt even for a second how I feel about you?"

I threw my hands up. "Because I'm standing practically naked before you and you won't fucking look at me!"

"We're both teetering at the edge of uncharted territory. After everything you've been through, I would rather die than hurt you."

"You hurt me more when you won't look at me or touch me," I protested.

With an agonized sigh, Rev finally allowed his gaze to rake down my body. There was no feeling of embarrassment or inadequacy. Just the look on his face warmed me from head to toe. "You're so beautiful," he murmured.

Tears stung my eyes from his adoration. "I am?" I questioned.

He smiled. "Every inch of you."

Closing the gap between us, I took his hands in mine. One I brought to my cheek and the other I brought to my breast. Rev and I both sucked in a breath as his fingers closed over my nipple. I cupped his face in my hands. "Please don't ever stop looking at me like you want me."

He shook his head. "Not wanting you sexually has never been an issue, Annabel. Every morning you lay beside me, I was hard as a rock. But I didn't want you to think I could only see you sexually— that I was some sort of animal like Mendoza. I wanted you to see I cared about what was inside." His chin jerked at the shower. "You better get inside before all the warm water is gone."

"Get in with me."

Although his hand remained firmly on my breast, his brows shot up in surprise. "Are you sure that's a good idea?"

"Warm me up, Rev. I need you." My hands went to the jacket of his tux. When I moved to slide it off his shoulders, he didn't protest. As my fingers worked at the buttons on his shirt, he began to unbutton and unzip his pants.

When he slid off his pants, he revealed that even with a tux, he was going commando. As I stood there, staring at him, my heartbeat roared so loudly in my ears I was sure Rev could hear it. God, he was so beautiful. A wall of muscle that was decorated with multicolored tattoos. My gaze slid down his washboard abs to take in the dark dusting of hair below his hips, but, more important, his already large manhood, which wasn't fully aroused yet.

At Rev's chuckle, I glanced up in surprise. "It's surprising that a lady like yourself would be staring at my package."

"I can't help it. I'm impressed."

His eyes gleamed with male pride. "I'm glad to hear that."

After I shimmied out of my panties, I stepped into the shower. Rev followed close behind me. The scalding water didn't feel nearly as good as having him so close or feeling his eyes on me.

We stood there, breathing hard and staring at each other, for a few seconds. "I swore if you took me back, I wouldn't move fast with you," Rev whispered to me.

"Once again, it's me putting the moves on you, isn't it?"

He flashed me a wolfish grin. "I would have to say I'm a very willing participant."

"All I know is what is happening between us or what is going to happen feels right. That's all we can go by, right?"

"Yes, it is."

Rev stepped behind me and turned my body into the full force of the stream of water. He brought his strong hands up to rub up and down from my shoulders to my wrists. Between the warm water and his touch, my chilled skin became inflamed. He placed a tender kiss on my shoulder blade, which caused me to arch my back against his lips. Gentle kisses feathered across my back to my other shoulder. He then kissed his way up to the back of my neck while his hands left my shoulders to rub around my waist and abdomen.

Resting my head back against his chest, I sighed in what could only have been extreme contentment or ecstasy.

Slowly Rev turned me around so that I was facing him. "Are you getting warm?"

I smiled seductively at him. "I'm on fire."

"Where?"

"Everywhere," I replied.

His hands came up to cup my breasts. "Here?"

As he rubbed the hardening nipples between his thumb and forefinger, I closed my eyes. "Mmm."

"You have beautiful breasts."

Never one to be satisfied with compliments, I argued, "They're not very big."

"Look," he commanded. When I opened my eyes, he gestured

to his hands holding my breasts. In a lust-filled growl, he replied, "They're a perfect fit for my hands."

"Yes. They are," I replied breathlessly.

"Maybe I should see how well they fit my mouth."

My heartbeat skipped at his suggestion. "You probably should."

Dipping his head, he closed his mouth over my right breast. As he sucked, his tongue twirled and flicked over the nipple, causing me to moan. My arms slid from his shoulders into his hair, my fingers tangling through the wet strands. When his teeth grazed my tight nipple, I gripped his hair even tighter, which caused him to groan. "Did I hurt you?" I panted.

He released my nipple with a pop. A sly grin appeared on his face. "No. It's more like I get hard as fuck when you tug my hair." To prove his point, he rolled his hips against me, letting me feel his erection.

I smiled at him. "I'll keep that in mind."

Rev shifted to my other breast, teasing and tasting me until I had to squeeze my legs together because of the growing ache. As if he sensed the tension in me, Rev snaked a hand between us and dipped it between my thighs. I gasped at the wonderful feeling. His forehead wrinkled with concern. "Is this okay?"

"It's more than okay. It's amazing." I then opened my legs wider to give him more room.

Over and over his calloused fingers teased my clit. When he plunged two fingers inside me, I cried out and gripped him tighter. As I worked my hips in rhythm with his fingers, I wanted more than anything to come. I wanted to come for Rev and his ability to turn me on, but more than anything, I wanted to come for myself, so that in a small way I could reclaim my sexuality.

I grew closer and closer to the edge, but I couldn't go over. And then Rev sank to his knees. Pushing my back against the tile, he spread my legs even farther apart. It took only the flick of his tongue against my clit to send me over into orgasm. As tears stung my eyes, I came, crying out his name over and over.

But he didn't stop. Instead, he waited for me to come down. Then his tongue and fingers went to work again. My legs began to shake, and they felt like they wouldn't hold me up, so I gripped Rev's shoulders to steady myself. It didn't take long this time before I was throwing my head back and experiencing sheer mind-blowing pleasure once again. "So fucking sexy," Rev muttered against my sex.

He rose from his knees. When his mouth met mine, I could taste myself on his lips and tongue. I don't know how long we stayed lip-locked, our hands running over each other's body. With my fingertips, I traced the bulging muscles of his biceps, his hard pecs, and his washboard abs. Although the large contours of his body could be frightening, I found myself feeling more and more protected. I was safe with Rev. He would never expect me to do something I wasn't comfortable with or that made me uneasy.

When the water turned cold, Rev tore his lips from mine. As he stared into my eyes, I knew we were once again teetering on the edge of a line—a line that would inevitably have to be crossed. "Make love to me," I whispered.

Conflict raged in Rev's eyes. I knew that in his mind he thought we had gone far enough with what we had already done. We didn't need to rush things—we had all the time in the world.

"Please," I murmured.

With a slight jerk of his head, Rev reached forward to turn off the shower. After he got out, he turned back to grip me by the waist. He hoisted me into his arms and carried me out of the bathroom, then eased me gently down on the bed.

When he turned and started back toward the bathroom, I propped myself on my elbows and gazed at his retreating form. "What are you doing?" I called. I hoped he hadn't changed his mind about giving in to me.

He returned with two large towels. Kneeling over me, he brought the soft cloth to my arm. After he dried me, he placed warming kisses on my skin. He repeated the process along my chest, taking extra time with my breasts, and then my other arm. By the time he finished with my lower body, I was drenched between my legs and aching for him. I'd barely given him time to dry himself off before I was grabbing his arm and dragging him closer to me. "What about a condom?"

I thought about all the testing I'd had in the hospital. Remarkably, my rapists and Mendoza hadn't given me any STDs. "I'm clean," I replied softly.

"So am I . . . as long as you trust me."

I smiled up at him. "Of course I trust you."

But when his body loomed over mine, a prickly panic crawled its way over my skin. Although I had managed to push my rapists out of my head, it seemed now that they had found a way to claw their way back in with the intent of ruining what I had with Rev. *I am safe. I have a choice, and I choose this.*

As if he sensed my growing panic, Rev rolled off me. When I started to protest that I wanted to continue, he gripped me by the hips and pulled me up to straddle him. "Take me, Annabel. You're the one in control."

Moisture tinged my eyes at his words and his offering. He wanted to do everything within his power to enable me to conquer this first time. I rose up to grip his erection in my trembling hand. When I brought it to my center, I momentarily faltered when I began to take him inside me.

Rev's hands sought mine. After intertwining our fingers, he said, "Look at me, babe. It's only me and you here. Only love."

Gazing into his determined eyes, I found the courage I needed. I eased farther down on his cock, taking him deeper inside me.

Once I was full of him, I sat for a moment, just staring at him. "I love you," he murmured.

"I love you, too," I whispered. As I looked into his beautiful blue eyes, I realized it was just the two of us in this room—him and me. Two people who loved each other with all their flaws and weaknesses. I wasn't having sex with a stranger; I was being made love to. It wasn't a harsh and vile act forced upon me without my consent. I welcomed the feel of his hands, his fingers, and his tongue on my skin. Most of all, I was taking his cock into my body, not having him take me. His expression wasn't cruel or vicious. Instead, it was filled with lust, love, and a possession of a different type. Because of all those things, I could do this. I wanted this.

I rose up and came back down on him. The feeling of being with him was overwhelming. It was a connection of mind, body, and soul on a level I had never experienced before.

As I sped up the tempo of my movements, I released Rev's hands so that I could place my palms on his chest. He groaned in pleasure as I rode him harder and faster. He was so beautiful laid out before me, his eyes closed, his teeth biting into his lip.

He raised his hips to meet mine, our slick skin meeting in a desperate rhythm. I had never come through sex before, and after what had happened to me, I doubted I ever would. But when Rev's hand came to stroke and tease my clit, I felt a building pressure I had never experienced before with a man inside me.

The harder I rode Rev, the harder he stroked me. I dug my fingernails into his chest as I felt the tiny shudders of an orgasm. It wasn't the same as the ones in the shower, but it was still momentous to me. Tears stung my eyes at the realization of how wonderful it had been. And as Rev's orgasm had him calling out my name and coming inside me, I collapsed onto his chest, my head falling against his rapidly beating heart.

EIGHTEEN

Rev

I had been with a lot of women. Most of them I knew, but then there were some whose names I didn't even know. I had also had all kinds of sex, but until I was with Annabel, I had never made love to a woman before. I'd never known the connection that could be made between two people through the joining of their bodies. If I could have, I would have stayed inside Annabel the entire night. Nothing had ever felt better than having her tight walls around me.

As we lay in the dark, I could tell Annabel's mind was spinning with thoughts. She had just conquered the mental equivalent of climbing Mount Everest. I knew she had gotten physical pleasure out of it, but the body can be convinced to react even if the mind is in turmoil. More than anything in the world, I wanted her to be okay with what had just happened to her and between us.

Turning to her, I asked, "What are you thinking about?"

"It's silly, really."

"Don't undermine your feelings that way," I argued.

She gave a little snort of a laugh. "You sound just like my therapist."

With a smile, I said, "Then tell Dr. Rev what you're feeling." Nudging her thigh with my leg, I added, "No matter how silly or strange you think it is." When she still remained silent, I couldn't help asking her about what was on my own mind. "Do you regret what we just did?"

Her eyes widened. "No. Never."

"I'll understand if you're having second thoughts."

Annabel shook her head. "That was the most fulfilling sexual experience of my life." She ducked her gaze from mine like something was embarrassing her. "The truth is that was the first orgasm I've ever had when a guy was inside of me."

While my chest swelled with male pride, I fought to keep my face clear of any dickhead smirking. "Really?"

Annabel grinned. "Go ahead. Pat yourself on the back. You know you want to."

I laughed. "My inner caveman is beating his chest." I leaned down to kiss her tenderly. "Most of all, I'm proud of you for conquering your fears and being able to enjoy yourself."

"Thank you, Rev. Thank you for everything, but most of all for loving me."

"Now, what was it you were so lost in thought about?"

She propped one of her hands on her elbow and stared into my eyes. "I was just wondering if you ever had to conquer sex like I just did."

"That's not a silly question at all. All victims of rape and molestation have to go through separating their past from their present, including me."

"What happened with you?" she questioned softly.

Although I really didn't want to dredge up painful memories of the past, I was willing to do it for Annabel. "I was always really shy and awkward around girls even before I was raped, so afterward, I kind of retreated into myself. Each time I wanted to ask a girl out, I would worry that I was a less of a man because of what had happened. When I was sixteen, I had yet to kiss a girl, so my father took it upon himself to have one of the club whores teach me about sex."

Annabel gasped in shock. "Like a prostitute?"

"Well, she didn't get paid for it, and she certainly *wanted* to deflower me." I chuckled when I thought back to being that scared but horny-as-hell sixteen-year-old. "Apparently there were a lot of the girls who wanted to get their hands on me, but she won the luck of the draw."

"Really?"

I nudged her playfully. "You act so surprised that I had women clamoring to get in my pants, yet you wanted to do me," I countered with a grin.

She giggled. "I didn't mean it to come out that way. I can certainly see why you had so many women wanting you." She leaned forward to bestow a kiss on my lips. When she pulled away, she blushed.

"What is it?"

"I was just wondering how it was."

"With the club whore?"

"Yes."

"For a sixteen-year-old kid who practically had calluses from jacking off, it was pretty fucking amazing."

"Ew!" Annabel squealed, wrinkling her nose.

"You asked," I countered.

"I kinda wish now I hadn't."

"Looking back, I can call it amazing, but at the time, it was also really awkward. Really the only thing that improved it for me was practice."

Cocking her head at me, Annabel asked, "Did you try practicing until you were perfect?"

"Hmm, you think I'm *perfect*, huh? I think my caveman is going to beat my chest in with pride."

Annabel giggled. "I think I've created an ego monster."

I grinned. "Let's just say after conquering that first time, I was back in the saddle pretty quickly." As I stared into her beautiful green eyes, my expression grew serious. "No matter how many times we do this, you don't ever have to explain if you're having a hard time with it. I'm a pretty good reader of your body language, but if we need to, we can come up with a safe word or something like that."

"We don't need anything like a safe word. You know me inside and out, Rev. I know that you'll never expect more of me in the bedroom than I can give, even if it means I have to convince you I'm ready to take things to another level. It's just one of the many reasons why I love you."

Her words caused my chest to tighten. I had never experienced absolute trust with a woman like I did with Annabel. I knew now why Mama Beth had said it was the most important thing in a relationship. After all that Annabel had been through, her giving me her implicit trust was one of the greatest gifts she could ever give me.

I had her heart, her mind, her body, and her soul, and she, in turn, held me captive in the palm of her hand.

Although sunlight streamed through the hotel curtains, I refused to wake up. I was having the most amazing sex dream of my life. Silky wet lips traveled up and down my hard dick. I groaned, bucking my hips. As I was suctioned into her warm, inviting mouth, I felt like I had died and gone to heaven.

And then my eyes flew wide open. This was no dream. This was all wonderfully fucking real. Gazing down, I watched as Annabel drew me in and out of her mouth. When she looked up at me, I fought not to blow my load right then and there.

I started to ease her off me, but she refused. Instead, she kept right on bobbing up and down, her tongue swirling around me. "I'm about to come, Annabel," I muttered. That statement only seemed to fuel her to go faster. Gripping the sheets with both my hands, I let myself go, jerking my hips off the bed as I came into her mouth. "Annabel!" I cried.

Once I had finished, she crawled up my body to lie beside me. "Good morning," she said with an impish grin.

I chuckled. "Good morning to you. That was a hell of a wake-up call."

"You were so attentive to me last night I wanted to repay the favor." She brushed her hand up and down my chest, her fingertips raking through my thick hair.

"I will always attend to you first. That's just the kind of man I am."

She giggled. "You'll get no protests from me."

Ducking my head, I leaned down to kiss her gently. When I pulled away, I stared intently into her eyes. "Are you okay?"

"Deliciously sore in all the right places," she replied.

I cupped her cheek. "Although I'm always concerned with your body, I think you know what I mean."

She sighed. "Yes, I do. And I'm fine." When I gave her a skeptical look, she countered, "Do you think I would have blown you this morning if I was emotionally fragile about us having sex?"

My eyes widened. "What a naughty mouth you have there, Miss Percy."

Annabel grinned. "You have firsthand knowledge of my naughty mouth."

Relief filled me that she was okay emotionally. I didn't know what it might be like for her in the light of day. We seemed to be moving at warp speed since last night, considering she'd run away with me and now we had taken our relationship even further by making it physical.

"I missed waking up next to you these past four months," she said softly.

"I missed it, too."

Annabel stared up at me. "What was it that made you finally come after me? I mean, the way you showed up at the party was like something out of a movie. After all those months, I thought you had forgotten me."

"You really don't get it, do you?"

"What do you mean?"

"You're the most amazing woman I've ever known. Strong, beautiful, kind, caring, and funny. No man in his right mind could ever forget you."

Her lip trembled at my compliments. "You really mean that, don't you?"

"I sure as hell do. As for me coming after you, I was pretty much miserable on a daily basis, but it was Willow who really helped me see the light."

Her mouth dropped open in surprise. "She did?"

"I swear that kid is one hell of an old soul."

With a smile, Annabel said, "I can't wait to see her again."

"She'll be thrilled to see you. Everyone will. They love you as much as I do."

"And I love them."

I brought her arm up from my chest to kiss her palm and then her scarred wrist. "I've been thinking," she said.

"Mmm," I murmured as I continued kissing along the scar.

"Since I'm going to be a biker's old lady, I think I need some ink."

I glanced up from her hand in surprise. "You do?"

"All of the girls have a tattoo but me, even Alexandra."

I was once again surprised. "She does?"

Annabel nodded. "It's somewhere hidden by her clothes. Somewhere only Deacon can see."

"Mmm-hmm, and is that the type of ink you plan on getting? Something somewhere that only my eyes will see?"

"Not exactly." She held her wrists up for both of us to look at. "I want to get the scars made into something beautiful. Maybe a butterfly on one wrist and angel wings on the other."

I smiled, since it was obvious she had been giving this a lot of thought, even when we were apart. "Why those specifically?" I asked.

Annabel pursed her lips thoughtfully. "Well, a butterfly has a beautiful rebirth when it comes out of its cocoon, especially since it seemed like its entire world was over."

"That's true."

"And then angel wings because it felt like at times I had an angel watching over me." She smiled. "Or maybe you're my angel."

I laughed. "I think I would be more of the fallen angel variety."

"I don't mind."

"I think you getting ink would be wonderful. I have just the guy to do it for you. I can make you an appointment when we get back."

"Thank you. I would appreciate that." She stared up at me with hopeful eyes. "Will you go with me?"

"Of course." I pushed a strand of hair out of her face. "We're a team now."

"I'm glad to hear that." She reached up to kiss me tenderly. Just as we started to get hot and heavy, my cell phone rang on the nightstand.

When I pulled away, she protested by gripping me tighter. "I need to get that," I murmured against her lips. "Tell the boys where I am."

"Okay."

I reached over and grabbed the phone. "Yeah?"

"You're in Virginia?" Deacon demanded.

"Are you tracing my phone now?"

He snorted. "No. But as your VP, I was just informed by a prospect that a very angry-sounding man by the name of Senator Percy called the roadhouse wanting to speak to you."

With a groan, I glanced over my shoulder at Annabel. When her brows rose questioningly, I said to her, "You need to call your parents." Then it was her turn to groan.

"Thanks, brother. I'll take care of it."

There was a moment of silence on the line before Deacon asked, "So you went after her finally?"

I smiled into the phone. "Yeah, I did."

"It's about fucking time."

With a laugh, I said, "I assume that means we have your blessing."

"It sure as hell does. Just get your ass back here ASAP so we can celebrate."

"We'll be there as soon as we can."

"Later."

"Bye." I then handed the phone over to Annabel. "Deacon sends his love."

She grinned. "He does?"

"Yeah, he's glad I finally came after you."

"That makes two of us."

When she crawled across the bed to wrap herself around me, I shook my head. "Call your parents."

"Then will you make love to me again?" she asked, her breath warm against my cheek.

"Babe, you don't even have to ask."

NINETEEN

Annabel

Getting home to Georgia took a little longer than we had expected. While I had bought some warm clothes and boots to make the drive, it was still blistering cold to be on the back of the bike for any length of time. But even with the extreme cold, I grew to enjoy riding with Rev. It didn't take too long to see the allure that it held for him—the freedom, the adrenaline rush. More than anything, I enjoyed wrapping my arms around him and squeezing him tight. Although I'm not proud to admit it, I might've played on his sympathies a bit with worrying about me and the cold. The truth was I wanted nothing more than to stay in bed with him for a few days.

I don't know who was more surprised by my insatiable appetite—me or Rev. But I couldn't seem to get enough of him. I loved learning all the little things about him, like what made him groan with need or pinch his eyes shut with passion. It felt like I was discovering sex for the first time. In some ways I was—at least the new Annabel was. I knew there was still a wolf looming at the door, and at any minute this newfound perfection could come crashing down through flashbacks. But for the moment, I chose to be optimistic and happy.

Three days later, we pulled up at the Raiders compound. I was never so glad to see a place in all my life. Still, I was more than a little surprised to see the twinkling Christmas lights. "Who would have thought bikers would be so festive," I remarked as I handed Rev my helmet.

He chuckled. "Trust me, we aren't. That's all for Willow."

When we walked through the front door, a roar went up in the room. "WELCOME HOME!" everyone shouted. At first I felt completely overwhelmed, but the feel of Rev's hand on the small of my back gave me the courage to smile and move closer to my new family.

As if they had been given a pep talk on how to treat me, they hung back and let me go to them. I was hugged and kissed by more people in the first few minutes than I had been in my entire life. At the back of the main room, Rev's blood family stood anxiously awaiting me. I couldn't hide my shock at seeing Mama Beth. She was never one to be in the roadhouse. I ran into her waiting arms. "I'm so glad you're home, sweetheart," she said, her voice wavering as if she was about to cry.

Her warm welcome and words caused tears to burn my eyes. "I am, too."

When I pulled away, there were quick hugs from Deacon and Bishop, and then a lingering one from Alexandra, whose enormous belly looked like she was ready to deliver at any moment. When I said as much, she shook her head. "I still have six weeks, if you can believe it."

"He's going to be a very big boy."

Alexandra smiled as she patted her stomach. "He already feels enormous when he's kicking me."

I then turned to a very impatient Willow who I was surprised had waited this long to give me a hug. "Wait until you see Poe. He's huge!" she said after she'd clung to me for several seconds.

"Thank you for taking such good care of him!"

"It was mainly Uncle Rev who took care of him, but I had to help because he was such a mess over missing you."

I couldn't help the laugh that erupted from me at the pint-sized girl talking about relationships like a grown woman. When I looked at Rev, he appeared to want to strangle his niece. "Well, I missed him pretty bad, too."

"I figured you did." She grinned up at me. "Did he tell you he loves you?"

"Willow!" Alexandra and Deacon admonished.

"What?" she questioned innocently. "You guys said you wondered if he did earlier."

While Deacon and Alexandra gave Rev and me sheepish looks, I couldn't help laughing at the situation. "Yes, he told me he loves me, and I told him I love him."

"Are you gonna get married?" Willow asked.

Now it was my turn to be speechless. Although there had been no proposal or discussion of marriage, the idea of Rev and me living the rest of our lives together seemed to be a given. While it seemed that we knew each other down to the deepest and darkest parts, there was still a lot of relationship building we needed to do before we thought of marriage.

"I think it's time we got you something to eat," Alexandra suggested.

"Yeah, that's a helluva good idea. Let's stick something in her mouth to shut her up," Deacon muttered under his breath.

Once Willow had been ushered over to the food table, Rev and I exchanged a glance. "Well, um, that was . . . intense," he said.

"Very. Who would have thought we would get the marriage question already?" I said, giving a laugh to try to ease the tension.

"I meant more the inquisition by Willow."

"Oh," I murmured. What did he mean by that exactly? Had he been thinking of marriage? I swallowed hard at the thought.

With a smile, Rev said, "I think I could use a drink."

"You and me both."

He took me by the hand and led me over to the bar. This time I settled on a Corona rather than my former buddy Jack Daniel's. The house band went up onstage, and it wasn't long before they were cranking out tunes, including some rock versions of Christmas carols.

After we finished our beers, Rev steered me over to the kitchen. The old ladies and other women had put on quite a spread of food. "All this for me?" I asked as I was handed a plate.

Kim grinned. "Of course. Especially since you decided to come home on the night of our annual Christmas party."

I laughed. "Lucky me that I didn't keep Rev gone another day."

Sweeping a hand to her hip, she said, "Yeah, about the trip home, missy. It doesn't usually take over a day. Just what caused you all to be so late?"

As I spooned up some lasagna, I couldn't fight the warmth spreading across my cheeks. "We just had to stop a lot because it was so cold," I finally answered.

"Mmm-hmm. I bet I can imagine just what kind of warming up went on, too."

"Easy there, Kim," Rev cautioned.

She grinned. "Like I couldn't tell you'd been fucking nonstop from the utterly satisfied looks on your faces."

While it was totally mortifying to have our sex life discussed, there was also a grateful feeling that accompanied it. No one was treating me with kid gloves or walking on eggshells when it came to the topic of sex. That meant I was no longer seen as just a victim, and that was certainly liberating.

As we ate dinner, we talked with different in- and out-of-town members who came by our table. Everyone was in the festive holiday spirit. I couldn't help thinking how different this party was from my parents' party.

At the thought of them, I wrinkled my nose. When I had spoken to them the other day, they had been utterly horrified at what I had done. Regardless of how they chided me, I was not about to change my mind about my decision. Even though they threw out words like "disinheriting" and "disown," they forgot I was just months away from my twenty-fifth birthday, when I would receive my inheritance from my grandfather. When I had told Rev about the half million dollars coming to me, he had nearly fallen off the bed in shock. While the money meant security for us, it would have no value to me without Rev in my life.

When the band shifted to a slow love song, Rev took my hand. "I think I owe you a real dance."

"What do you mean?"

"That night when we got drunk together, we danced in my room."

At first my eyes widened at his words, and then the memory came back to me. "I remember that," I murmured.

Rev smiled as he wrapped his arms around my waist, drawing me flush against him. I would never get enough of being this close to him, especially being able to press my ear against his chest and listen to his heartbeat. "I love you," I said loud enough for him to hear me over the music.

"I love you, too. I know this all seems to be happening very fast—"

I shook my head. "We built a strong foundation for it the month we were together."

He smiled. "I agree. With that said, it's been a whirlwind of a couple of days. But it still doesn't keep me from wanting to do this."

I stared dumbfounded at him as he pulled away from me. When he sank onto one knee, I began trembling all over. In times past, though, I had trembled with fear and anxiety, but now I felt a wonderful sense of anticipation. Whistles and catcalls went up around the room. The roar of Rev's brothers became so loud it almost deafened me.

After digging into his pocket, he produced a glittering diamond. "Annabel Lee Percy, would you make me the happiest man alive by marrying me?"

"Get it, Rev!" Bishop shouted.

"Oh my God," I whispered.

"That's not quite the response I was hoping for," Rev mused.

I licked my suddenly dry lips. "Are you really sure about this?"

"I think this fat diamond should illustrate how very certain I am."

"It's just so . . ."

"Sudden?"

I nodded. "A little."

"I bought the ring before I went to Virginia because I knew if you accepted my apology, there was no one else in the world I wanted to share my life with. And while we could live together, I'm an old-fashioned guy and would prefer you to be my wife."

"That's understandable," I murmured breathlessly. Staring into his earnest dark eyes, I couldn't help feeling totally undeserving of him. "Even with all of my baggage?"

Rev smiled. "We both have baggage. I'll help you carry yours, and you can help carry mine. How does that sound?"

The tears that flooded my eyes caused his image to grow wavy before me. Even though it was sudden, I couldn't fathom loving Rev any more than I did at this moment. He had been it for me since he had bared his soul to me that day in the hospital bathroom. He had spent nights by my side giving me the strength of his silent comfort. He had spent countless hours talking with me, laughing with me, and offering me a depth of friendship I had never experienced before with anyone—male or female. He had given me the greatest gift anyone ever could by bringing me into his blood and MC family, which set me on the path of the healing and acceptance I so desperately needed.

I had spent four miserable, heart-wrenching months without him, so I knew I wanted to be with him for the rest of my life. He was my heart, mind, and soul.

"Yes. My answer is yes."

Rev beamed before slipping the ring on my finger. I jumped into his arms to bestow kisses all over his face and neck. I was once again rushed by Rev's brothers and their families. Pitchers of beer, rather than champagne, appeared for us to toast with. Everyone was genuinely happy for us, especially Rev's blood family.

Once the hoopla had died down, Rev and I once again found ourselves on the dance floor. Gazing up at him, I smiled. "Take me home and make love to me. I won't even mind if you fuck me, just take me home."

At my use of the f-word, Rev's dark brows shot up. "With a request like that, how can I say no?"

Taking my hand, he led me away from the other couples dancing. When we started for the back door, Deacon called, "Where you two sneakin' off to?"

When I glanced over my shoulder at him, he winked at me. "It was a long ride, and I'm really tired," I answered.

Bishop hooted with laughter. "Ha. More like you're planning on some long ridin' in the bedroom."

"Shut your trap, asshole," Rev growled, which caused me to laugh. It was obvious he wasn't used to his brothers ribbing him about a girl. When I nudged him playfully, he did manage to give me a smile.

As soon as we were out the door and out of sight of his brothers, Rev couldn't keep his mouth or his hands off me. It took us longer than normal to get down the hill because we kept stopping to grope each other in the dark.

Even though it was freezing outside, we were already stripping each other as we started up the porch stairs. We tumbled in the front door in just our underwear. I don't know how we made it back to Rev's bedroom. As we collapsed onto the bed, I couldn't help thinking of all the times I had slept with Rev in this bed. Now we were finally going to have sex in it.

Without unfastening my bra, Rev pushed the cups up to bare my breasts. His mouth went to work, sucking and licking my nipples. As I wrapped my legs around him, he began to rub his growing erection against my panty-clad core. They were practically drenched within seconds. "Rev, please," I urged.

"Please what, baby?" he asked, his warm breath hovering over my breast.

"Get inside me."

"With my tongue or my dick?"

I pursed my lips at him. "Aren't you being a dirty talker tonight?"

He gave me a teasing smile. "You bring it out in me."

"I could say the same for you."

Rev rose to his knees. He jerked off his underwear and then relieved me of my panties. It had taken a few times before I was comfortable with him on top. Now it was my favorite position because it meant I could wrap my arms around him and feel his skin on mine. He didn't need to do anything else to prep me because I was more than ready.

When he thrust inside, I gasped with pleasure. "You feel so fucking amazing," he murmured.

As he settled into a pounding rhythm, I brought my hips up to meet his thrusts. When my fingernails raked up and down his back, Rev groaned. The next place my hands went was his hair, which I knew was a pleasure spot for him. He reciprocated by dipping his head to nuzzle the tops of my breasts. I arched up to give him access to my nipples.

He pulled back to sit up on his knees. With his hands gripping my hips, he worked them as he thrust hard in and out of me. Our bodies became covered with a sheen of sweat from our efforts. After a few minutes, he pulled me up to where I could wrap my arms around him. I was once again riding him in a way, but I loved it more because we were chest to chest and face to face.

It was wonderful coming with his eyes locked on mine, sharing in the emotions and feelings. Rev followed me a few seconds later. When he eased me onto my back again, I cradled his head to my chest. My fingers naturally went to the long strands of his hair. "So we're engaged now," I mused once we had finally caught our breath.

"Yep. I'll need to get you a cut of your own that says 'Rev's Property' on it."

"You're not serious?"

He raised his head up to grin at me. "I sure as hell am. Haven't you seen them on the other women?"

"I haven't noticed Alexandra wearing one."

"I don't think they come in maternity sizes."

"What would you say if I said I didn't think I liked the idea of wearing a cut?"

"I would say I would be very disappointed and sad that you didn't want to share that part of my life." His serious tone took me by surprise.

"It really means that much to you?" When he nodded, I sighed. The feminist in me wanted to tell him where he could shove his little "property of" patch, but then I realized that relationships were all about compromise. He might've been the president of an MC club, but he wasn't the type of Neanderthal to demand things of me. I appreciated him for that. "If I only have to wear it within the compound, then I'll be happy to."

Rev's face lit up. "You mean it?"

"Yeah, I do."

"Mmm, let me show you just how happy you make me."

When his head dipped between my legs, it was him making me very, very happy.

TWENTY

ANNABEL

Things continued to speed along with absolute perfection for Rev and me. A few days before Christmas, we got our first tree together—hand cut by Rev himself from the woods behind the house. We spent Christmas Day at Mama Beth's, where both Alexandra and I helped her prepare a huge feast. As I sat around the table so full of delicious food that I couldn't breathe, I once again had to thank God that going through hell had led me to the most divine existence I could ever imagine.

As New Year's Eve approached, Rev and his brothers were busy planning a huge party at the roadhouse. I found myself at home sitting around the tree while working on my admissions essay to the veterinary program at the University of Georgia. I had already talked to an adviser, who, after reviewing my transcripts and work experience, put me at ease about having missed almost a year of school after what had happened to me.

When Rev suddenly burst through the front door, I didn't have to ask what he was doing home. His darkened expression told me something bad had happened. "What's going on?" I demanded as I rose off the couch.

He didn't even stop to look at me. From the kitchen he called, "I need to you pack up enough clothes and personal items for a week or two."

I didn't bother arguing with him that most of my possessions were still en route from Virginia. My parents were more than happy to have some of the maids box up my belongings.

As he blew around the house, snatching and grabbing things, my chest tightened with worry. "Rev, please talk to me."

At my pleading tone, he set the items down on the kitchen table and turned to me. "The club is going on lockdown." When I stared blankly at him, he asked, "Do you know what that is?"

"Like on campus if there was a threat of a gunman we were put on lockdown in classrooms until the police could get there?" I said.

He nodded. "It's somewhat like that. When the club receives a threat, we go into protection mode where everyone comes together in the compound, including wives and children."

My mind whirled as I processed what was happening. "If we stay within the compound, why can't we stay here?"

"We just can't risk it."

"But why?"

Rev's expression darkened. "Because the last time we thought our houses were safe, Case got blown up and killed."

I didn't have any response to that.

Once again, I remained rooted to the floor as I tried not to be overwhelmed with this aspect of Rev's life. Then a thought came to me—one that made me shiver. "What was the threat?"

"Nothing you need to worry yourself with."

When he refused to look at me, I closed the gap between us. "Rev, who did the threat come from?"

The moment his haunted eyes met mine, I knew. *Mendoza.* Rev's involvement with my past had come back to haunt his club. His family. "Please tell me everything. We've been through too much together not to be honest with each other now."

After jerking his hands through his hair, Rev sighed. "The El Paso Raiders' clubhouse was attacked today and two guys were killed."

I gasped in horror and felt sick. I couldn't help thinking of the Raiders who had come to the hospital to see me. They had been so kind to me. "One of the ones we knew?"

Rev shook his head. I could tell our conversation was having an effect on him. He was becoming visibly rattled. "No. It wasn't one of them."

The relief I felt was fleeting. "How did they know it was Mendoza?"

When Rev shifted uncomfortably on his feet, I knew I needed to brace myself for more horrible news. "One of Mendoza's men called. He said unless they gave up the information where Roja was, more of them would die."

Hearing Mendoza's demand caused my knees to buckle. I would have sunk to the floor if Rev hadn't reached out and caught me. He eased me down onto the couch. Although I hated myself for my weakness, I began to sob uncontrollably.

"Shh, Annabel, it's going to be all right."

Jerking my head up, I stared at him in disbelief. "How can you possibly say that? Two innocent men were killed today because of me. They could just be the tip of the iceberg if Mendoza gets his way. Some of them could be your brothers. . . . It could even be Deacon or Bishop."

Rev brought a hand up to cup my cheek. "Listen to me. You are not to blame for what happened today. You never asked to be kidnapped or to be Mendoza's slave. Rescuing you was the right thing to do. This was all done to you, not by you."

"I wish I could feel that way."

"My Raiders brothers and I aren't going to just sit back and let Mendoza win. We've been in church since the call came through from El Paso." At what must've been my questioning look, Rev replied, "Church is what we call our meetings."

I nodded in understanding. There was still so much of his world I had to learn about. "So you have a plan?" When Rev only nodded and didn't seem ready to fill me in, I growled in frustration. "Be honest with me, dammit! This is your life and mine we're talking about here."

"Fine. You want to know all the details? Then here it is. Mendoza is a lieutenant for the Rodriguez drug cartel. If anyone can make him listen or take him out, they can. To get them on our side, we have offered them all our gun trade. The supplier we used to run guns for would simply ship to Texas and then go on to them in Mexico. At no charge."

"Isn't that bad for the Raiders businesswise?"

"It cuts us off at the knees in one way, and then in another it ensures that we go legitimate."

"You're willing to do all of that just for me?"

Rev smiled. "I would do all of that just for you, but in this case, it's for all of us. We've been working to go legitimate for several months. It was a promise Deacon made to Alexandra to get her to marry him. It was also something we all wanted to do to honor Case's memory."

As I stared into Rev's handsome face, I couldn't help feeling like my love for him would overflow beyond the confines of my physical body. He was so loyal, so strong, and so honorable. I wanted their plan to work so much for him, for his brothers, and for me. Most of all, I wanted to stay strong for him.

Rising off the couch, Rev said, "You just have to have faith. In the meantime, we all need to lay low in case Mendoza knows more than he's letting on." He held out his hand. "Now hurry up with the packing. I need to be back to the roadhouse to supervise as soon as I can."

When I stood up, Rev drew me back into his arms for a moment. "The only thing you need to be worrying about right now is how well you'll handle being cooped up with a crowd." He stared intently into my eyes. "Mendoza will never hurt you again. I swear."

As I brought my lips to his, I wanted to believe him, but I just couldn't seem to drive away the dark feeling of foreboding that enveloped me.

Three days into the lockdown felt like thirty days. Although I loved my new MC family, it was hard being cooped up together with tension weighing heavy in the air. I also couldn't help feeling like people were staring at me because I was the source of the trouble. I didn't bother voicing my concern to Rev because I knew he would say I was just being silly or paranoid.

Considering how laid-back everyone usually was, life during lockdown ran on a pretty strict schedule. There had to be order to ensure that everyone got fed, showered, and slept. Most of the men were housed down at the warehouse, since it was poorly insulated and heated. Rev and I barely had time alone since Bishop slept on the floor in our room with his flavor-of-the-week club whore. His bedroom had been given to Mama Beth, who was bunking with some of the older women.

It was also Alexandra's first time on lockdown, and she wasn't handling being cooped up any better than I was. Of course, she was also dealing with swollen feet, backaches, and exhaustion from being pregnant. At breakfast, she had appeared utterly spent and kept rubbing her lower back. She had excused herself in the middle of the meal and gone to lie down. After that, I was surprised that she insisted on helping out the officers' old ladies who were in charge of meals.

We were all hard at work preparing the chicken and rice when Alexandra said, "Shit. I think we need more rice."

I held my hand up to stop her. "Take it easy, mama. I'm on it," I said as I headed into the giant pantry just off the kitchen. As I reached for the bulk-sized box of rice, I heard the door close behind me. I didn't think much of it until a hand snaked around my waist, drawing me against a hard, familiar body. Although his intent was clear, I asked, "What are you doing?"

Rev's reply came in the form of his warm tongue sliding up the column of my neck, causing me to shiver in pleasure. One of his hands slid from my waist up to cup my breast. When he squeezed it, I gasped and tried to turn toward him. His breath scorched my ear as he whispered, "I need you."

"So badly you have to molest me in the pantry with your brothers' old ladies outside?" I teased.

He rubbed his erection against my backside. "I need you," he repeated, his voice deep with desire.

I turned slowly in his arms, making sure to rub every one of my curves against his body. In the dim glow from the lightbulb overhead, I could see the evidence of his desire in his face. His deep blue eyes were hooded, his strong jaw clenched. He made me feel so beautiful in moments like these, so wanted, so complete. Never defiled and degraded because of what I had been through.

Bringing my lips to his, I savored his rough and rugged handling of me. My arms came up to wrap around his neck, my fingers tangling through the strands of his long hair. His tongue slid across my lips, opening my mouth to allow him inside. Our tongues danced along together. When I tugged his hair, he groaned into my mouth.

His fingers came to fumble at the button on my jeans. Once he had them undone, he jerked the zipper down. And then one of his hands slipped inside, cupping me over my underwear. "Rev," I moaned when his fingers delved into my panties to stroke me. My hips bucked against his hand, desperate for more friction. Back and forth his fingers slid over my clit, rubbing it, teasing it, and driving me mad when he wasn't even inside me. I rubbed myself even harder against him, not caring that I'd positively soaked him with my need. And then I came faster than I ever had before. Eyes pinched shut. Legs giving way. Crying his name so loud that I was sure anyone in the next room could hear.

Rev pulled his hand out of my panties and jeans, and with eyes burning with lust, he proceeded to lick me off each one of his fingers. I grunted with frustration before reaching out to undo his jeans. "Quit teasing me and get inside me."

He gave me a lazy grin. "If that's what you want."

I gripped his erection tight in my hand, causing him to suck in a breath. "Yeah, that's what I want, and I'm pretty sure that's what your dick wants, too."

His eyes widened. "Annabel Percy, what a mouth you have on you."

Smiling, I replied, "Being around bikers has been a bad influence."

He chuckled. "Then a part of me hopes that lockdown doesn't end anytime soon."

I shoved his jeans down over his buttocks while he worked at tugging mine down my thighs. It probably would have been easier just to undress ourselves, but there was something much hotter about taking care of each other.

Once our pants and shoes were in a rumpled pile on the floor, Rev's firm hands lifted me up to wrap my legs around his waist. He didn't ease in. Instead, one powerful thrust had him filling my core. I gripped his shoulders hard, grinding my hips against him.

As he pounded in and out of me, we crashed back against one of the shelves, strewing boxes along the floor. Over and over, he surged into me. Each time he seemed to go deeper, reaching the perfect spot that caused me to moan and shudder. I gripped his shoulders tight, anchoring myself to him. He was always my lifeline—in and out of the bedroom.

Although I'd once had such a hard time coming with a man inside me, Rev knew exactly how to make me shatter around him. I cried out his name once again, burying my face in his neck. He began pumping harder and harder, and within a few moments, he was filling me with his warmth.

Once his hips stopped jerking, he stared at me intently. "I love you."

I smiled. "I love you, too."

He gave me a tender kiss. "I wish we could stay like this forever."

"Locked in a dusty pantry?" I asked teasingly.

"Smart-ass," he muttered as he playfully smacked my bottom. "I meant, I wish I could stay inside you like this. The two of us joined as one."

He had a way of melting my heart with his words. Sometimes it was still hard to believe such sensitive and tender things could come out of his mouth. I swept his hair out of his face and stared into his soulful blue eyes. "There's nothing I want more than to be with you. Always."

We had just started kissing again when a knock came at the door. "Annabel? Are you in there?" Alexandra asked.

"Um, yeah."

"We really need the rice."

"One sec!"

Quickly, Rev and I went about getting dressed and smoothing down our mussed hair. When Rev opened the door and I thrust the box of rice at Alexandra, her eyes widened, and she appeared flustered. "Sorry," I mumbled.

She took the rice and backed slowly away from me. "No, I'm sorry to have interrupted."

I quickly ushered Rev out of the pantry and closed the door. After taking in Rev's and my guilty faces, Kim busted out laughing. "Were you two just fucking in the pantry?"

Rev and I were both so mortified we couldn't reply. Kim patted my back. "Oh, honey, just about every one of us has fucked in there at least once before. Most of the time, we didn't even have the excuse of being on lockdown." She jerked her chin at Alexandra. "I even got an eyeful of Deacon's bare ass when he had her up against the racks."

"Kim!" Alexandra hissed, her face turning crimson.

"What?" With a wink at me, she added, "It's a mighty fine ass, too. Maybe I should get a look at Rev's to compare."

It was then that the absolute absurdity of the moment overcame me, and I burst out laughing. I found that I couldn't stop, and I ended up bent over, with tears streaming down my cheeks. When I finally recovered, everyone else had joined in laughing with me.

After wiping my eyes, I wagged a finger at Kim. "Sorry to disappoint you, but no one but me gets to see Rev's ass."

Rev's eyes flashed with pleasure at my comment, while Kim only grinned. "I get it, sister. You've staked your claim. I'll just have to settle for flashbacks of Deacon I guess until I get a peek at Bishop's."

While slowly stirring rice in a giant boiler, Alexandra said, "I'll be the first to admit that Deacon has a very nice ass." She threw a wicked glance at us over her shoulder. "Very firm when you grab or spank it, not to mention being very lickable."

Rev groaned. "Do you mind? The last thing I want to hear is a description of my brother's ass."

While Kim and I laughed, Alexandra grimaced. The stirring spoon in her hand fell to the floor as she clutched her stomach. At her whimper, Kim, Rev, and I rushed forward.

"What's wrong?" Kim demanded.

"I . . . I think my labor might be starting," Alexandra replied in a hoarse whisper.

"But you're not due for another three weeks," Rev argued.

"Have you been having any back pain?" I asked.

Alexandra nodded. "A little. Not a whole lot more than usual."

Kim's eyes looked concerned as she asked, "Any blood?"

"Maybe a little in my underwear this morning."

"Oh shit, you had your bloody show," Kim replied.

"My what?" Alexandra questioned.

"It means you're in labor. Hell, you've *been* in labor. God only knows how far you're dilated." Kim grabbed hold of Rev's shoulder. "Go call Breakneck. Tell him to get his ass here ASAP." She then turned to me. "Go find Deacon."

When Alexandra cried out in pain again, I knew we were in trouble. Her contractions were coming pretty quickly. Although my scientific knowledge of birth was limited to animals, I knew from a few early anatomy courses that labor could take days or mere hours.

"Come on. Let's get you to bed," Kim instructed.

Once she recovered from the pain, Alexandra shook her head. "I need to get to the hospital."

"Besides the fact you're progressing way too fast, we're on lockdown, sweetheart. You're having this baby here."

Alexandra's dark eyes widened. "I want Deacon. Now."

With a nod, I turned and fled the kitchen to find him. I had no idea where on the compound he might be. After glancing around the main room, I didn't see him. At the back door, Archer was standing guard with Crazy Ace. "You guys seen Deacon?"

"Down at the warehouse."

When I started past them out the door, Crazy Ace grabbed my arm. "Where the hell do you think you're going? No women are allowed outside, least of all you."

"I have to get Deacon," I protested.

"We'll get him. You wait here," Crazy Ace replied.

"You better run like hell for him. Alexandra is in labor."

Archer's mouth gaped open. "Holy shit." He glanced at Crazy Ace. "I'm faster. I'll go get him."

Crazy Ace nodded, and then Archer tore out the back door. The entire main room went silent as a tomb when Kim led a hysterical Alexandra out of the kitchen and down the hall to the bedrooms. Just when the conversation started up again, Deacon blew through the door.

He and I then raced across the main room and down the hall to his and Alexandra's roadhouse bedroom. When he threw open the door, we found Alexandra stretched out on the bed, weeping uncontrollably, while Kim stood by, helplessly wringing her hands.

Deacon went to Alexandra's side. "Babe, I'm here. It's all right." He took her hand in his and squeezed it.

Alexandra stared up at him. "I don't want to do this here. We need to go to the hospital."

Deacon's expression grew grim. "We can't. It's not safe."

"But it's not safe to have this baby here. I need my doctor and nurses."

"Breakneck will be here. He's delivered lots of babies."

"Please, Deacon. Don't make me do this here."

"Babe, I'm sorry, but we just can't risk it. We're already taking a huge risk getting Breakneck here," Deacon argued.

Another contraction had Alexandra contorting her body in agony. When she recovered, tears streamed down her face, but she managed to shout, "I hate you!"

"Alex, please."

She shook her head wildly back and forth. "You promised me that the club was going to go legit. You promised me that Willow and I and the baby would be safe. If anything happens to my son, I'll never forgive you!"

Tears welled in Deacon's eyes. "I'm sorry. Jesus, I'm so sorry."

"Get out! Get out of my sight, you lying bastard!" When

Deacon reached for her hand to try to calm her, she slung him away. "I said get out!" she screamed, then broke down into hysterical sobs, which were so hard they shook the bed.

With an expression of defeated agony, Deacon fled from the room, the door slamming behind him. Kim and I exchanged a look of horror, at a loss as to what we should do next. Although my experience was completely limited to animals, I knew it wasn't good for Alexandra to be so emotional.

I went to her side and took her hand. "Alex, look at me."

It took her a few moments to calm down enough to stare into my eyes. I held her gaze, stroking her forehead with my other hand. "It's going to be all right. You're going to be all right, and the baby is going to be all right."

At my words and touch, her entire body seemed to relax. She sighed deeply and squeezed my hand. "Thank you, Annabel."

Breakneck burst into the room, followed by Rev. The good doctor had his standard black medical bag, along with a rolling suitcase. I guessed he had raided the maternity ward at the hospital for all the necessary supplies.

He then went to work, assessing Alexandra and barking orders to Kim and me.

Breakneck handed me a basin. "Go fill this with boiling water. Tell the women to keep a pot constantly boiling."

With a nod of my head, I hurried out of the room. When I got outside, I almost tripped over Deacon, who was sitting with his back against the wall.

He raised his haunted eyes to mine. "Is she okay?"

"She's fine. Breakneck is with her, and things are progressing as they should."

Deacon nodded and then hung his head. I knelt down beside him and took his hand. "She isn't going to stay mad at you, Deacon. Pain does things to you, makes you say and do things you don't mean."

"If something happens to her or the baby because of me, I'll never be able to forgive myself."

"Listen to me. Alexandra is young and strong. She's had a perfectly healthy pregnancy. She will be fine." I rose to my feet. "I have to go get the water."

Without another word to him, I sprinted to the kitchen. Thankfully, Boone's wife, Mary, had had the presence of mind to have a pot of water already heated up.

When I returned with the boiling water, Rev was seated beside Deacon, his arm slung over his brother's shoulder. I gave him a fleeting smile and then hurried back into the room. Mama Beth had replaced Kim at the bedside. She sat on the edge of the bed, holding Alexandra's hand and keeping her as calm as she could.

Everything seemed to start happening at a whirlwind pace. I tried to help Breakneck when he asked me, but I felt completely and totally clueless. Some moments felt like the hands on the clock were spinning out of control and others seemed to drag by.

"And there's the head. You need to keep pushing now." A beaming smile lit up Breakneck's face. "He's got a head full of gorgeous hair."

"He does?" Alexandra asked.

"Yes, dark hair just like you and Deacon."

At the mention of Deacon's name, Alexandra's eyes filled with tears. "Oh, Deacon," she murmured, then turned to me. "Please get him for me! He didn't get to be there when Willow was born, and I don't want him to miss seeing his son come into the world."

I spun on my feet and dashed to the door. As I flung it open, I prayed that Deacon was still just outside and hadn't gone to do something stupid like get drunk. My heart leapt at the sight of him still sitting beside Rev with his head buried in his hands. "Deacon, come quick. Alexandra is asking for you."

I had never seen anyone move so fast. He was on his feet in a flash and by my side. He didn't wait for me. Instead, he barreled on inside and went to Alexandra's side. "I'm so sorry. I'm so, so sorry," he murmured over and over again as he bestowed tender kisses all over her face.

"It's okay."

"No, it's not. I'll give Rev my cut right now if you want me to leave the club."

My head spun over to the doorway where Rev stood in open-mouthed disbelief at his brother's suggestion. We then both looked back to the bed to await Alexandra's response.

She gazed up at Deacon. "How could I ask you to do that? This club is your life."

"You and our children mean more to me than anything in the world," he replied.

"Let's just leave things as they are for right now. How's that?"

Deacon brought his mouth to Alexandra's and kissed her passionately. "God, do I love you."

"I love you, too. But I need to push now."

He immediately stood upright. "Okay. What do I need to do?"

She laughed at his bewildered expression. "Just hold my hand and talk to me when the pain gets bad."

"I can do that."

Now that Deacon was taking care of Alexandra, I went over to Rev, who still stood in the doorway. I wasn't sure if we should stay in or go, but when Alexandra met my gaze, she said, "Stay."

"If you're sure."

"You've already seen the worst part. Might as well see the best. Besides, it makes sense for his godparents to be in the room."

Together, Rev and I smiled at her. It was an honor to be a part of seeing life come into the world. It was a double honor to be named the baby's godparents. So Rev closed the door behind him.

When things got dicey for Alexandra with the pain, Rev would squeeze my hand. I knew in some ways he could imagine me being in that much pain, which would kill him. Deacon certainly wasn't faring well at seeing Alexandra hurting.

The mood in the air shifted, and with a hearty cry, Deacon and Alexandra's son came into the world. After cleaning his lungs and cutting him free from Alexandra, Breakneck held the wailing baby out to me. I momentarily froze.

"Annabel, aftercare for infants isn't terribly different from aftercare for animals. Prepare the baby for Alexandra to hold." At his encouraging look, I grabbed a waiting blanket and took the baby into my arms.

"Shh, it's okay, sweetheart," I murmured to him as I wrapped him up.

As Breakneck dealt with the afterbirth and made sure Alexandra was okay, I took the baby over to the tub of warm water and began to gently clean him. At the contact with the water, his cries grew louder, and Deacon came to my side. With a smile, I glanced at him over my shoulder. "I promise I'm not hurting him."

"That's not what I thought at all," Deacon replied, but I could tell his fatherly instincts to protect his son were kicking into overdrive.

Once the baby had been washed and dried, I took a fresh blanket and wrapped him snugly in it. When I turned around, Deacon was staring expectantly at me. "Ready to meet your son?"

"Hell yeah," he replied with a smile.

I passed the baby over to his waiting arms. Then Deacon did something I would never have imagined. Cradling his son to his chest, he broke down into quiet sobs. When I glanced from Deacon to Rev, I saw the same expression of disbelief on Rev's face that I was sure I had on my own.

Deacon quickly recovered and dragged his free arm across his wet eyes. "Look at you, little man," he murmured.

"Does he have a name?" I asked.

After glancing at Alexandra, who nodded, Deacon smiled. "It's Wyatt David Malloy."

"Nice choice," Rev replied.

Deacon went over to Rev. "He's handsome, isn't he?"

Rev grinned. "Very handsome. Although I think he's going to favor his mother."

With a slight frown, Deacon eyeballed his son. "Yeah, I think you're right."

"Don't sound so sad about it," Alexandra joked.

"He should be honored to take after his mother, as good-looking as she is," Deacon said, and then he winked at Alexandra.

"Well, everything looks good. I think it's time this mother got to hold her baby," Breakneck said.

As Deacon started to take Wyatt over to Alexandra, Rev leaned down to place a tiny kiss on the top of Wyatt's head. The simple gesture was my undoing. All the emotions of the day converged in me at that moment. I knew I had to get out of that room.

Without a word to Rev or the others, I hurried to the door. I don't know how he made it so fast, but he was at my side before I got it open. Taking me by the hand, Rev led me into our bedroom. Thankfully, it was empty. He went to the bed and lay down, pulling me down beside him. "I know that had to be hell for you, so cry all you want to."

But the tears didn't come. Instead, I looked at the amazing man before me in disbelief. "I'm such a selfish asshole."

Apparently Rev hadn't been prepared for my response because he burst out laughing. "No, you're not," he replied.

"Yes, I am. This is such a happy day for you, not to mention we're in the middle of lockdown because of Mendoza." I shook my head. "You're too good to me. In fact, you shouldn't marry me."

"Just because you think you're a selfish asshole?" he asked almost teasingly.

"No. It's just . . . the way you kissed Wyatt's head . . . the way you are with Willow." I exhaled an agonized sigh. "I can't give you the children you want . . . the children you deserve."

"We don't know what the future holds."

I shook my head. "I can't have a baby, and we can't adopt. No judge would give us a child with your background."

"Hmm, so I guess we're both a little to blame?"

"I didn't mean it like that," I protested.

Rev wrapped his arms tighter around me. "Annabel, none of us know what tomorrow holds. But I do know that we'll have a child one day." When I started to argue, he said, "I've done a lot of reading on surrogacy, and I've talked to some of the girls in the club. When the time comes, we'll have a baby. You have to believe that."

I jerked my head off his chest to stare into his eyes. The conviction in them gave me hope. I shouldn't have been surprised that he was already thinking ahead for us—that was just his way—but his confidence gave me hope.

Just like we would weather the Mendoza storm together, we would make it through building a future and a family together as well. Somehow, some way. I just had to have faith.

TWENTY-ONE

Mendoza was close. So very, very close. Roja would soon get what was coming to her. As his car crossed the state line into Georgia, the ever-present mix of rage and desperation surging through him reached a volatile new level. The one thing that had pushed him through the bullshit of the last few months was revenge. Revenge against the man who had taken Roja. Revenge against Roja for daring to leave him.

The months had melted into a blur of false leads and dead-end roads. He'd called in favors to gain information, and he'd had to end the lives of a few less-than-cooperative people as well. He had poured more money into this quest than what he had anticipated—some of the money he had owed to Rodriguez and the cartel. At the time he hadn't given a fuck about the cost.

But in the last two days he had gotten wind of a plan that caused his desire for revenge to escalate further than he had ever imagined.

This Hells Raiders biker—this *chingada madre*—had not only

dared to infiltrate his compound, but had cut him off at the knees by having him alienated from his cartel brothers. Who the fuck did he think he was to approach Rodriguez for protection for his club, for himself, and, most important, for Roja? And who the fuck did Rodriguez think he was to betray one of his lieutenants for gringo biker scum?

Oh yes, the cocksucker would pay. He would pay with his life and with Roja's, but only after he had been tortured to where he would pray for death. And Roja would watch every blow until the time came for her to suffer her own dose of justice.

TWENTY-TWO

REV

Two days after Wyatt's birth, I had Boone and Crazy Ace open up the main gates on the compound. Deacon, Bishop, and Mac, our club secretary, followed me as I zipped out onto the main road. I had received a call the night before from Hector Rodriguez himself. He was more than willing to take the guns off our hands, and he had set up a meeting with us at noon with some of the men in his operation. As vice president, Deacon would be there as my second-in-command, and we needed Mac to record what was agreed to verbally. Of course, Bishop, as sergeant at arms, was along as well for any needed muscle.

Although the January cold bore down hard on us, I couldn't help enjoying the sunshine and the freedom of being outside of the compound. Our contact point was about two miles from the compound, which Rodriguez had chosen to put us Raiders at ease of not being far from home. We pulled into the parking lot of a rather run-down Mexican restaurant, which I'd previously had no idea was involved in any dirty dealings.

When we stepped inside the restaurant, I quickly scanned the room. A waitress hurried up to us. "Come with me," she said.

"Guess she knows we're not here for the food," Bishop mused.

We were led to a back room that had once been used for private parties. Two men sat at one of the tables. They rose to their feet at the sight of us. "Please come in. You're very welcome," the older of the two said.

When I stood before him, he offered me his hand. "I'm Hector's cousin, Juan. He flew me in to meet with you."

After shaking his hand, I introduced him to Deacon and the others. As we sat down, beer and bottles of tequila appeared from several waitresses. I took a beer to ease some of the tension I couldn't help feeling.

Since you never wanted a paper trail of your dealings, everything was done verbally. Your word was your bond, along with a handshake. "So I'm to understand that the Georgia chapter of the Raiders will no longer deal in guns to other sources. Instead, your shipments will come to us in Juárez via your brothers in the El Paso club," Juan said.

"We're going legitimate."

Juan's eyes widened. "Interesting. Too much bloodshed or too much heat from the authorities?"

"Too much blood."

"Although I cannot totally understand your desire, I greatly appreciate it, since it will benefit our organization."

I smiled. "I'm glad you see it that way."

Juan glanced at the still-nameless man at his side before turning back to me. "I understand you ask for no money in return."

"That is true."

"Your generosity comes in the form of the elimination of one man. Manuel Mendoza."

I shifted in my seat. "I never asked for his termination. Merely for protection."

"He killed two of your El Paso brothers, did he not?"

"Yes. That is true."

"And he is your fiancée's rapist, true?"

Sucking in a harsh breath, I tried to still my emotions. Juan had hit a raw nerve by mentioning Annabel. "Yes. He is," I spat out through gritted teeth.

"So tell me why this man deserves to live."

Before I could respond, Deacon growled, "We came to make a deal, not to be fucked with!"

Juan's lips quirked up in a smile. "My apologies."

I cleared my throat. "Excuse my brother. He is very protective."

"It is understandable. I was merely feeling you out on the subject."

"You would take out one of your loyal lieutenants for a deal?"

"Members of our organization are expendable. They know that when they join." Juan narrowed his eyes. "To say that Mendoza is loyal would be far too complimentary. He's always had his own agenda. But that stays within these walls."

"I understand," I replied.

Juan extended his hand. "So do we have a deal?"

As I stared at his hand for a moment, I couldn't help thinking of my old man and of Case. I hoped that what I was about to do would have made them proud. Even if we went legitimate, we would never disband the Raiders brotherhood.

I reached for Juan's hand. "It's a deal."

He smiled. "I'm very glad to hear that. I will phone Hector and let him know everything is taken care of."

"Including Mendoza?" Bishop asked.

Juan nodded. "He is no longer a threat to you."

"My club, as well as my El Paso brothers, appreciate that."

After Juan had shaken hands with the others, we headed out of the back room. When we got outside the restaurant, I exhaled the breath that I felt I had been holding since Mendoza had reared his head again.

"How does it feel to be just a regular old biker?" Bishop asked.

Deacon snorted. "Until we unload the gambling at the gym, we're only half-legitimate."

With a grin, Bishop asked, "So we're basically a bastard?"

"You're always a bastard," I replied.

"Har fucking har," he muttered, as he slid across the seat of his bike.

After putting on my helmet, I gunned my bike's engine. We then rode out of the parking lot, me speeding ahead of my brothers. I couldn't wait to get back to Annabel.

Just as we rounded the curve about a mile from home, the unmistakable sound of gunfire rang out. Glancing over my shoulder, I saw Deacon and Bishop spin out, their bikes crashing onto the pavement. When Mac tried to miss their combined heap of metal, he overcorrected, sending him careening into the ditch. When they didn't move, I didn't know if it was from the bike wreck injuries or if they had been shot. I started to turn my bike around when a bullet hit my back tire, and it was my turn to slide along the asphalt.

After struggling until my bike came to a stop, I lay on my back trying to catch my breath and heard squealing tires. Turning my head, I watched as a car came speeding toward us. Furiously I started trying to pull myself out from under my bike. The car screeched to a stop, and a man jumped out just as I wiggled free. I had no time to reach around my back for my own gun before the muzzle of a pistol was pointed at my head.

Although I had never laid eyes on him, I knew who it was. Mendoza stared down at me with lifeless black eyes. Then with one kick of his steel-toed boot, the world around me went dark.

TWENTY-THREE

ANNABEL

Pacing around Deacon and Alexandra's bedroom, I kept an eye on the nightstand clock as well as the light blue bassinet in the corner. Rev had left two hours ago for his meeting with the Rodriguez cartel, and by now I was beginning to get antsy. As a novice in the MC world, I had no idea how long such meetings should take.

While she waited for Deacon to return, Alexandra had slipped into the shower while Wyatt slept peacefully. I had offered to watch him to put her at ease. Although it had initially been hard being around Wyatt, I had grown to enjoy being with him, feeling his soft skin, smelling his sweet smell.

Digging in my pocket for my phone, I checked to see if there was a call from Rev that I had somehow missed. When there wasn't, I decided to be the overbearing fiancée and call him. After the voice mail connected, I said, "Rev, I hate to be a nag, but could you please give me a call? I love you."

Loud, panicked voices and heavy boots stomping down the hallway caused a chill to run down my spine. I hurried over to the door and threw it open. I gasped at the sight of Deacon and Mac carrying Bishop into his room. I ran into the hallway, forgetting all about watching Wyatt.

Boone stopped me before I could go into Bishop's room. "What's happened? What's wrong with Bishop?"

With a grimace, Boone replied, "He's been shot. Breakneck's on the way."

Craning my neck, I surveyed the group of men in the hallway. Rev was nowhere to be seen. "Where's Rev?" When no one answered me, it felt like I was free-falling off the edge of a cliff, my arms and legs pinwheeling madly. *"Where is Rev?"* I demanded again, my voice growing shrill.

Deacon appeared in the doorway. His face and arms were torn with ragged cuts, and dried blood crusted over the deep scratches. With legs that shook so hard they could barely support me, I lunged at him.

"Where is Rev?"

"We were ambushed on the way home from our meeting. He took Rev."

I didn't have to ask who had taken Rev. I knew without a shadow of a doubt. "Oh my God," I murmured.

Deacon's arms reached out for me, pulling me against him. "We're going to get Rev back, Annabel. Mendoza took him for a reason. If he didn't plan on making demands of us, he would have killed Rev then."

"You don't know Mendoza," I whispered. Flashes of his vicious eyes, his volatile temper, and his never-ending cruelty raced through my mind.

Tilting my head to cause me to look at him, Deacon said, "Mendoza is pretty much fucked. He has both us and now the Rodriguez cartel on his ass. He's not going to win this one. We're already working on tracing his phone to find him."

I wanted to believe Deacon. I couldn't bear the thought of living in a world without Rev. After all, he was my world—the sun, the moon, and the stars. I knew I needed more security than just what the Raiders could do.

"We need help."

Deacon's brows rose in surprise. "Excuse me?'"

"I don't want to take one chance when it comes to Rev's life."

"I said we would—"

"I'm calling my father. I want the FBI or the ATF or whoever the hell takes out men like Mendoza to make sure Rev gets out of this alive."

A collective intake of breath came from the other members of the Raiders. Deacon's expression darkened. "We don't work with the feds."

With adrenaline pumping obscene amounts of courage into me, I stood toe-to-toe with Deacon. "You might not work with the feds, but I do." When Deacon growled with frustration, I countered, "Think about it for a minute. Mendoza would never imagine you coming at him with the feds, would he?"

"Probably not."

"I think it's pretty clear what Mendoza is going to demand when he does reach out to you."

Deacon winced. "I imagined as much."

"Then I think if I'm the target it's only fair I get a say in this."

"She's right," Alexandra said behind us. Outfitted in a robe, she stood at the entrance to her bedroom. "It's just like with me and Sigel. You have to come at them where they least expect it."

"I'm not sure when women started having a fucking say in the way this club runs, but it sure as hell needs to be stopped. Fucking pronto," Deacon grumbled.

Holding up my phone, I said, "Sometimes you don't have to have a dick to come up with the best plan."

Deacon stared openmouthed at me before slamming his hand against the wall. He breathed heavily for a few seconds. "Fine. Call your father and the feds. You just make sure that nothing blows back on the Raiders since we're going legit."

"You're such an asshole," I muttered as I started dialing my father.

"Damn straight, babe," Deacon replied.

TWENTY-FOUR

❧

REV

Oh, sweet Jesus, the pain. Fiery torrents of it plagued every inch of my body. It pulled me out of the depths of unconsciousness. The smell of burning flesh assaulted my nose. It took a few seconds for my brain to process that it was my own skin being burned.

My eyes shot open to see Mendoza standing before me with a blowtorch in his hands. When I tried to jerk away, I found my hands were bound and my arms were stretched above my head. I had been stripped of my shirt to give him better access to torture me.

"Glad to see you're back with me. I was almost afraid I had kicked you too hard. I didn't want you to miss out on the fun."

"Fuck you," I spat.

He rewarded my outburst by singeing my bare lower back until I couldn't bite back my screams. I panted and heaved as I tried to stay upright. When I moved, it felt like the entire layer of skin on my back was peeling off as it blistered and bubbled.

"You know you deserve much worse for what you and your men did to my camp. Do you know the money you cost me?"

I didn't answer him. I knew if I opened my mouth I would throw up from the searing pain biting my flesh. Instead, I focused my energy on staring him down.

Mendoza met my glare. "But the worst thing you did was taking my Roja from me."

Gulping down the bile rising in my throat, I grunted through gritted teeth, "She isn't yours. She never was."

Burning agony engulfed my chest. Pinching my eyes shut, I tried riding out the pain. I bit down on my lip so hard that blood ran down my chin. When Mendoza finally let up, I couldn't speak. I could barely think. All I could do was try to focus on my breathing. As long as I was breathing, I was still alive. I had to stay alive for Annabel.

"Did you enjoy fucking her?" Through my tormented agony, I opened my eyes. When he saw I was looking at him, a cruel smile curved on Mendoza's lips. "She's one of the finest pieces of ass I've ever had. And the way her pussy tasted when I stuck my tongue deep inside her." He licked his lips. "I can't wait to taste it one last time."

I jerked against my bindings, desperate to get free so I could tear him apart. The thought of him reminiscing about the way he had tortured Annabel made me as rabid as a feral dog. As I focused on Mendoza's throat, I envisioned ripping it out with my teeth.

Mendoza's next words chilled me to the bone. "I'm about to call her to make a deal." While I stared at him in disbelief, he said, "I'm going to lead her to believe I will trade you for her. What a beautiful little fool to be willing to risk her life for the man she loves. Some would think I would be stupid to trust her, but I know my Roja. She is honorable to a fault. Took the worst fucking beating of her life just to keep a ring one of the whores gave her."

I hung my head and my chest tightened as I remembered that it had been Sarah who gave her the ring. Surely my brothers wouldn't let Annabel come for me, even if it meant my death.

Mendoza jerked my hair so I had to look at him. With a sinister gleam in his eyes, he said, "When she gets here, I'm going to fuck her one last time in front of you. Then to truly devastate her, I'm going to kill you in front of her. For the big finish, I'll slit her throat."

Holding up my phone, he smiled. "Let's get the party started."

TWENTY-FIVE

ANNABEL

Regardless of the way I had left things with my parents, I believed they wouldn't completely abandon me. Of course, it didn't hurt that my life was in danger once again by the man who had enslaved me. Within minutes of our call, my father's connections had us patched in with the Georgia branch of the ATF, and after just a half hour, they had two teams heading to our area. I also had my phone being tracked for my location as well as to trace incoming calls. If I had ever doubted the power my father possessed, I would no longer do so.

All that was left was to wait for Mendoza to reach out. I once again resorted to pacing around the main room of the roadhouse. Thankfully, Breakneck had stitched up Bishop's bullet wound to the back. Luckily it had narrowly missed nicking one of his kidneys. Breakneck had gotten Deacon and Mac cleaned up as well.

The eerie silence in the roadhouse was interrupted by my phone ringing. I would have ignored it had it not been Rev's ringtone. Snatching my phone to my ear, I said, "H-Hello? Rev?"

There was a pause on the line before I heard the voice from my darkest nightmares. "Roja, how lovely to speak to you. I've missed you. Haven't you missed me?"

A chill ran over my body at the sound of his voice in my ear. I had been haunted by it for months. Flashes of his rapes instantly tormented my mind, but I fought with everything in my being to push them out. I had to be strong and focus on the here and now to get Rev back.

"Where is Rev?" I demanded.

"Ah, I would assume you're speaking of the biker trash you spread your legs for."

"Tell me where he is!"

"You have been away from me for far too long, Roja. You should know better than to speak to me that way," he admonished.

Refusing to let him ever intimidate me again, I snapped, "Cut the bullshit and tell me what you want!"

"That should be clear. I want you."

I closed my eyes as a wave of revulsion ran through me. "So you are willing to trade me for Rev?"

He chuckled. "You're already trying to negotiate a deal. This man must mean a lot to you."

Thinking of what Deacon had said, I replied, "You obviously took him for a reason instead of killing him. So tell me what to do so we can end this."

"I don't give you any directions until I know you're away from the Raiders."

"Fine. I'll leave the compound now."

"I'll give you ten minutes. If you're not alone then, I'll start taking out chunks of your lover."

My stomach churned at his words. "I'm on my way."

Deacon and the others stared expectantly at me. "He won't tell me where he has Rev until I'm away from the compound." I then related to them what he had said about giving me ten minutes or he would hurt Rev.

"So that's it? We're just supposed to let you walk out of here alone?" Deacon demanded.

"I won't be entirely alone. I'll have the ATF with me then."

With a roll of his eyes, Deacon said, "That makes me feel so much fucking better."

"I can't argue about this anymore. I have to get out of here."

"If something happens to you, Rev will never forgive me," Deacon said.

I smiled sadly at him. "This isn't his choice; it's mine. I'm doing what I feel I have to do to save him—and to save me."

After shaking his head, Deacon gave me a quick hug. "You be careful, okay?"

I nodded. "I'm a lot stronger than I look."

"Trust me, I know that."

I got halfway across the room and stopped. Whirling around, I said, "I don't have a car." It was the one part of the plan I had overlooked.

Boone came over and handed a set of keys to me. "It's the Mustang outside."

My brows shot up in surprise. "Are you sure?"

He nodded. "It'll get you to Rev faster."

I gave him a quick hug before racing out the door. After cranking up the car, I roared out of the roadhouse parking lot. Of course, I had no idea if I should go right or left. All I knew was Mendoza would phone with instructions.

With just a minute to spare before my ten minutes were up, the phone rang. With a shaky hand, I reached for it. "Hello?"

"Go to the old rock quarry off Route 19. Come around to the back of the barn."

"But I don't know—," I started to protest.

"You'll figure it out." Mendoza hung up.

"Son of a bitch!" I shouted. Pulling the car off to the side of the road, I Googled a rock quarry. Amazingly enough, the route pulled up. It was only fifteen minutes away, but it was in the other direction than I had come out of the roadhouse. After turning around, I gunned the engine. Even though they were tracking my phone, I wasn't taking any chances with the ATF. I dialed Agent Hollis's number that I had programmed in my phone earlier. "I'm supposed to meet him at a barn beside the old rock quarry on Route 19."

"We are only a few minutes from the location. When you arrive, stall for a few moments in the car before you go in. We do not want too much time to elapse before you go in the barn and before we come in."

"Okay. I can do that."

"I know you can. We have every confidence in you, Annabel," Agent Hollis said.

I wished that his words made me feel better, but sadly, they didn't. While I might've looked calm and collected on the outside, I was a fucking basket case on the inside. I had stared down death once before, so I wasn't afraid of being killed. More than anything, I didn't want to lose Rev.

Veering off the road onto Route 19 caused my stomach to churn. Rolling down the window, I threw up the contents of my stomach. With a nervous laugh, I thought about how Boone would regret loaning me his car when it came back with puke down the front door.

When I saw the barn, my heart started beating so hard it felt like a cannon's blast inside the car. I eased around the back of the building, craning my neck to see if anyone was around. Just one car was parked there, and I knew it had to belong to Mendoza.

Once I turned the engine off, I tried to collect myself. My arms and legs trembled uncontrollably with nerves. But then I focused on the image of Rev's face and it gave me the strength I needed. Opening the car door, I slowly got to my feet. I took small steps from the car, taking as much time as I could.

When I got to the back door, it opened before I reached for it. The next thing I knew I was being grabbed and dragged inside. Then I was thrown to the ground. "So glad you could come," Mendoza greeted me.

I started to glare up at him, but then something to my left drew my attention. Rev was strung up to one of the lower hanging barn beams. His arms were jerked at a painful angle over his head, but the worst thing was the burns on his chest. "Rev!" I cried as I started to scramble to my feet.

But then I felt the familiar bite of a belt slamming across my back. I couldn't hold back the scream that tore from my lips. Grabbing me by the hair, Mendoza jerked me to my feet. With a cold glare, he asked, "You didn't think you could just waltz in here without being punished, did you?"

Another crack of the belt had me shrieking. "You wanna beat someone, you beat me, you cocksucker!" Rev shouted.

"You don't get to call the shots." He licked his lips as he drew me closer to him. "Right now I think I'll make her scream for another reason."

Mendoza grabbed one of my breasts, kneading it harshly. At my whimper of pain, a cruel smirk curved on his lips. "That's nothing compared to what I'm going to do to you, Roja."

At that moment the barn door burst open and four agents came crashing through it. "Freeze! Drop your weapon. Now!" an agent shouted. After recognizing his voice, I knew it was Agent Hollis.

"You lying cunt!" Mendoza spat before lunging at me so hard that we both fell to the ground. He started punching and kicking me until he was wrestled off me by one of the agents.

"Are you okay?" Agent Hollis asked.

My sides and stomach screamed in agony where Mendoza had kicked me. When I tried to sit up, I couldn't. I seemed to be working overtime to catch my breath. But the sound of Rev screaming my name had me struggling to my feet with some help from Agent Hollis.

After I wiped the blood off my busted lip, I nodded. At that point, I didn't care about the pain. All I could think about was Rev. As I limped over to him, I met his haunted gaze. "Oh, Rev," I murmured. Turning back to Agent Hollis, I said, "Get him down. Now!"

As he worked to cut the rope that held Rev in place, I brought my hands to Rev's face. "I'm so, so sorry, my love," I murmured.

"Not your fault," he gasped. He tried to lean closer to me, but he couldn't reach. I leaned in and brought my lips to his. "Thank God you're okay."

With a smile, I said, "I feel the same way about you."

Agent Hollis eased the rope so that Rev's arms could come slowly down at his side. I started working at getting his hands free of the rope. Suddenly, one of the agents shouted in alarm. When I glanced over my shoulder, I saw Mendoza push out of one of the agents' reach and grab the agent's extra gun from his chest holster.

Mendoza then whirled around toward me and Rev and pointed the gun. As the blast went off, Rev shoved me out of the way. After I fell to the ground, I glanced back to see Rev's body contort in pain as blood spewed out of a wound in his stomach. "No, no, NO!" I screamed.

Rev collapsed on the ground at the same moment the agents tackled Mendoza. I crawled over to Rev, cradling his head in my lap. He stared up at me, his eyes glassy.

"Been gut-shot," he gasped. "Not good."

"Don't say that!"

"I love you, Annabel."

I shook my head. "Don't you dare act like you're saying goodbye. You're going to marry me, remember? We're a team—you and me against the world." Tears streamed down my cheeks and fell onto his face.

One of the agents dropped down beside us and started working on compressing Rev's wound. "Ambulance is on the way," he said to me.

"You hear that, Rev? The ambulance is coming, so you have to hold on until it gets here."

With a weak smile, he reached up to cup my cheek. "My beautiful Annabel Lee." Then he closed his eyes.

"Rev, stay with me. Please . . . please stay with me." I buried my face against his, unable to stop the sobs that overtook me.

TWENTY-SIX

REV

A pulsing white light filled with peaceful energy enveloped me from head to toe. As I gazed around, I realized the light was filling me up and healing me. I no longer felt any pain from the gunshot wound. I brought my hands up to pat around on my gut. No blood. No wound.

"What the . . . ," I muttered.

In the distance, a figure began walking toward me. As it got closer, I blinked several times to make sure I was seeing clearly. When I still saw the person in front of me, I decided I must be hallucinating because it simply couldn't be possible. "Pop?" I questioned.

Preacher Man smiled at me. "Hello, son."

"What are you . . . ? What am I . . . ?" I questioned lamely.

"I'm here to tell you that it isn't your time, and you have to go back."

I frowned in confusion as everything floated along in this trippy consciousness. "Are you trying to say this is heaven?" I swallowed hard. "Like I'm dead or something?"

"Maybe it is or maybe you're just hallucinating this from a

temporary lack of oxygen," Preacher Man suggested with a sly smile. He reached out and placed his hand on my shoulder. "Just know I'm proud of you, son. Regardless of what happened to you, it never broke you; it only made you stronger." He squeezed my arm. "You're the man I wish I could have been."

Although breaking down was the most unmanly thing I could do, I let the tears flow freely. "Thank you, Pop."

"No—thank you, son."

As he faded away, a jolt of electricity rocketed through my body, sucking me out of the white light and slamming me back onto a stretcher in the back of an ambulance. A paramedic held the crash cart paddles in his hands and I heard him say, "He's back. We have sinus rhythm."

I gulped in the oxygen from the mask on my face, trying to still my out-of-control heart rate. I started to bring my hand to my gut to see if my wound was real again, but the other paramedic grabbed my arm. "Easy there."

Once he released me, I moved my hand up to my face. At the feel of moisture on my cheeks, the world grew dark around me again.

When I came to, I was in a bed at the hospital. Blinking my eyes, I took in my surroundings. Machines beeped on and off, but I was grateful to find I just had an oxygen mask, rather than a breathing tube. It felt like there was some sort of cool sheeting on my back— it must've been something to deal with my burns. They must've been giving me some good drugs because I wasn't in any pain.

As I looked around the room again, I saw that one entire wall was covered with balloons, flowers, and cards. Jesus, how long had I been out of it? Turning my head, I saw something that made my heartbeat speed up on the monitor. Annabel slept in one of the uncomfortable chairs next to my bed. Her disheveled hair and the dark circles under her eyes told me she hadn't left my side. Not that there was any doubt about my feelings for her, but her true devotion made me fall in love with her all over again.

I eased the mask off my face. "Annabel?" I croaked.

At the sound of my voice, she shot upright and almost fell out of the chair. "Rev! Rev, you're awake!" she cried as she dove for the bedside. She bent over to bestow kisses on my cheeks and then my lips. Just when I could barely catch my breath, she pulled away, tears flowing. "I love you. I love you so, so much."

Smiling up at her, I replied, "I love you, too."

She pushed my hair back from my face. "I thought I had lost you. You came so close to dying."

An uneasy feeling prickled over my skin. "I did?"

Annabel nodded. "They said you crashed in the ambulance on the way here. You went into emergency surgery as soon as you got here. The doctor said you were lucky to be alive."

Slowly, I began to remember the bright light and seeing Preacher Man. I didn't like thinking how close I had come to leaving Annabel and my brothers and Mama Beth.

"It wasn't my time," I murmured.

"What?"

Realizing I had said Preacher Man's words, I shook my head. "It's nothing."

"Deacon and Bishop have taken turns staying the nights with me."

"Nights?"

"You've been unconscious for five days. Well, most of them you were kept in a medically induced coma to let your burns heal."

"Holy shit."

Annabel laughed. "The doctor said you would come around when you were ready. Of course, that didn't mean that your mother and I didn't worry to death about when that might be. But thankfully, there's no lasting internal damage. You might have some scarring from your burns."

My mind went back to Mendoza and his sadistic use of a blowtorch. Then a sobering thought hit me. "What happened with Mendoza after he shot me?"

"The ATF took him in. I've been assured he won't get out of prison."

"He won't," I said adamantly.

Annabel's expression became unreadable at my words and tone. Gazing down at the blanket, she hesitated before asking, "Does that mean you'll have him taken care of in prison?"

I reached forward to grab her hand. "He won't be coming out alive, you can rest assured of that. But before it's done, he'll suffer."

A tremor ran through Annabel's body. "I suppose the thought of you having him tortured should disgust me, but it doesn't. I think of what he did to me and then what he did to you. . . . He deserves everything he gets."

Squeezing her hand, I said, "That's an old lady talking right there." She shook her head, but then smiled in spite of herself. As I stared into her eyes, I thought of what she had gone through to save me. "You were so strong and so brave. I'm so very proud of you, Annabel. Proud and honored to call you my future wife."

Tears once again shimmered in her eyes. "It was my love for you that gave me the strength." She bent down again to kiss me. I brought my hand up to tangle through the strands of her long auburn hair. When she pulled away, she smiled. "I'd better call your mother and Deacon. They'll want to see you."

"They can wait. Why don't you lie down with me for a while? I want to feel you close to me."

She narrowed her green eyes at me. "Nathaniel Malloy, I certainly hope you're not trying to get fresh with me just a few minutes after regaining consciousness. I'm sure the doctor will be in here any moment."

I laughed. "No, Annabel Percy, I merely want to hold the

woman I love close to me since there was a brief moment when I didn't think I would ever get the chance again."

Annabel's expression softened. "We have to be careful, though."

Sliding my body over in the bed caused more pain than I had anticipated. At my sharp intake of breath, Annabel started to move away from the bed. "Oh no, you don't," I muttered through gritted teeth.

Gently, she eased up onto the mattress and stayed practically hanging off the edge to ensure that she didn't hurt me. I took her hand in mine and brought it to my cheek, enjoying the softness of her skin and the warmth of her touch.

Somehow two broken people had found their other half that completed them and made them whole. The worst of circumstances had brought us together, but some of the greatest loves in the world were born of tragedy.

As I kissed her palm, I thanked God that I had gotten a second chance to love and be loved by this woman—this Annabel Lee.

TWENTY-SEVEN

ANNABEL

Sunlight streamed through the heavily tree-lined woods, warming even the shadowy parts. With the hem of my dress clutched in my hand, I carefully made my way through the uneven terrain. I dodged tree limbs and shrubs that might nick my dress. After all, I didn't want to do anything to ruin my appearance, considering it was my wedding day.

I'm sure it seemed a little unorthodox to be tromping through the woods on the most important day of my life, but at the same time, there was no other way to reach the wedding venue. Rev's near death at Mendoza's hands illustrated to us both how precarious life can be, and made it seem a little ridiculous to wait to get married.

So a month to the day after Rev had come home from the hospital, we were becoming man and wife. Because we were on a tight schedule, most of the venues were booked up. In the end, the most obvious choice was right before our eyes . . . or at least a mile into the woods. Our ceremony would take place on the banks of *tohi a-ma*.

When I stumbled over an exposed tree root, Deacon's arm shot out to catch me. "Easy there, sister. I don't want you face-planting before we can get you to the altar," he said, his voice laced with amusement. Behind us, Bishop snickered.

"Thanks. I'll keep that in mind," I replied with a smile.

Deacon and Bishop were not only escorting me to the service; they were also giving me away. Although my father had come through for me when I needed him, he would have never consented to me being married anywhere but in a church, outfitted in a twenty-thousand-dollar Vera Wang dress, with tons of reporters following the ceremony, making him look like father of the year. I didn't want anything to ruin my day, so I planned on calling my parents from my honeymoon to tell them I had eloped.

When we reached the clearing, the gentle strumming of a guitar floated back to me. As the woods melted into the green grass, the pathway was strewn with rose petals. I couldn't help smiling because it wasn't a detail I had asked for. The beautiful soul of my hard-core biker fiancé had added that romantic touch.

As if he could read my thoughts, Bishop muttered, "What a pussy."

I elbowed him in the ribs. "You could learn a little something from your older brother," I countered.

He wrinkled his nose in disgust. "No fucking thank you. Hell, Rev's always been a sensitive fucker, but since he fell for you, it's like he's grown a vagina."

When Deacon snickered, I shot him a death glare before turning back to Bishop. "Let me set you straight on one thing. There is nothing unmanly about Rev, especially not in the bedroom. And you can't have a vagina when you're that well-endowed." At Bishop's openmouthed, wide-eyed look, I said, "Just in case you're not sure what 'well-endowed' means, it means your brother has a giant dick and knows how to use it."

I bit back a laugh at how I'd shocked the hell out of both of my future brothers-in-law. With a wink at them, I said, "That last comment was to show you that I'm not too uptown to be a biker's old lady."

Both Deacon and Bishop hooted and snorted with laughter. I couldn't hide my surprise when Bishop reached over and kissed my cheek. "I don't ever have any doubts about you being a good old lady, Annabel."

I smiled at him. "Thank you, Bishop."

Once we rounded the bend of the clearing, I could see all my wedding guests—my new family—standing on the banks of the glittering water. Outfitted in a frilly pink dress, Willow was our impromptu flower girl. She stood next to Alexandra, who held baby Wyatt in her arms. Mama Beth was beside her, keeping a watchful eye on her grandchildren. Kim and her five children were in attendance, including her eighteen-year-old daughter, Cassie. Our newest miracle had come in the form of the beautiful, intelligent girl. She wanted to be Rev's and my surrogate in exchange for help with paying the tuition to college that her family couldn't afford. It had seemed almost too good to be true, but after lengthy discussions with Cassie and Kim, we came to see how serious she was about it. So after we enjoyed a few years together as just man and wife, we would take the next step to becoming a family.

My heart skipped at the sight of Rev. Just as I was dressed in a simple white sheath dress with spaghetti straps, Rev wore simple black pants, a white shirt with the sleeves rolled up, and his cut. I wouldn't have had it any other way. He wasn't a tux kind of guy, and I was no longer couture.

When he caught sight of me, a broad smile stretched across his handsome face, making warmth spread over my body. In a way, it was so surreal that I was marrying a man like Rev—a man I wouldn't have given a second glance had it not been for my tortured past. As

I gripped the bouquet in my hands tighter, I thought of how blessed I was that something so wonderful had come out of something so horrific.

The guitarist began strumming "Here Comes the Bride," and although we grew closer and closer to Rev, I couldn't get to him fast enough. I fought the urge to grab up the hem of my dress and start running. When I finally stood before him, I couldn't keep my hands off him. I threw my arms around his neck and pressed myself against him.

A chuckle rumbled through his chest. "I don't think we've gotten to this part yet," Rev murmured into my hair.

I pulled back to smile up at him. "I couldn't help myself."

"I'm not really complaining." Rev ran his thumbs across my cheekbones. "You look so, so beautiful."

"Thank you. You look pretty handsome yourself."

The minister, an out-of-town Raider road-named Fuzz, cleared his throat. "I think we oughta get this show on the road."

"You just want to get back to the roadhouse for the beer and cake," Rev challenged with a good-natured smile.

Fuzz grinned. "Can you blame me?"

I shook my head. "No, we can't." I pulled out of Rev's embrace, and we took our appropriate places in front of Fuzz.

"Dearly beloved, we're gathered here in the sight of God and these witnesses to join this man and this woman together in the bonds of holy matrimony. . . ."

As we began the official part of the ceremony, I kept my eyes locked on Rev's. I couldn't fight the tears that stung my eyes. But they weren't sorrowful tears—they were tears of pure happiness. A happiness that had been hard won. To the outside world, we were such an unorthodox pair. After all, what bride-to-be received a wedding present from her groom in the form of the death of her rapist and torturer? While Mendoza might have escaped into custody the day that Rev had been shot, he met a horrific end in jail. So horrific that Rev refused to give me any details about what had happened to him before his throat was slit.

Pushing those macabre thoughts out of my mind, I focused instead on the bright future that lay before me as Rev's wife. The old Annabel was a former debutante who lived in a world of excess in every area but love and affection. While she was ripped violently from that world, she came to find solace and healing among bikers, and a happiness that the old Annabel never knew existed. This was where I belonged.

Don't miss Bishop Malloy's story in

LAST MILE

Coming from Signet Eclipse trade in February 2016

For the hundredth fucking time, I felt eyes on me, stalking my every move. Casually, I glanced over my shoulder to take in the crowd. The Raiders clubhouse was at full capacity for a Saturday night. The house band was cranking out tunes, and couples were in the middle of the floor, bumping and grinding. With Rev and Annabel gone to Virginia to visit her family, and Deacon off on a fucking Brownies camping trip (of all things) with Willow, I was the only Malloy in residence.

Even without looking, I could have guessed who was eyeballing me. Three weeks ago, a new mechanic had started at the garage I was working at. His name was Marley, and he was former Army. Once he learned who I was, he expressed an interest in becoming a hang-around for the Hells Raiders. It was a way to prove yourself for moving into a prospecting position. After everything that had gone down with Mendoza, we were looking to bring in a few new guys to steady things until the heat wore off. We were still slowly and surely moving toward being legitimate. Marley appeared to be just the kind of guy we could use.

From his table across the room, Marley worked on draining another beer. But he wasn't the one looking at me. He hadn't glanced in my direction all night. No, it was the fine-as-hell woman beside him who had been doing her best at eye-fucking me who'd drawn my attention.

Tonight was the first night I had had the pleasure and the pain of meeting Marley's girlfriend. She had at least five years on me, and that fact made me want to volunteer to be her cougar cub. If there was one word to describe her, it was exotic. Sure, she was probably more of an ethnic mutt, but it made for one hell of an attractive combination. One moment, she looked more Hispanic than anything, while the next, she took on an Asian appearance, thanks to her almond-shaped eyes. She had turned the heads of more than one of my brothers.

When she realized I was looking at her, a catlike smile curved her ruby-red lips. She tossed some strands of her silky, jet-black hair over her shoulders. Marley, sitting beside her, didn't act like he noticed anything that she was doing.

Even though he wasn't a patch-wearing brother, I still shouldn't have been giving her the eye. You didn't fuck around with other guys' women. It usually led to trouble of the fist-flying kind. And even though there were more than enough hot pieces of available ass here tonight, I couldn't help letting my mind wander to places it shouldn't with this woman.

My ears perked up at the sound of a baby's cry. I knew the cry very well—it belonged to my nephew. As I headed across the main room of the roadhouse, I could see Alexandra in the doorway to the kitchen, walking around, trying to pacify the fussy baby.

"What's wrong with the little man?" I asked.

Alexandra huffed out a frustrated breath. "I have no idea. He's just been fed and had his diaper changed, but he insists on being whiny." She kissed the top of her son's dark-haired head. "Truth be told, I think he's sick of me. With Deacon gone camping with Willow, he's had no one else to amuse him the past three days."

"Here, let me take him."

Alexandra's brows rose in surprise. "Really?" When I nodded, she passed him into my waiting arms. He immediately dried up the sniffling and gazed into my face. "Who knew you were so good with babies," Alexandra mused.

With a wink, I added, "Nah, it's more about the fact he's had too much tit time. He needs to be with some men for a while."

"You're terrible," she replied, smacking my arm playfully.

"You love me, though," I teased.

Alexandra leaned over and planted a kiss on my cheek. "Yes, I do. Very much." Patting Wyatt's back, she then said, "Bring him back when you get tired of him or he gets tired of you."

"Sure thing."

As I walked Wyatt around the main room, several of my brothers stopped to talk to us while their old ladies or girlfriends cooed at Wyatt. Although he was all Alexandra when it came to the looks department, Wyatt was like his old man in that he knew how to work a crowd. He grinned and waved his hands, drawing smiles from everyone we talked to.

"What a little cutie," a voice said behind me.

I turned around to find my eye-fucker standing behind me. "Thanks."

"Is he yours?" she asked.

"Oh hell no. He's my brother's."

She smiled as she reached out to stroke Wyatt's chubby cheek. "I take it you don't have any of your own."

"That would once again be a hell no."

"You're awfully good with him."

"I like kids just as long as they belong to someone else," I answered honestly. When Wyatt reached for her, she looked at me to gauge my response. "Sure. You can hold him."

Wyatt happily dove into her waiting arms. "Aren't you a charmer?" she murmured.

"I don't think we've met," I said as she sweet-talked Wyatt.

"I'm Samantha. But you can call me Sam."

Extending my hand, I said, "I'm Bishop."

"Nice to meet you."

I knew with her introduction that she had to be new to this whole lifestyle. Most of the women knew that when introducing themselves, they were to say which man they belonged to. "You're with Marley, right?"

She nodded. "This is my first MC party."

"And what do you think about it?"

"It's . . . interesting?" she answered honestly.

I laughed. "Sounds like you're trying to be nice. Trust me, this one is pretty tame. Wait until you go to a rally." At her wide eyes, I added, "It has to be seen to be believed."

"Somehow I don't think I like the sound of that."

"You'll get used to it. Especially if Marley becomes a prospect and then a patch member."

At that moment Marley showed up behind us. "Hey, Bishop. I see you got to meet my girl."

Deep inside, I wanted to snarl at his reference to Sam being his girl. Of course, I had no fucking reason to do that. Hell, I didn't even know her. Yeah, she was one hell of a looker who got my dick up and running, and she seemed to have a sweet side when it came to the way she was interacting with Wyatt. But that was it.

"You're a lucky man," I finally replied.

Marley grinned and planted a smacking kiss on Sam's lips, which caused her to step back slightly. But then she gave him a beaming smile. "I guess I'd better hand over this cutie," she said. After I took Wyatt back from her, she said, "Thanks for letting me hold him."

"Anytime."

She then slid her arm around Marley's waist and they moved away from me. Just as they got halfway across the room, she glanced over her shoulder at me, giving me that catlike smile again.

When she turned her head back, I groaned, which caused Wyatt to glance up at me in surprise. I smiled at him. "Little man, your uncle is in deep shit."

Katie Ashley is the *New York Times* and *USA Today* bestselling author of the Proposition series and the Runaway Train series, as well as several New Adult and Young Adult titles. She lives outside of Atlanta, Georgia, with her daughter and her two very spoiled dogs. With a BA in English, a BS in secondary English education, and a master's in English education, she spent eleven years teaching middle school and high school English until she left to write full-time.